WHISKEY PAIN

VIKTOROV BRATVA
BOOK 2

NICOLE FOX

MAILING LIST

Sign up to my mailing list!
New subscribers receive a FREE steamy bad boy romance
novel.

Click the link below to join.
https://sendfox.com/nicolefox

ALSO BY NICOLE FOX

Vorobev Bratva

Velvet Devil

Velvet Angel

Romanoff Bratva

Immaculate Deception

Immaculate Corruption

Kovalyov Bratva

Gilded Cage

Gilded Tears

Jaded Soul

Jaded Devil

Ripped Veil

Ripped Lace

Mazzeo Mafia Duet

Liar's Lullaby (Book 1)

Sinner's Lullaby (Book 2)

Bratva Crime Syndicate

Can be read in any order!

Lies He Told Me

Scars He Gave Me

Sins He Taught Me

Belluci Mafia Trilogy

Corrupted Angel (Book 1)

Corrupted Queen (Book 2)

Corrupted Empire (Book 3)

De Maggio Mafia Duet

Devil in a Suit (Book 1)

Devil at the Altar (Book 2)

Kornilov Bratva Duet

Married to the Don (Book 1)

Til Death Do Us Part (Book 2)

Heirs to the Bratva Empire

Can be read in any order!

Kostya

Maksim

Andrei

Princes of Ravenlake Academy (Bully Romance)

Can be read as standalones!

Cruel Prep

Cruel Academy

Cruel Elite

Tsezar Bratva

Nightfall (Book 1)

Daybreak (Book 2)

Russian Crime Brotherhood

Can be read in any order!

Owned by the Mob Boss

Unprotected with the Mob Boss

Knocked Up by the Mob Boss

Sold to the Mob Boss

Stolen by the Mob Boss

Trapped with the Mob Boss

Volkov Bratva

Broken Vows (Book 1)

Broken Hope (Book 2)

Broken Sins *(standalone)*

Other Standalones

Vin: A Mafia Romance

Box Sets

Bratva Mob Bosses (Russian Crime Brotherhood Books 1-6)

Tsezar Bratva (Tsezar Bratva Duet Books 1-2)

Heirs to the Bratva Empire

The Mafia Dons Collection

The Don's Corruption

WHISKEY PAIN

Someone stole my baby.

But Timofey Viktorov thinks it was *me*.

I took my loved ones and ran.

What other choice did I have?

But somewhere out there, some monster has the baby I've come to love as my own.

Timofey comes after me.

He finds us—because duh, of course he does.

Now, I'm in the fight of my life. Can I make him believe me?

Or will the pains of our past blind him to the truth:

That the only way we'll rescue our son is if we do it together.

WHISKEY PAIN is Book 2 in the Viktorov Bratva duet. The story begins in Book 1, WHISKEY POISON.

1

PIPER

The last time I was in Noelle's apartment, I had a clay mask on my face and 90s rap music was blasting through the speaker on her kitchen counter.

"Is my skin supposed to be burning?" Ashley had asked, poking at the hardened layer of green clay on her face.

I examined myself in the mirror hanging above Noelle's couch. "Why is it drying all wrinkly? I look like a swamp monster."

"Would you two stop complaining? Beauty is pain." Noelle carried out a tray of fresh cut fruit and cheese with two wine bottles fitted precariously between her fingers. "Time for the monthly session of Whine and Wine to commence."

Ashley lunged for the wine. "Be careful with these! This is the only reason I'm here. If you drop them, I'm leaving."

She laughed, but we couldn't quite bring ourselves to. She was "California sober," to use one of her pet phrases, which basically meant not sober at all. Three weeks later, Ashley would have an overdose scare and end up back in rehab.

At the time, I thought it was the worst thing that could happen to any of us.

Now, I know better.

Because now, I'm standing in the center of Noelle's dark apartment with a flashlight, and I'd kill to go back to that night. Back to bailing Ashley out of jail, rather than hunting through Noelle's personal files for evidence that she committed a white collar crime. Back to complaining about my coworkers instead of fighting my feelings for a known criminal who, more and more, is turning out to be the only person I can trust.

I sift through the drawers of Noelle's desk. Yellow light from the street is streaming in through the slats of her blinds. Her laptop is closed on the corner of her desk, but I leave it be. Almost everything is online these days. I highly doubt she'd use her personal email account to plot with the Albanians.

"You're smarter than that, Noelle," I mutter, flipping through the pages of her daily planner. "You know how to keep things hidden."

Although, come to think of it, she didn't really do such an amazing job at keeping this hidden; I just ignored half a dozen obvious signs. I didn't realize the news headlines about Noelle's company and the recent audits could have anything at all to do with her. When I saw a few articles pop up on Twitter, I didn't even ask her about it because she only worked in a subsidiary of the larger parent corporation. It seemed so unlikely for one of my best friends to be involved in fraudulent activity—*especially* Noelle—that I never entertained the possibility for a second.

That blind faith oversight nearly killed me.

Worse, it nearly killed Timofey and Benjamin.

The thought of Benjamin in danger nearly steals my breath. I've only been his nanny for a few weeks, but I couldn't help but fall in love.

With Benjamin? asks an obnoxious voice in my head. *Or his adopted father?*

I ignore the question from the peanut gallery and press my hand to my heart to slow its racing. "Timofey has Benjamin. He's safe… for now."

I do not miss the irony that I once wanted nothing more than to get Benjamin away from Timofey, and now, I'm comforted by the fact that they are together. Irony is all I've got left these days.

It's just that Timofey would never let anything happen to Benjamin. He'd tear apart the world to save the people he loves.

And after everything you've been through, you gave up that security. You gave up Timofey.

I shake my head, trying to shake the traitorous thoughts loose once and for all. Timofey didn't love me. Our relationship was for show. The only thing I gave up when I walked out on him was the illusion we'd created.

But my feelings for Benjamin are no illusion. I have to do whatever I can to save him from whatever Noelle and the Albanians have planned.

First things first, though: I need to find the proof.

Noelle may be one of my oldest friends, but she committed a crime and justice should be served. Honestly, that's what's best for her, too. Prison is going to be kinder to her than the Albanians will be.

I set Noelle's planner aside and move to the recycling bin under her desk. Maybe she tossed something with the expectation that no one would ever see it. It's not exactly normal for people to break in and raid your trash, after all. She couldn't be blamed for thinking it was fine to throw something incriminating in there.

I'm separating the bin into receipts, bills, and junk when someone pounds on the door.

The knocking is so loud that I instinctively duck, expecting wooden shrapnel to start flying.

There's a beat of silence before the knocking starts again. The window behind me rattles in the frame. The door might not explode, but whoever is on the other side will be bursting through it in a second.

And I have nowhere to run.

"Shit!" I hiss, swiping all of the papers back into the bin and sliding it back under the desk. Whoever it is, I don't want them to see any sign that someone is in the apartment.

I consider making a run for the bedroom. There's a fire escape on the back of the building, but I'm not sure if I can even get to it.

"If there ever is a fire in this place, I'd probably die in a fall through those rusted-out stairs," Noelle said once, after the building's fire alarm went off in the middle of the night. "If I could even get the window open. It's been painted shut since I moved in."

I snatch Noelle's craft scissors from the desk drawer in case I need to chip the paint away. I take one single step towards the bedroom when there is a final, resounding knock.

But it isn't just a knock.

It's an apocalypse.

The entire door snaps off the hinges and falls into the entryway with an ear-splitting *boom*. As the dust settles, I drop to my knees and scramble back under the desk. Noelle's apartment is one square living space with an adjoining kitchen, but I'm in the corner closest to the door. Which means I haven't seen whoever broke down the door and they haven't seen me.

I pray it stays that way.

I slink back under the desk, hoping the shadows are enough to keep me hidden. Maybe if the intruders move to the bedroom, I can haul ass through the front door.

Then again, if it's the Albanians, they will have brought plenty of backup. So maybe I'll hide in the closet with the trash chute at the end of the hall. Then, when I'm sure they're gone, I'll come out.

Plans and backup plans and backup-to-the-backup plans formulate in my mind. I'm prepared to use the lamp next to the couch as a weapon, if need be. I can scream and try to wake the neighbors. Maybe the intruders aren't with the Albanians after all, and they'll be spooked by a crazed woman shrieking at the top of her lungs.

But the moment I see him step into the living room, all that dissolves like smoke.

I don't breathe. I don't move. I'm rooted to the floor, frozen in place with shock and confusion.

His confident footsteps move closer. A knee plants itself on the hardwood floor in front of me. A smell I remember. Smoke and mint and musk. A shadow. A bulk. A presence.

Before I can even decide if I need to scream, Timofey grabs me by the hair.

2

PIPER

I bite back a scream and struggle to my feet.

"I thought I might find you here," he growls. He shifts his hand from my hair to my neck. His fingers bite into my skin, and I can feel the pressure building in my head.

I squeeze my eyes closed, trying to quiet the thrumming in my ears so I can think. "What are you doing here?"

"You stole my question, Piper. But that's not the only thing you stole, is it?"

I try to turn and look at him, but he forces my head down, keeping me in submission. "I don't understand. What's going on?"

A frustrated growl rumbles through his chest. Then he shoves me forward, and I catch myself on the arm of the couch. Air whooshes out of my lungs.

"It's simple. Sit down and I'll explain it."

Every word out of his mouth is gritted between clenched teeth. When I shift into a seated position and can actually look at his face, it is so twisted with fury that I almost don't recognize him.

But those eyes... I'll never be able to forget those.

It's there in the familiar depths of his eyes that I catch a glimmer of the man I know. I reach out for him. For *that* man —not the one yelling at me, but the one who saved me in a dark alley. The one who opened the door of that panic room with his heart in his throat, desperate to know if I was safe. That's the man I reach for. That's the man I need.

"Timofey," I breathe, "I know you're upset with me for walking out the way I did. I was—I was angry with you, but I shouldn't have left. We both said things we didn't mean, and I think we can—"

"Can what? Make up?" His eyebrows furrow. "Maybe we'll hold hands and let the past be the past. Is that what you want?"

The question sounds like a trick, but yes. That's exactly what I want.

He can't really be this angry, can he? Right now, I can forgive him. Our fight felt like a big deal at the time. Now, I know there are bigger issues, Benjamin's safety being a huge one. But Timofey was still in the wrong. He lied to me and threw money around to get my father out of my life. If either of us has reason to be upset, it's me.

"We can move forward." I swallow down my nerves and jump into the vulnerability. "I don't want things between us to be fake, Timofey. I want to be with you. I want to make things work."

He grabs my chin and tilts my face up. I want to stand up so we're at eye level. So I can see if what I've said is landing, if it's breaking through his battle armor.

Then his hold turns to iron, and all I want is to get away.

I try to pull back, but he follows me. He shifts forward, wedging his knee between my legs and pinning my head against the back of the couch.

"Timofey. Please. I don't understand."

"It's going to be a little hard for us to make things work," he bites out. "I'm not sure I'm ready to *move on* from the fact that you kidnapped my son."

I blink up at him. "But I never—what? I didn't write up the CPS report. Did another caseworker come to the house? I never recommended you be removed as Benjamin's guardian."

"Of course you didn't. Why would you need to? You knew you were going to take matters into your own hands anyway." Faster than seems possible, he grabs my wrists and spreads my arms along the back of the couch. He pins me down and leans over me, his breath hot on my face. "Where is he, Piper? *Where the fuck is my boy?*"

I struggle against his hold for a second before it's painfully clear there will be no escape for me. In a battle of strength, Timofey will win every time.

"What are you talking about?"

His hands tighten around my wrists to the point I'm sure there will be bruises. "Tell me where Benjamin is. Now."

I inhale sharply. "You don't know where Benjamin is?"

Noelle. That's my first thought. Blunt and stupid and obvious. She wanted me to get Benjamin away from Timofey. She has to be involved here.

But it's only been a few hours since I saw her last. Surely she couldn't have done anything since then, right?

It's not as if the Bratva doesn't have enough enemies. If the Albanians could get Noelle to turn on me, then they could have hired someone else to kidnap a baby.

No. It couldn't have been her. She wouldn't.

Would she?

"Tell me where he is!" Timofey roars when I take too long to answer.

He slides his knee further between my legs. My lower back is pinned to the couch, but as he stretches my arms further apart, I'm forced into an uncomfortable arch. The muscles in my back are burning from the position.

A whimper forces its way out of me. "You're hurting me. Please."

"I'm going to do a lot worse than this if you don't tell me where he is."

My shoulders are screaming. There's so much happening inside my head that I can't sort through it.

"Maybe…maybe…" Then it hits me. An epiphany that almost brings a smile to my face. "Rodion! It's Rodion. He did this, Timofey. I didn't trust him before, and now he is—"

"Dead."

My face falls. "What?"

"Rodion is dead," he repeats slowly. "A bullet blew his head open an hour ago. His body is still in my entryway."

Hope drops like an asteroid in my stomach, cratering whatever semblance of calm I still have left.

Timofey will do anything for the people he loves. Including murder. I knew that. I *know* that.

Now, like Rodion, I'm about to experience it firsthand—and I can't say I blame him. I'm doing my best to shove aside the painful horror that Benjamin is missing, but it gnaws at my insides nonetheless.

"Timofey, please." I search his eyes for some small part of him that cares for me. That *believes* me. "I really have no clue—"

"You're in her house, Piper," he hisses. "Noelle came to see me tonight. She claimed to have some information for me about Emily. Next thing I know, Benjamin is gone. Explain that."

I frown. "She came to see you?"

His top lip curls. "Don't act like you don't know."

"I don't! I didn't!"

"You're sitting here waiting for her. You and one of your best fucking friends worked together to kidnap my son. I want him back. Now."

"No. No! That isn't what—I'm not here to see her," I stammer. "I came here to…"

The words die in my throat, along with my hope.

Timofey killed Rodion in cold blood. They'd known each other for years—practically grew up together—and he still killed him without hesitation. How much worse would he treat Noelle?

If I tell Timofey that Noelle is working with the Albanians, he'll kill her. Forget the information the FBI has on her. Forget a jury or a trail. Timofey will execute Noelle without a second thought. She may have betrayed me and she may have committed fraud, but she isn't a kidnapper. She wouldn't hurt a *baby*.

I can't let what happened to Rodion happen to her.

"Came here to what?" he hisses. "Having trouble coming up with a lie?"

I shove aside my fear and lift my chin, meeting Timofey's cold blue eyes. "No, I'm saving my breath. You won't believe a word I say anyway. So I might as well save my energy. I get the feeling I'm going to need it."

His nostrils flare and his breathing hitches like he's going to say something. I brace myself for the verbal onslaught. For words that will hurt worse than anything his hands could do.

But it won't matter. Timofey will do anything for the people he loves, but I can endure anything for the people I love. I know because I've been doing it most of my life.

So let him try to hurt me. I won't break. I can't afford to.

But instead of saying anything, Timofey lets me go. There is a moment of relief before he hauls me to my feet, shoves me across the room, and pushes me into the closet.

I catch myself from smashing into the back wall with both hands, and then Timofey presses in after me. He squeezes in, taking all of the extra oxygen with him, and closes the door.

Even in the dark, I see the sadistic snarl on his face.

"Well, this is cozy," he says. "You, me, and your claustrophobia should fit nicely in here, don't you think?"

I open my mouth to answer, but no words come out.

It's hard to speak when you're dying.

3

TIMOFEY

It's only been a minute and Piper is already wheezing.

Her breaths whistle in and out of her as if my hand was wrapped around her throat. Like I'm crushing her chest.

But I'm not even touching her. I'm leaning against the closed door, watching her fall apart.

"I don't know," she whimpers. "If I did, I'd tell you."

"Lies won't free you, Piper."

She squeezes her eyes closed and forces a shaky breath through her lips. "Neither will you. I know you better than that."

"Apparently not."

She cracks an eye open, peering up at me.

"I should kill you," I muse.

I don't mean to say it, but the thought is so loud inside of my head that it forced its way out.

It's what a don should do. It's what the job title requires.

Ruthlessness. No mercy.

"I gave you the chance to tell me the truth; instead, you denied everything. You should die for that."

If she was anyone else, she'd already be dead. I don't want to unpack why she's still breathing.

But if I give *that* any thought, especially right now, Benjamin is as good as gone. I need to maintain control. Absolute control. It's the only way to get enough information to track him down.

The moment I admit to myself the real reason why Piper is such an exception to every rule I've ever known, that control is gone.

Just one more thing she's stolen from me.

Piper bangs her head back against the wall. The single bulb in the center of the closet casts her closed lashes in long shadows across her cheeks. "I'm already dying."

"It's a closet, not a coffin. Relax."

I brought her in here because I knew she wouldn't be able to relax. That was the point. She needs to be uncomfortable. I shouldn't be trying to comfort her.

But the sight of her chest heaving with every breath, her lips parting as she inhales and exhales slowly… All of it is making it hard to remember why we came in here in the first place.

It's the way I felt with her pinned to the couch, arms spread, back arched.

I wanted to touch her.

A change of scenery hasn't lessened that desire. If anything, the cramped space is amplifying the feeling.

She's so close.

Her eyes are still shut when I cross the distance between us. My hand snakes around her neck, and she stretches onto her toes.

I press my lips to her ear. "Where is he?" I close my eyes at the way my voice manages to crack with the pain I can't— *won't*—let her see.

"I don't know." She starts to shake her head, but stops when I squeeze.

Desire and anger brew a toxic cocktail in my gut. Her life is in my hands, and I'm not sure what I want to do with it. I could do what any other don would do in my stead. Or... I could do what *I* want.

She fights for a breath, but I only let up just enough for it to shudder through. Old instinct wars with new. Yet another problem I don't have the time to face.

When I do release, she collapses against me. She's gasping for oxygen with her forehead resting on my shoulder. I can see straight down the front of her shirt. Her chest rises and falls, and I feel my breathing synchronize with hers.

I'm as breathless as she is.

Fuck.

"Tell me the truth, Piper," I rasp.

She looks up at me. Her eyes are glassy with unshed tears and her brow is furrowed. "What are you going to do to me, Timofey?"

I push her against the back of the closet, my hand returning to her neck. "Whatever I want."

"Are you going to kill me?"

Her throat bobs. I feel the vibration of her words against my palm, and I squeeze tighter. Just enough to warn her, but nowhere near the level of ruthless I should be.

A small kind of yelp bubbles between her lips, and I want to swallow it down. I want to seal her mouth with mine so she can't make another sound.

Her hands slide around my shoulders. But she doesn't push me away; she draws me closer.

This isn't what I had planned when I shoved her in the closet. But then again, there's more than one way to torture someone. There's a power in this. Anyone who disagrees isn't doing it right.

Piper won't give me what I want.

So I'll take it.

I slide my hand down the front of her pants and find her hot and damp. Her hips buck against my palm as I hiss into her ear, "When I'm done with you, death will feel like a blessing."

As much as I need to destroy Piper, the minute our lips touch, I can practically hear my control fly out the window. Her mouth is hot and hungry against mine. Desire roars inside of me like a fire, all-consuming and inescapable.

The kiss shifts from heated to an inferno in seconds. She digs her fingers into my skin as I crush her against the wall. Our bodies press and seek in violent, clumsy movements.

Distantly, I hear hangers rattling to the floor and things shifting around us, but I don't give a fuck. The goddamn earth would have to open up and swallow me whole before I cared.

Piper is straddling my thigh, dragging herself up and down the length of my leg. She moans. "Timofey."

I pull back. "Naked. Now."

There's uncertainty in her green eyes, but her response is immediate. Piper strips off her shirt and her bra. By the time she's reaching for the waistband of her jeans, I can't wait. I shove her hands aside and yank the material down around her knees.

I cup her warm center, stroking my fingers over the lacy material of her panties. Then, with a quick rip, she is bare against my palm.

"You can't lie about this." I swirl my finger in the moisture pooled between her thighs. She is slick and ready. "You like it rough, don't you? You're desperate for me to destroy you."

She trembles when I circle her clit. Her lower lip is pinched between her teeth and her eyes are closed.

"Look at me," I bark.

She blinks and meets my gaze. Color is rising in her cheeks, and she's breathing heavily for a new reason now.

"It's a simple question. Do. You. Like. This?"

I curl two fingers into her. She rises onto her toes for a second and then tries to spread her legs. But the jeans around her thighs have them pinned closed. Soft, pleading sounds work loose from her, but no words.

"Answer me."

Her lips stay stubbornly closed until I stroke into her once and then twice, massaging her quivering insides as my thumb circles her clit.

Then I add a third finger.

She gasps and her eyes flutter shut.

I grip her chin, and they snap open. "Piper," I growl, pumping my hand into her again and again. "Do you like it?"

She doesn't want to say, but then her body goes rigid and she has no choice. "Yes!"

That's when I pull away.

Piper's shaky legs nearly collapse underneath her. She looks up at me with murder in her eyes. "Wh-why did you stop?"

I grab her shoulder and spin her around. Her legs are still bound by the denim wrapped around her knees, so she can't resist or brace herself. All she can do is fall against the wall where I place her.

Then I free myself and slide into her ready wetness.

Piper cries out and presses her palms flat against the wall. Curses bloom and die on her lips before she ever gets the chance to spit them at me.

"I never said I'd stop." I wrap a hand around her waist, lifting her hips to me for better access. I can't swallow back the groan when I feel myself sink even deeper into her velvety heat.

Fucking perfection.

She grunts with my every thrust. It makes me want to fill her again and again. Harder. Faster. "This is insane," she gasps.

I fist her hair and tug. "This is happening, Piper. Soak it in."

She curses softly under her breath when I sink every inch deep inside her and grind. "I was crazy to think I could trust you. I should have known you'd use my weakness against me."

I kiss her neck and taste the salty sweat that's blooming across her skin. "Remind me of that weakness."

"You already know."

"That's right," I whisper, biting the velvet smooth skin of her earlobe. I do know; I just refuse to acknowledge it. "You're weak for toe-curling, earth-shaking fucking." I give her another solid thrust just to underline my point.

She tries to laugh, but it comes out in a breathless pant. "Someone has a high opinion of themself."

"Prove me wrong, then." I slide my hand between her thighs. "Don't come."

I stroke her inside and out until her body is a tight ball of tension in my arms. I can feel her quaking with the effort to fight off her orgasm.

"You're as dirty and broken and fucked up as I am, Piper. Give into it. Life will be better."

She reaches back and claws my thigh, meeting my thrusts. "I'm a good person, Timofey."

"You're a liar. A kidnapper." The words coming out of my panting mouth are the complete opposite of the words hammering inside my head. It's my rage fueling my tongue, and it's driving me to finish what I started. It's keeping the part of me that might actually believe her silent and buried. "You're a whore for the Albanians, seducing me to do their bidding."

She groans and tips her head back. "You don't believe that."

"Yes. I do."

Now, who's the liar?

I stamp that thought—that weakness—out the moment it appears.

She rests her head back on my shoulder, her body bowed to the breaking point. From this angle, I can see her breasts shake with every thrust. I palm them and pinch the hardened points of her nipples. She surges around me, and again threatens to steal my control.

"You don't," she moans, writhing against me. "If you really believed that, I'd be dead."

"I wish you were dead," I growl.

Life would be so much easier if I never met Piper. Hell, life would be so much easier if I didn't try to do things the legal way in the first place when it came to adopting Benjamin. It would have been easier to just pretend he was mine. No agencies, no house visits, no maddening social workers to seduce me into submission. Benjamin would be home safe right now. I wouldn't be torn in half, fighting duty and desire because of whatever siren song exists inside of this woman's pussy.

Life would be simpler if Piper was gone.

"Then get it over with. Kill me." She grips both of my hips and rolls herself onto me, moving in torturous circles. She quickens her pace, moaning and crying out until I feel her entire body tighten around me. With a deep shudder, she clamps down, pulsing around me with pure pleasure.

And I can't hold back.

I pump into her, filling her with every drop of my rage and hunger and confusion.

I manage to ignore the way I hold her in my arms when I do.

Piper sighs and slumps against me. "Timofey, that was... I feel so..."

Good.

This woman kidnapped my son, and I just made her feel good. It wasn't torture. It wasn't punishment. It was lust, pure and simple. And I prioritized it over my own son.

What the fuck has this woman done to me?

"You couldn't have done that if you didn't believe me," she says, sliding her jeans up over her hips.

She still has her back to me. Her limbs are still trembling in the afterglow, and I silence the part of me that wants to hold her close until she stills. I've given both of us far too much lenience already.

"If you really thought I had something to do with Benjamin disappearing, you'd have me chained to a chair, not naked in a closet.

I ignore her. She's trying to lure me in, trying to blur the line I've drawn in the sand between us.

I can't let her. I won't.

She snaps her bra into place with delicate fingers and then reaches for her shirt. As she bends down, I'm tempted by yet another craving for her. Seconds since we finished and I already want more. But I ball my hands into fists so tight my nails threaten to pierce my skin.

This meant nothing, I tell myself. *I used her the same way she used me.*

"I want to help," Piper says, standing tall again. She sways slightly, losing her balance. "I want to—Benjamin is—"

I'm ready to tell her off, even shove her hard back out of the closet, when Piper turns to me suddenly.

Her eyes are glassy and unfocused. The color I just fucked into her cheeks is gone. She is a deathly shade of white I've never seen on a living person before.

"Piper?"

She glances down at my clenched fists. Her brows knit together. But by the time her green eyes make it up to my face, they are rolling back in her head.

"Timofey," she wheezes.

Then she drops to the floor.

4

PIPER

Between each blink and the next, my world shifts.

There is darkness and the woodsy, cinnamon scent I know as Timofey.

Then the world is rumbling beneath me. My cheek is pressed to smooth leather, and I hear Timofey's voice.

"Have a room ready the fucking second we get there," he growls.

A room? A torture chamber, he means. Maybe a prison cell.

I try to ask if we're in a car and where he is taking me. I'm not sure if my mouth even manages to form the words before it's black again.

Another blink and there is blinding light. It paints my eyelids white and prickles like static electricity across my skin.

I keep my eyes closed. Opening them is too difficult, anyway. They're heavy and I'm heavy. My limbs are weighted down, but I also feel like I'm floating.

Is this still from the orgasm I had in the closet? I shouldn't have let Timofey touch me—not when he was so angry and I was so confused—but we are magnetic. We fit together like we were made for each other.

Then he pulled out and I turned around. I saw the way his fists were clenched so tight, his knuckles were white. Then I saw...nothing.

I wish you were dead.

My heart thumps in my chest. I invited him to do it.

Then get it over with. Kill me.

Did he try? Is that what's happening? I'm in some bright white waiting room on the other side because Timofey did what I dared him to do, at the same time as the unbearable release he gave me was still pulsing deep within my core?

That'll be a tough one to explain to the Big Man Upstairs.

"Piper."

A voice cuts through the noise in my head. I turn towards it.

God? Only if God is a woman.

"Piper?" the voice calls again, soft and low. "Can you hear me?"

I blink repeatedly, my eyelids peeling open bit by bit until I'm staring up at a blurry silhouette above me.

"There you are," the voice says. "I thought you were awake."

"Where am I?" My throat is sandpaper.

Something touches my lips, and I flinch back.

"It's just ice water. You can take a drink. Here's the straw."

Either Timofey hired a kind woman to staff the interrogation dungeon beneath his mansion, or I'm not in a dungeon.

I take a long drink and try again. "Wh...where am I?"

My vision is becoming less blurry by the second. The shape next to my bed forms into a tall, thin blonde woman with an equally tall, thin nose. She's middle-aged and has a glittery purple stethoscope around her neck.

"You are in one of the best hospitals in the city receiving the best possible care," she says with a smile. "We were threatened within an inch of our life to make sure of it."

I take another drink. "How long have I been out? Am I okay?"

"A few hours. You were dehydrated when you came in. You are doing great now, so don't worry about that. It looks like you're just a little iron deficient."

There is an IV in the back of my hand and a heart rate monitor beeping along behind my bed. I'm not sure how I didn't hear it before. Now, it's almost all I can hear.

The woman says something else, and I have to plug the ear closest to the monitor to hear her. "Sorry. What did you say?"

"Naps," she repeats. "I'd recommend working a daily nap into your schedule and some relaxing practices. Light exercise works, if you're up for it. If not, meditation is great. Anything to help you stay calm."

I frown. "So naps and meditation will help with the iron deficiency?"

She chuckles. "No. I'm afraid that's just something that comes with the territory. Lots of women end up being anemic. You'll be on iron supplements for the next seven or so months. Your doctor will monitor those levels and let you know if anything changes."

"I—What?" I struggle into a seated position and take another drink of water. "I'm sorry. I guess I'm a little confused. I thought—I passed out, right?"

"Correct. You were admitted after fainting. We ran some tests, and your iron levels came back low. You are now classified as 'anemic.'"

"And that will just go away after seven months of supplements?"

She shrugs. "Sort of. Really, it will go away with delivery. That's when most women see their iron levels return to normal."

"Delivery? Of what?"

The nurse snorts and then seems to stifle it, trying to be professional. "Delivery of the baby. Your baby is growing rapidly right now, so that can lead to exhaustion, fatigue. Even fainting spells."

I stop hearing anything after she said "baby."

She's saying something else when suddenly, she stops and reaches for the blood pressure cuff hanging on the wall. "Your heart rate is climbing a little quick for my liking. Are you feeling okay?"

No.

I'm not okay.

Nothing about this is okay.

This woman just told me I'm pregnant.

She wraps the cuff around my arm and blows it up until it's uncomfortably tight. Then she releases it, her eyes pinned on the clock on the wall.

"Blood pressure is a little high, but that's to be expected." She pulls out the paper tracking my heart rate. "You're in a bit of a spike right now. Can you take a few deep breaths for me, Piper?"

"Easy for you to say." I inhale and exhale slowly. "You didn't just find out you're pregnant."

Now, it's the nurse's turn to freeze. She turns to me, eyes wide. I have a feeling if her heart rate was being tracked, it would spike right now, too.

"What?" I ask, suddenly worried. "Am I okay? Is something else wrong?"

"You didn't know?"

I shake my head. "I guess we didn't use… But I was on birth control. I have been. There were a few days I missed, here or there. That happens, though. I just double up the next day and everything works out. I… shit, I don't know."

She closes her eyes and presses a hand to her forehead. "I'm so sorry, Piper. I thought you knew."

"Are you sure? Maybe we should take another test. Those little stick tests can be wrong. Can't they? Maybe this one is wrong."

I try to think back to the only other time I've taken a pregnancy test. The booklet of information inside the box said something about false negatives or false positives. One of them is more common than the other, and now, I can't remember which one.

"It was a blood test. They are ninety-nine percent accurate."

Scratch that then.

The nurse drags a hand across her head, smoothing down her ponytail. "The doctor wrote the results down on your chart, but there was no date. Blood tests usually take a few days, but if it was rushed because of your—I just assumed it was a known pregnancy."

It's strange to be on the verge of an emotional meltdown myself and still be worried about someone else, but I reach out and touch the woman's arm. "It's okay. You didn't know."

"Neither did you, apparently!" She manages a shaky laugh, her face flushed several shades of sheepish. "I'm so sorry. This is not how anyone should find out."

I briefly try to imagine what the alternative would look like. Maybe I would have experienced symptoms. Nausea, cravings, heartburn. I would have run to the store for a test and then crowded myself into the cramped bathroom of wherever I was staying.

Would I have anxiously counted down the minutes before revealing the test? Or maybe I would have stared at it for every single one of the passing seconds, waiting for the lines to reveal themselves.

And when they did…what then?

Excitement? Relief?

No. Definitely not.

"Believe me," I tell her, "there is no way discovering this news would have been easy. Maybe this was for the best. You ripped the bandage off."

She ripped it off, alright. Tearing off all the hairs and a good bit of skin from what I thought my future would look like.

A baby.

With Timofey Viktorov.

As if she can read my mind, the woman leans forward, her hands braced on the plastic side of my bed. "Your husband, er, boyfriend—I don't know who he is to you, but I recognized him. When he brought you in."

"Timofey?"

She nods. "Everyone here knows him. He assaulted a doctor in pediatrics a few months ago."

I can tell by the way she whispers the words and eyes me that she is waiting for a crack in my façade. For me to crumble in fear.

Timofey Viktorov assaulted a doctor. He must be an abusive monster.

I should kill you.

Actions speak louder than words, right? God knows I've seen that on enough motivational posters in my lifetime. Timofey said some horrible things, but none of them were backed by his actions.

To be fair, neither were mine.

"There's more to the story," I try to explain to her. "He was going through a difficult time. He'd just lost his family. He isn't usually like that."

She doesn't look even slightly convinced. But the mention of his loss does soften the hard edge around her eyes. "Yeah, well, he didn't seem at all interested in being a father when he left the baby here. What is he going to think about *this* news?"

Timofey only decided to raise Benjamin because of his love for Emily. Because he wanted to do right by his sister.

But me? He wishes I was dead.

I can't imagine he'll be thrilled.

Dread coils tight in my stomach, and I feel lightheaded all over again.

"Piper?" The nurse stares worryingly up at my heart rate monitor.

I hear it beeping frantically in the corner, betraying the storm raging inside of me. "Don't tell him," I blurt. "About the baby. Don't tell him."

She stares at me for a long, silent moment. Then she nods. "Of course. It's our secret."

It's our secret, I think. *But for how much longer?*

5

TIMOFEY

"I didn't think smoking was allowed in hospitals." Akim leans through the door of the small waiting room and scans the ceiling, presumably for any signs of a smoke detector.

I tap my cigarette on the arm of the chair next to me. Ash and embers fall like dark snow into the only other chair. "Take a seat."

"You're chipper. I'm guessing I shouldn't mention that we don't usually bring the people we 'interrogate' to the hospital?" I glare up at him, and he holds his hands in surrender. "Don't kill the messenger."

"You have to deliver a message to be considered a messenger." I wave him on with my fourth cigarette in the last hour. "So fucking get on with it."

"Kreshnik found Arber's body. Not that it was hard to find, exactly." He shrugs, biting down a proud smile. "I had the guys arrange it in one of the adirondack chairs on the porch. He was holding onto his own head. It was pretty artistic, actually. I think I have an eye for this kind of thing after all those years of making your plates."

On another day, I might've laughed. Today is not that day.

I grimace. "Remind me not to give you time off. You go crazy when you aren't cooking for me."

"We all have to have our hobbies." He drops into a silence that stretches across several drags of my cigarette. He's trying to avoid the minefield of off-limits topics between us right now. Finally, he drums his fingers together. "So… when will I be cooking for you regularly again?"

I glance over at him.

Akim walked in on the scene back at the house. He knows Rodion is dead. He knows Sergey escaped. He knows Benjamin is missing. He knows the Albanians are a threat.

He knows almost everything, but I don't have the energy to fill him in on the rest.

"Did you buy the tickets?" I ask instead.

He drags a hand through his hair. He looks tired. "Yeah. Yeah, I got it all sorted. You're good to go."

"Okay." I nod. "Then you know it will be a while before I'm eating in my own kitchen."

"I figured, but there wasn't a return date. Is now really a good time to leave? You didn't ask, but Kreshnik is—"

"It will be war now that he knows Arber is dead. I know."

I can only imagine how furious Kreshnik is that his only son has been murdered. Though my imagination can get pretty close—he's probably as angry as I was to discover my only son has been kidnapped. More than that, as angry as I was to discover the woman I let into my life and trusted is the one responsible.

Without meaning to, I crush my cigarette in my fist. There's a sizzle of heat against the palm of my hand, a flash of pain, but I just brush off the cigarette debris and light up another one.

Akim leans in, voice low. "How is she?"

He doesn't have to say her name, and I'm glad he doesn't. There's no one else he could be talking about. He knows I went looking for Piper. Now, we're here.

I know what he's probably thinking, but what I did was a lot worse than torture. I don't want him to know what happened in that closet.

"Is she…?" *Alive.* "Did you…?" *Kill her.*

Before I can answer, someone approaches.

"Mr. Viktorov?"

I stand up the moment the nurse says my name, and she shrinks back. She scans my face and the cigarette in my hands. Her mouth tightens in disapproval. I guess my reputation precedes me.

"Ms. Quinn is awake now," she says. "You can go in and see her."

Without another word to Akim, I leave. I crush the embers of my cigarette beneath my boot on the way out.

6

TIMOFEY

Piper is a lot more than awake when I walk into her hospital room.

She's packing up.

There isn't much to pack, but her hospital gown is folded on the table and she's dressed in her own jeans and t-shirt again. She's sliding her phone into her back pocket as I enter.

"It looks like you're trying to run off without me."

She stiffens and slowly turns. I expect anger in her green eyes, but instead, there's a wariness I haven't seen in a long time—since the day we met, actually. It's almost like she isn't sure what to do with me.

This is what happens when you shove a woman in a closet and tell her you wish she was dead while you fuck her brains out. Shit gets complicated.

I want to tell her I didn't mean it. But I dismiss the idea.

"I'm not running. But I *am* leaving."

"Without saying goodbye?"

"Stop it," Piper snaps. She walks over to the bed and pulls the blankets up, as if the nurses aren't going to strip the bed and disinfect this entire room before the next patient. "Just stop. Stop acting like that. Stop playing games. You came in here for something—fuck knows you don't do anything without getting something out of it for yourself—so what is it? What do you want?"

She wants to get straight into this? Fine. We'll get straight into it. She seems strong enough to handle going toe-to-toe with me.

"Tell me the truth."

She lifts her hand from her side. For a second, it flutters awkwardly in front of her stomach almost like a metal detector wand. Then her hand claps back to her side and remains glued to her thigh. "About what?"

A nurse rattles down the hallway with a talkative patient who is complaining about getting three cups of orange yogurt and no red. I kick the door closed with the bottom of my foot.

"I thought we were done playing games. You know what I want to know, Piper."

"I already told you I don't know where Benjamin is. If I did, I would have mentioned it before I passed out in a hot closet."

I arch a brow. "Is that what we're calling it now? A 'hot closet?' Did the *heat* make you pass out?"

Her face flushes. It reminds me how she gasped and panted and arched her back as she rode my fingers, her face flushed the same way.

Blyat', I need to focus. I'm supposed to have the upper hand right now. Instead, I'm getting hard just by remembering what my hand did only a few hours ago.

"You can't keep me here."

"I can do whatever I want." *Whoever I want. And* I want *right now. Fucking hell, there's so much I want.*

"Okay, then why not leave me in that closet? What's the point of bringing me here to make sure I'm all patched up?"

"You're no use to me dead."

"Someone sounds just like dear old Dad," she says bitterly. "People are only as good as their usefulness to you."

Even the suggestion of Sergey is enough for me to see red. If Piper realized how close she was to the edge of my patience, she'd back off. "When it comes to my enemies, yes."

"Am I your enemy?"

"Refuse to cooperate and you'll have your answer," I growl.

She shakes her head. "You care too much about your reputation. That's why we pretended to date in the first place. If I turn up dead, all signs will point back to you."

"I pretended to date you so you'd help me keep my son. Now that you've done the exact opposite of that, I couldn't care less about my 'reputation.'"

Piper looks deep into my eyes and sees how serious I am. Her jaw works side to side as she thinks. "But then you won't ever get Benjamin back."

Blood is thrumming in my ears. I move to the center of the room, chest tense with anger. "That better not be a fucking threat."

She frowns in confusion. "Oh—No. No, I didn't mean—I don't know where Benjamin is."

I meet her eyes, staring into their emerald depths for a long moment. Finally, I manage to look away. "You're a better liar than I thought."

"I'm not lying!" she cries out. "I didn't mean that I would keep Benjamin away from you. I'm just saying, if you start running around town kidnapping women and killing people, you're going to get caught. You can't raise a baby in prison."

"Oh, so you're just worried about me then." I sigh in disbelief. "Yeah, that's believable. And I'm not a don; I'm a philanthropist. All I want is to make the world a better place."

"Is that what you were doing when you killed Rodion? 'Making the world a better place'?" The abrupt change of subject stops me short. My brows pinch together, and Piper rolls her eyes. "Sure, right. You kill so many people you've already forgotten who Rodion is. I get it. But be serious. Did you kill him because you found out he is the one who killed Emily?"

She doesn't know.

She actually doesn't know.

Plotting behind the scenes apparently doesn't give you the benefit of grade A information. Because Piper is miles behind the plot. She has no clue Sergey killed Emily and Rodion. I, for one, have no intention of filling her in. The more dangerous she thinks I am, the more likely she is to tell me what I want to know.

I stare at her, and the longer I stare, the more uncomfortable she becomes. Piper shifts from foot to foot. Then her fingers twitch on her thighs. Finally, her hand lifts again in the same way it did before. But then she slaps her hand back down.

She's nervous.

"Okay, so you can kill a man but you can't talk about it?" she asks.

"Since when do you care about Rodion?" I start to ask.

Then an idea strikes.

The moment the words are out of my mouth, I follow them across the room. I move so quickly Piper doesn't have time to back away or protect herself. She just flattens against the wall as I shove my hand down the front of her jeans.

"What are you—" She slaps at my arm and kicks at my ankle. "Get off!"

I don't feel anything, so I yank her shirt up. Her stomach is flat and bare. "You're not wearing a wire."

She squeals and squirms until I let her shirt drop. Her hands settle protectively across her stomach. "Why in the hell would I be wearing a wire?"

"To get me sent to prison. You have the connections. Your friend's boyfriend is in the FBI."

"She isn't—" The words die on her lips, and I know there is something she isn't telling me. Several somethings, I'm sure. "Noelle has nothing to do with this."

Piper tries to slide out from between me and the wall, but I brace my arms on either side of her head. "It would be a shame if you were trying to frame me, but you implicated her instead."

"I'm not trying to frame anyone!" she shouts as I slide my hand across her shoulder and down, tracing the swell of her breast. She goes rigid. She stares at me with wide eyes. "What are you doing?"

"I can't trust you. You say you're not wearing a wire, but you also say you don't know where Benjamin is. How can I be sure until I check every inch of you?"

She grabs for my wrist, but I twist away from her and drag my hand lower. My fingers edge under the hem of her shirt. If I actually believed she had a wire on, I'd do a full strip search. As it is, making her a little uncomfortable serves my purposes just about as well.

"I'm telling the truth. About everything." She presses herself flat against the wall, her arms folded over her waist. "Do you believe me?"

"No. I don't. And it's too bad." She sags in disappointment, but I immediately press her flat with the weight of my body. "Because Ashley and your grandmother are going to suffer because of you."

Color leeches out of her face. "I am telling you the truth. I don't know—"

"Enough with the same fucking lie. At least be original," I growl. "Don't Ashley and Gram at least deserve that much from you?"

Her hands fist in my shirt. Then, all at once, she lets go. Piper shoves against my chest, and I let her. I back away a few steps, giving her just enough room to pace back and forth like a caged animal.

"You can't..." She drifts off, not finishing the thought right away. "You can't find them. They're gone."

"Is that so?"

She nods, growing more smug. "Yeah. I put them in hiding weeks ago. I knew this would happen. I knew I couldn't trust you."

"Just as I knew I couldn't trust you." I hold up two fingers, a wide fake smile on my face. "Two tickets to Mexico in the middle of trying on dresses for our first date. It seemed a little early for you to be planning a romantic trip for the two of us."

I watch her, letting the meaning settle like a fine mist. Horror creeps across her face. "You're… you're lying."

"No," I say. "I deal in the truth, no matter how ugly. And the truth is, you have until my plane lands in Mexico to tell me where Benjamin is. If you fail, I'll find Ashley and your grandmother. Once I do, they are dead."

I turn for the door, but Piper claws at the back of my shirt. "No. Wait. No, I—Noelle! Noelle is working with the Albanians. She is the one who—"

"Throwing one friend under the bus to save another? Yet you say I'm the one who can't be trusted."

"It's the truth!" she says through gritted teeth. "I was lying before, but now—"

I wave a lazy hand in the air. "You were lying before, but I should trust you now. How convenient. Maybe I should start writing these down so I can keep up with all of your lies, Piper."

"I'm serious!" She comes close to shrieking her words in my face. Her hands move to grip my arms, and the touch almost makes me hesitate.

Almost. But it's not enough to erase the facts: my son was kidnapped and she's the reason why.

I shake her off of me and she crumples to the floor. She's a mess. A shuddering, sobbing mess. Seeing her on her knees like this fills me with conflicting emotions.

"If you really wanted to save them, you'd tell me where Benjamin is."

"I can't! I don't know!" Her voice crackles with something that sounds like heartbreak.

Some deep, dark, insane part of me wants to believe her. It's the part of me that keeps growing despite every attempt to kill it. I want all of this to be some big misunderstanding. I want Benjamin to be safe in his crib, in my home. In *our* home.

I want Piper to think I'm a great father.

But she doesn't. She thinks I'm so ill-equipped to handle raising a baby that she is willing to put other people's lives in danger just to keep Benjamin away from me.

That fact would sting if it didn't make me so fucking angry.

"Until the plane lands in Mexico," I remind her. "If you don't reveal where he is by then, your friend and grandmother are dead."

Her face cracks wide with despair. If I stayed, she'd probably beg. Maybe she'd make a deal.

But the time for that is over. Now, it's time to catch a plane.

7

PIPER

Ashley and Gram are half a continent away from me. That was the entire point of sending them to the Yucatan Peninsula. It's what I wanted. What I *thought* I wanted, at least.

Now, it's the worst thing in the world.

How can I protect them when they are half a continent away?

The idea hits me all at once. One second, I'm crumpled on the hospital floor, my face pressed to tiles sticky with mop water. The next, I'm on my feet with my phone to my ear.

"Does my phone plan include international calls?" Ashley asks in lieu of a greeting. The line is a little fuzzy, but otherwise, it sounds like she's in her fifth floor walk-up ten minutes from my office. "Because if not, you're gonna have to hang up and text me."

"I'll cover the charge. Ashley, listen—"

"Oh, hold on," she says. There's a staticky sound like she's covering the receiver. Then I hear distant voices, followed by Ashley laughing long and loud. When she comes back, laughter is still fresh in her voice. "Sorry about that. Mateo was picking up the kids."

Kids?

"Who's Mateo?" *And what kids?*

"Our neighbor," she sing-songs. I can tell immediately she likes him. "His wife is out of the picture and he needs help watching his kids occasionally. They're seven and five."

"You hate kids."

"I hate *most* kids," she corrects. "But Mateo's kids are great. He's great."

Shit. All at once, it hits me that I'm about to drop a huge, steaming pile of my drama on top of Ashley. After I already sent her to a new country with nothing but a few scant explanations and a wad of pesos.

"You two have friends there already?" I ask.

She hums in the affirmative. "Gram is good friends with the couple who run the bed and breakfast. They've been introducing us to the neighbors. I guess most people don't stay as long as we have. It's a nice little community. I have a bread guy now. He makes this amazing sweet bread over an open flame. It's so amazing with a cup of coffee. You'll have to visit and try some."

Just like that, I have a plan.

Timofey said that when he landed in Mexico, he'd *find* Ashley and Gram. That means he doesn't know where they are yet. *That* means I still have time to head him off at the pass. He won't listen to me. Not now, not here. But maybe, if I can surprise him in Mexico, he'll have cooled off long enough to listen to me.

I'll tell him about Noelle and the Albanians and Benjamin. The thought of that sweet little baby being in danger still makes my chest ache and my eyes sting with tears.

This is for him, too.

I can save Benjamin, Ashley, and Gram without having to worry them. Telling them Noelle is a fraud in bed with an organized crime syndicate and Timofey is...well, a leader of an organized crime syndicate... who wants to kill them wouldn't change anything right now. It certainly won't help things no matter which direction this all goes. They can't hide from him, and Timofey can't hide who he is from them for much longer..

Especially if he's literally holding guns to their heads.

The image curdles my stomach, and I blow out a breath. I'm the only one who can stop this.

"Ashley, I-I'm glad things are going well. I have to go, okay?"

"But wait. You just called. What's going on with—"

I hang up before she can ask the question. Despite what Timofey thinks, lying doesn't come easily to me.

I leave the hospital and take a taxi straight to the airport. The driver is a young guy with shaggy blond hair and a wispy goatee. "Are ya picking someone up?"

I blink away from the blur of buildings and people passing by the window. His brown eyes are framed in the rearview mirror. "What?"

"Are you picking someone up?" he repeats. "If you are, I can wait and drive you both wherever you're going."

I'm not sure if he's too young to realize that would be a terrible business decision for him or if he's trying to hit on me. I don't need to check my reflection to know I look haggard. My guess is it's the former.

It also occurs to me: I don't have any luggage. I forgot that detail in my rush to save lives.

"Thanks, but I'm actually catching a flight."

"You don't have any bags, though." He echoes my thoughts out loud, which is more irritating than it should be.

I cross my arms over my chest, feeling suddenly vulnerable. "It's a short trip."

"Real short if you're not even taking underwear." He laughs nervously, and I get the sense he's as uncomfortable with mentioning my underwear as I am. I decide not to hold it against him.

"Yeah. I'll buy what I need when I'm there."

Thank God I set some cash aside from each of my paychecks from Timofey. The irony isn't lost on me that even when he's trying to ruin my life and kill my loved ones, he's still—in his own sick and twisted and manipulative way—taking care of me.

He hums, nodding his head to a nonexistent beat for a while. Then he sits tall and makes eye contact in the mirror again. "Make sure you hold onto your cash and passport."

"I plan on it." I'm not sure anyone purposely loses their money and only means of returning home. Ever since I bought the tickets for Gram and Ashley, I moved my passport to my wallet. I wanted to be able to leave at a moment's notice.

Today, I'm grateful for Past Me's forward planning.

"Good," the driver mumbles. "My cousin went to Mexico last summer and lost everything. It was a whole mess. He ended up sleeping on a beach for a few nights after he ran out of money. He came home all bitten up by bugs and stuff. Got an infection."

"Oh." I smile. "Yeah. Thanks."

"You're just too pretty to sleep on a beach. Or get an infection." His eyes widen, and he snorts. "I mean—I just... Be careful."

When I first climbed into the cab, I had my suspicions about the driver. He was parked directly in front of the hospital, almost as if he was waiting for someone. And when I stepped up to the curb, *he* waved *me* down.

Did Timofey plant him here? Did he suspect my next move and make sure he was in control of the variables? Timofey is a powerful man, but that seemed like an overreach even for him.

Now, I'm positive this man is not a plant. If he was working for Timofey, he'd know better than to flirt with me.

Suddenly, I'm much more sympathetic to his nerves.

I chuckle. "Thank you. I will be. I'm meeting some family there. They'll take care of me."

He nods, relieved. I settle back into the uncomfortable leather seat. By the time we make it to the airport, I'm at ease.

As at ease as I can be, given I'm rushing to another country to stop my fake boyfriend/ex-boss from hurting or killing my best friend and grandmother.

The driver hops out of the cab and opens the back door for me when we arrive at the airport. "I'd help you with your bags, but you don't have any."

"Is that how you earn your tips?" I tease.

"For you, I'd do it for free." Emboldened by my joking, he winks.

Definitely not a soldier for Timofey.

"Safe travels!" He waves from the driver's side of his cab, and I wave back as I step through the sliding doors into the airport.

I head towards the ticket counter, oddly optimistic after an encounter with a random, kind human. Maybe that's why, when a security agent approaches me seconds after the clerk hands me my ticket, I don't clock it.

"Ma'am, we are doing heightened security checks for this flight," the man in the black TSA uniform says. "I need you to come with me."

8

PIPER

The redhead behind the ticket counter is already helping the next customer, but the fact that she doesn't seem bothered by a TSA agent this far from security makes me feel better.

"I don't have any luggage."

"That's fine." He herds me towards a frosted glass door. I can see the silhouettes of more people waiting in the small room. "This will only take a second."

I try to make out the human shapes behind the glass, but there are no discernible features. They are only dark shadows. "I thought security happened...well, at Security." I laugh nervously. "I haven't been on a plane in a long time, though."

"Some passengers get chosen for an additional screening. It's randomized."

"This is what I get for buying a last-minute ticket," I joke. Though the good humor I had in the cab is fading quickly.

Do I need to tell this man I'm pregnant? I know I shouldn't get X-rayed, but the machines at security are metal detectors. Is that the same thing?

I'm debating asking when the glass door opens. Another man in a black uniform is standing just inside. He greets me with a straight face and a nod.

"Hello." My voice sounds small. It feels even smaller when I turn and see two more TSA agents standing like sentries on either side of a table. They are so large that it makes the already tiny room feel even smaller.

"Take a seat," my escort says.

I squeeze between the two muscled agents and drop down into a rolling chair. The wheels squeak and I smile in apology.

No one returns the gesture.

The agent who brought me here sits down across from me and folds his hands in front of him. "Where are you headed, Miss Quinn?"

I hold up my ticket. "Mexico."

"Mexico is a big place. Where, specifically, are you headed?"

I glance at the three other men in the room. Having four sets of eyes on me feels like overkill, but I try to be kind.

They're just doing their jobs.

"I'm flying into Mérida."

He nods tersely. "And where are you going from there?"

The answer is on the tip of my tongue when the first alarm bell sounds in my brain.

"You're with TSA, not Border Patrol, right?" I smile again, but it's thin this time. Like tea so weak you can see straight to the bottom of the cup. I'm sure they can sense my unease now.

"Just answer the question," the man in the corner barks. He crosses his arms and shifts in front of the door. I can't shake the feeling that he's sending me a subliminal message, blocking my way out. *Answer, or you aren't getting out of here.*

I want to ignore the not-so-subtle threat, but not being able to see the door makes the room feel even smaller. Panic clamps around my chest, and I have to work hard to inhale. "I'm going to meet up with some friends."

"Where?"

"I'm not sure yet." It's getting harder to speak between my stiff lungs and clenched teeth.

Alarm bells are ringing. Red flags are waving.

Something isn't right.

"You are going to another country without an idea of what you're doing when you get there?" He arches a skeptical brow.

"I guess I'm living on the edge."

My answer doesn't exactly endear me to these men. I'm pretty sure nothing I say will endear me to them. In fact, I'm pretty sure they are very specifically working against me.

I just don't understand why.

"Now is not the time to be cute." My interrogator scowls. "Who are you going to see when you arrive in Mérida?"

"I told you. Friends."

"Do these friends have names?"

My heart is racing and my hands tremble. It's getting hard to tell if I'm feeling this way because of claustrophobia or because something in this situation is seriously wrong.

Maybe I'm overreacting. Maybe this is normal. Even as the thoughts enter my mind, though, I dismiss them.

No. This isn't normal.

"I don't understand why you need their names," I tell him as evenly as I can. "They aren't getting on a plane. I am. My name is—"

"Piper Quinn." The man by the door winks when I look up at him, which is a jarring change of pace from how this has gone so far. "We know your name, sweetheart."

"Okay." I grasp the arms of my chair and brace to stand. "I'm done answering questions. I want to speak to your manager. Or supervisor. Or...whoever."

Nice. Very smooth. Very authoritative.

Still, I hold my head up high, meeting each of their eyes as I stand. "This is not appropriate or warranted. I want to speak to someone else."

The first "agent" hooks his arm around the back of his chair. He's grinning at his cohorts. "Did you hear that, boys? She wants to talk to the boss."

"I'll bet she does."

"She'd like that, wouldn't she?"

I don't understand the joke. I definitely don't appreciate it. But I'm losing steam as the old, familiar fear starts to squeeze my throat closed.

Their voices are coming from every direction now. The room is blurring before my eyes, and I inhale and exhale deeply, trying to clear my vision. Panic is taking over. In a second, my vision will narrow to pinpricks. I'll be bent over, gasping for breath. I won't stand a chance against whatever these agents—if they even work for the TSA—have planned.

"I'll call the—the p-police." I pull my phone out of my back pocket.

As soon as the screen flickers on, it's gone. Whisked out of my hand before I can blink.

The man across from me is holding it between his thumb and forefinger like it's a carrot he's dangling in front of me. "You aren't calling anyone. We're the only people you're gonna talk to."

"Now," the man in front of the door barks, "tell us where the fuck you are going, and who you're meeting. Names. Now."

Air hisses in and out of my tight lungs. I count the breaths. *In, two, three, four. Out, two, three, four.* It doesn't help, but deep breathing keeps me from talking. The less I talk, the better. It won't take much more of this before I'll say almost anything to get out.

The walls of the room seem to be pressing in from every direction. The deep male voices blend together into a single cigarette-and-coffee-stained rasp. I can't hear any one of them distinctly.

"Let me out," I whisper. "Please."

I can't tell what they're saying, but I know they're taunting me.

Why are you doing this? I'm not sure if I say the words out loud or not. *Maybe I should tell them. I'm going to see Ashley and Gram. They're in a bed and breakfast. They're in danger. But I'm in danger, too. I'm going to suffocate in here.*

Darkness is creeping into the edges of my vision, and I'm going to break. I'll say whatever I need to say to get out of here.

But before I can open my mouth, there's a loud knock at the door.

There's some murmuring amongst the men. The one by the door cracks it open. I see a sliver of a leg. Hear a muffled voice.

Then the men leave.

As each man exits the room, I feel the oxygen in the space increase. My head clears. My vision returns. My heart is still racing, but I'm better. I'm safe.

I'm okay.

Then: "I'm disappointed in you, Piper."

I hear his voice before I see him. All at once, the panic returns.

I'm not safe. I'm not sure I'll ever be safe again. Not so long as he's after me.

My vision narrows on the doorway just as Timofey steps into the threshold, a cruel smile on his beautiful face.

9

TIMOFEY

"She's losing it."

I almost detect a bit of sympathy in Akim's voice. I'm not wholly surprised. He has said numerous times he would never slaughter his own meat.

"We had chickens when I was a kid. I like them. So chickens are off-limits," he told me once. "And cows are too big. Those guns that shoot bolts into their heads? Hard pass. Maybe I could kill a bird, but…. No. Definitely not."

It's funny, considering how much death he has experienced. Still, if given the choice, Akim avoids the slaughter at all costs.

I've been around long enough to know that, sometimes, you don't have a choice.

"Everything will end the moment she gives me the information I need," I tell him.

Piper is fuzzy and pixelated when seen through the feed of the shitty security camera in the interrogation room. But I can't take my eyes off of her.

Her white teeth shine when she smiles, but it's going to take more than a pretty face to sway these TSA agents. I'm paying each of them more than they could make in a year to interrogate her.

Akim shifts behind me, mirroring the agent who just shifted in front of the door. "Maybe she really doesn't know. She loves Ashley and her grandma. She wouldn't risk their lives."

"You don't know that. People are capable of terrible things."

Like me, I think. *Here I am, emotionally and psychologically tormenting a woman less than an hour after she got out of the hospital. A hospital I put her in. After I fucked her.*

"Does Piper strike you as the kind of person who does terrible things?"

I finally look away from the screen, snapping around to stare up at my friend. "You're the one who wanted to come with me. Can you fucking handle yourself or not?"

He frowns. "Your soldiers make enough jokes about me being too soft. I don't need it from you, too."

"Then be quiet and let me do what I need to do."

I turn back to the screen, and things are dissolving quickly. Piper is bent over and bracing against her chair. She isn't answering questions anymore. Her mouth opens with a long exhale before she sucks in a new breath, filling her chest with air that I can tell even from here isn't enough to calm her stampeding heart.

"I'm not bothered by your methods," Akim says. "I just don't think they're necessary."

"What do you know about any of this?"

He edges into my peripheral vision, but I don't look away from the screen. "I know *you*, Timofey. I know you're punishing Piper because you care about her. You're punishing yourself because you care, too."

"I'm punishing her because she kidnapped Benjamin." I don't bother entertaining the second point.

"If that was true, she'd be dead already."

He's right. *Why isn't she dead already?* I try to drum up some feasible answer, but there isn't one. Not one I like, anyway. Definitely none I'll admit aloud.

"Let me out. Please."

Piper's voice crackles through the speakers and it's like she's whispering in my ear.

I'm on my feet before I know what I'm doing.

By the time I can consider it, it's too late to change course. I blow past Akim and wrench open the door. Then I take two steps, stopping just outside the next room over, and knock.

When the door opens, I tell the man on the other side of the room to leave. "All of you. Now."

They file out. The man at the desk is last. He leans in as he passes. "The bitch is ripe now. She'll tell you whatever you want to know."

I paid this man to break Piper, but now, I want to knock his front teeth in. I clench my fist and step into the room, which is identical to the one I just left. Except this one smells like vanilla.

"I'm disappointed in you, Piper."

Lies. I'm actually somewhat impressed. I expected her to break by now, but she surprised me.

She doesn't need to know that.

Her green eyes settle on mine, but they're like full moons hanging in the sky. Close enough to touch, but hundreds of thousands of miles away.

Her hands are flat on the table, fingers trembling. She bites her lower lip and then releases it in a shaky exhale.

In and out. In and out.

"Piper." I say her name once with something akin to tenderness before I remember Akim is in the other room, watching this unfold. I stomp around the table and yank her to her feet. She wavers, and I crush my hands around her thin arms. "Relax. Now."

She looks up at me, dark lashes flicking with surprise. Her cheeks are flushed with the heat of her panic. Her lips are parted as her gasps settle—somewhat—into steadier, whimpering pants.

Will this woman ever not have a vise grip on my cock? I should want to kill her, but all I can think about is spreading her out over this table and devouring her from thigh to thigh.

"Calm down," I order. I repeat it in my head for my own benefit.

She narrows her eyes. It's a relief to see some of that familiar fire from her. "Gee, thanks. How helpful. I'm cured."

I release her arms and take half a step back. "I live to serve."

She snorts, but it comes out like a weak wheeze. "What are you doing here?"

"I told you I was coming to the airport. The question is, what are *you* doing here?" I wave it away as soon as I ask it. "Actually, I already know. But I'd like to hear it from you."

Her breathing grows more regular and less labored by the second. Maybe I really am the cure for her claustrophobia after all.

"I'm here to stop you from wasting my time."

"*Gee, thanks,*" I flip back to her.

She grimaces in frustration. "You're wasting your time here, Timofey. You won't find anything in Mexico."

"I'll find exactly what I mean to find in Mexico. Wherever you sent Ashley and your Gram, I'll find them."

She swallows audibly. "I know you will. I'm just saying it won't help. They can't tell you anything."

"I don't need them to tell me anything," I explain. "You're the one keeping secrets, Piper."

"You need to look into the Albanians. Find out who they are working with."

"You."

She fists her hands and pounds them on the table. It's stainless steel, so she quickly winces and grabs at her knuckles. "I'm not working with them. I would never do that to you."

"It's not like you don't have a history. The only reason you agreed to work for me is to get close to Benjamin and steal him away from me."

She sucks in her cheeks, staring at me but refusing to speak.

"Well?" I bark. "Defend yourself. Feed me some more sweet lies."

"I'm not lying!"

"Yes, you fucking are!" I slam my hands down on the table right where she did the same. I feel the same vibration through my bones Piper just experienced, but I hold the position and her gaze.

She jerks back, her rolling chair slamming against the wall.

With one shove, I slide the table forward so she's pinned between the edge of the table and the wall. "You think I'm such a shitty father that you are willing to work with a dangerous crime syndicate like the Albanians to get my child away from me."

"*You're* a dangerous crime syndicate!""

I choose to ignore that point. "I should have trusted my instinct with you," I continue. "You and all these other CPS agents out here, kidnapping kids. It's a habit for you now. You can't help yourself."

She struggles against the table. When she realizes it's hopeless, she glares at me. "When you aren't being a stubborn, pig-headed asshole, you can be a great dad. A great man, even."

I shouldn't care what she thinks of me, but the words wiggle in my ear. And my chest.

It's extremely fucking annoying.

"Maybe…maybe at first I thought that," she admits. "But you changed my mind, Timofey. All of the times that you took care of the people you loved, the times you sacrificed your own safety for Benjamin—for me. All of that changed my mind. Every minute you spend going after me instead of the people actually responsible for Benjamin's kidnapping, though? That's undoing all of that good."

"I don't give a fuck what you think of me," I tell her succinctly. "I care where my son is."

"If that is true, then you should care what I think," she snaps back. "Because I'm trying to help you. If you want to be the father I know you can be, you need my help."

I stare at her, searching her face for something I can't find: signs of deception.

All at once, I pull the table away.

Now freed, I can see Piper's arms are folded across her stomach protectively. She uncrosses them quickly and stands up. "So do you believe me?"

She walks around the table, and I grab her by the arm and haul her against my body.

"Fuck no." *Maybe yes.* But I need to keep my friends close and my enemies closer, and I'm still on the fence about where she ranks between the two. It's best to make sure she doesn't know she has valid points—or that I'm unable to *not* consider them.

"Then—" Her chest heaves against mine. I fight the urge to look down the front of her shirt. "Then what are you doing?"

I don't know.

There is no rulebook for this. No plan.

All I have is a lifetime of experience and my instincts. And right now, my instinct is to keep Piper as close as humanly possible.

"Move." I push her towards the door. "We have a plane to catch."

10

PIPER

I wake up to a muffled voice and darkness.

Then light slices through my eyelids like a knife. I wince, covering my eyes with my arm.

"Rise and shine, princess," Timofey croons in my ear. "We're about to land."

I blink slowly and glance over to him. He's sitting in the seat next to me. *Of course he is.* His clothes seem completely unruffled after our ten hours of travel, but his eyes are bloodshot.

I don't even want to guess what I look like.

The pilot's voice crackles over the intercom, but my high school Spanish is limited to *"Donde está el baño?"*, and even that is shaky some days. Point is, I have no idea what he's saying.

"I fell asleep." Good Lord, my mouth feels like it's been stuffed with cotton balls.

"Lying really takes the energy right out of you." It almost sounds like he's joking, but I know better. I think.

I take in his appearance again. His clothes are pressed and flawless, but the rest of him isn't. The bags under his eyes are heavy enough to classify as carry-ons, and I don't think the redness is from lack of sleep. When I speak, my words slur because my mouth is dry as hell. But when *he* speaks, his words melt on the warm breeze of some first-class tequila. And he's slouching. I don't think I've ever seen this mountain of a man slouch.

"Are you drunk?" I blurt in shock.

A flight attendant clears her throat and hands me a covered plate. "Pancakes and orange juice, ma'am."

Pancakes have always been my favorite breakfast food. Right now, the sight of them makes me want to vomit. I take the plate anyway because I'm not rude. "Thank you."

Timofey waves her off and turns his bleary glare to the window.

As soon as she's gone, I lean in. "Are you drunk?" This time, I whisper the question.

He snorts. "Go ahead and ask the attendant for a pen. You can make note of it in your CPS report."

I bite my tongue and exhale my frustration. If the wooziness of his enunciation is any sign, he must have started drinking the moment the plane took off. Right after I fell asleep.

I thought maybe I'd be able to surprise Timofey in Mexico and tell him the truth. Now, I'm not sure what I'm going to do. A drunk Timofey is even less likely to listen to me than a sober one.

"I'm not worried about the stupid report, Timofey."

I'm worried about you.

But those words stay buried deep down inside.

If I wasn't being held against my will in a foreign country, I'd be gushing over the luxurious amenities in our hotel room.

I don't know why I'm surprised; Timofey doesn't exactly lead a low-key lifestyle. Still, the full bar we're actually allowed to drink from, the huge private balcony with a view of the city, and an equally huge jacuzzi tub make this the nicest hotel room I've ever been in. Never mind the beautifully patterned mosaic tiling beneath my feet or the lush foliage wrapped around the arched columns that separate the living room from a dining area.

"There's a fireplace," I gasp. "We're in Mexico. Who needs a fireplace in Mexico?"

Timofey has been quiet since we left the airport. He tossed back a bottle of water in the car and another from the lobby downstairs before we came up to our room. I get the sense he's trying to sober up.

"Is there anything else I can get for you, Mr. Viktorov?" A young man with a clean-shaven face and a burgundy uniform stands in the doorway to the bedroom, his hands tucked behind his back.

"Extra pillows," Timofey orders. "And towels."

"They've already been placed in the linen closet in the hallway. I'll leave a note for the maids to replenish the stash after they clean."

"Take the room off the cleaning schedule. I'll request it when necessary."

"Of course, sir." The man nods. "Anything else?"

Timofey doesn't look at me, but I feel his attention shift in my direction nonetheless. "Send up some food first thing in the morning. Bagels, cream cheese, and fruit."

The man nods again, and Timofey slides a wad of money in his hand.

Well, he *won't be any help to me,* I think. *I should have factored in buying off people for information and loyalty into my budget.*

When it comes to forging allies, my sob story isn't as strong a currency as the cold hard cash in Timofey's wallet. He paid off the TSA, for crying out loud. I'm sure the going rate for a bellboy is a lot lower. So if I can't even afford *that,* I'm in for a world of hurt.

Then the door closes, and we're alone, and the price of buying a bellboy's loyalty is suddenly the least of my concerns.

The air crackles with a tension I don't know how to dissipate. I decide not to try.

"I assume we'd rather not see each other." I gesture to the living room behind me. "I can take the couch."

"That won't be necessary."

I look at the only other option: the master suite. It's visible through the double doors straight ahead. There's a canopy bed draped in gauzy, almost sensual fabric, and of course it has another private balcony.

"You're going to give me the master?" It's a stupid question, I know. That room was built and decorated for one particular purpose. I just don't see Timofey utilizing that purpose while he's still wanting to throttle me and murder my loved ones.

"I'm not giving you anything. You've taken more than enough," he snarls. "We're sharing."

Then again, I could be wrong.

He turns to me slowly. His dark hair glistens in the silver moonlight pouring through the window. It still looks like he could use a nap and a pot of coffee, but even on the wrong side of a bottle of tequila, Timofey is undeniably handsome.

It's what makes him deadly.

I can't help but be drawn in.

"What on earth makes you think I want to sleep anywhere near you?"

"Believe it or not, Piper, this isn't about what you want."

I sneer at him. "How could I forget? Everything in life is about what *you* want."

He rolls his eyes and spins towards the mini bar. Or, in this case, the not-so-mini bar. There are three shelves of alcohol and a pyramid of tumblers ready to be filled. "If my life was all about what I want, things would look a lot different. For instance, you'd be naked in that bed."

My skin prickles with heat and awareness. I start to cross my arms over my stomach and then shift them higher, covering my chest. "That's all you think I'm good for? Sex?"

"You were there, too. You tell me."

"Fuck. You." I chew on each word.

"Is that an invitation?" I flip him the bird, and he chuckles humorlessly. "You'd be naked because you'd be the woman I wanted you to be. A woman I could trust. But since that isn't possible, you're lucky you're still alive."

I wish you were dead. I can still hear the tortured way he spoke those words in the closet. It was a confession as much as a threat. I thought Timofey always got what he wanted, but maybe the fact I'm still breathing is proof that he doesn't.

"If I'm not the woman you want, it's only because you're impossibly far from the kind of man I want," I hiss. "Because you're too stubborn and blockheaded and selfish to accept the truth when it's not what you want to hear. My words don't matter to you. I certainly don't matter to you. Fuck if you matter to me."

Timofey is reaching for a liquor bottle when his hand freezes in the air. He turns to me with fire in his icy blue eyes. "There you go lying again."

"I'm not lying!"

Maybe I am, though. Just a little. Maybe.

He shakes his head. "You are. Because we were both in that closet."

He keeps moving closer, edging me to the back of the couch, until there is nowhere for me to escape. This room is large, but he's standing between me and the front door. So I try to pivot away from that corner, but he's too distracting and my footing is all wrong and it's all I can do to not stumble back against the wall.

"That wasn't desire or...or anything good. What happened back there was a mistake."

"A mistake that you wanted," he clarifies. "Admit it, Piper. For once, tell the fucking truth."

I meet his glare with my own because I've got no other maneuver out of this. "You're the one lying. You say you want me dead, but *you* came onto *me* in that closet. Then you took me to the hospital. Why not just leave me to die?"

He's only a few steps away now. He's huge in front of me, all broad shoulders and corded muscles. But he's never felt more out of reach.

"I do wish you were dead," he whispers with barely restrained rage as my back hits the wall. He closes the distance, caging me in with his arms. "Because if you were dead, maybe the ache of wanting you would go away."

I inhale, and it's the warm chocolate skin of his breath, mixed with alcohol, laced with his words. If he hadn't drank so much on the plane, he wouldn't be saying this.

I wish he wasn't.

But as he leans closer, pressing his nose to my neck, I realize something: *I don't want him to stop.*

"Because what I want goes against my best interests," he continues in a growl. "*Who* I want threatens everything I hold dear: my Bratva, my son, and my loyalty. So yes, I wish you were dead, Piper. Because wanting you is killing me."

11

PIPER

I wish you were dead. Because wanting you is killing me.

Those last words are whispered against my shoulder. His lips brush against my collarbone, and I'm no longer breathing.

I'm perfectly still, frozen in place. Afraid to move and draw too much attention to this moment.

Timofey grips my waist and slides his hands down to my hips. He cups my ass for a second, drawing me against him so I feel the hard length between his legs.

Then, all at once, he lets me go.

My heart is thundering in my chest as Timofey retreats backward two steps and spins around. He holds something over his shoulder. It takes me a second to realize what it is.

"Hey!" I pat my back pocket and glare at him when I feel it's empty. "You stole my phone!"

"Maybe I wouldn't have been able to if you'd been paying more attention. Then again, you seemed a little distracted."

My cheeks flush with embarrassment. I was so preoccupied with his lips on my neck and his hands on my ass that I didn't even feel my phone slide free. "Give that back."

He shakes his head. "Can't have you alerting Gram and Ashley to my plans. Maybe I should make sure you haven't already."

"You may be a thief, but I doubt you're a hacker."

But as the words leave my mouth, Timofey presses his thumb to my phone and then shows me my home screen. My mouth falls open.

"Pavel had the tech guys give me access when you were living with me. Just in case."

"And you say *I* can't be trusted? Apparently, while I thought we were working together and getting along, you were setting up backdoor ways to spy on me. Who is dishonest now?"

Timofey pretends to think about it for a second. Then he arrives at his sarcastic conclusion: "Still you, darling."

He taps on my phone and scrolls around. His eyebrows lift when he finds what he wants. "There we are. Your text thread with Ashley."

Whatever Timofey is looking for, he won't find it in my conversation with her. That doesn't mean he won't find a lot of other things out, though.

Without thinking about it, I lunge across the room and make a mad grab for my phone.

Timofey shifts so I collide with his shoulder. He holds my phone above his head, a foot out of my reach, and scrolls through the thread.

He takes up a terrible imitation of Ashley's voice. *"'Noelle is crazy. I say, if you can get with someone as hot as Timofey, you ride that train as long as you can. And by 'train' I mean—'"* Timofey glances down at me. "Does that eggplant emoji mean what I think it means?"

I swipe wildly for the phone. "Give it here!"

"Hm. I guess it does." He laughs. "You took her advice to heart. Should I tell her how we fucked in Noelle's closet? Ashley is a gossip. She'd love that."

"You're a disgusting excuse for a—"

"That's what you said to Ashley, too. *'You're gross, Ash. I work for Timofey. It's not about sex.'* Once a liar, always a liar."

"I'm not a liar!"

He ignores me and reads Ashley's response. *"'With a Greek god impersonator like that, it's always about sex. How can you look at those biceps and thick thighs and think of anything else? It's a shame he has a kid; otherwise, I'd try to get with him.'"*

Timofey looks down at me again. "You should've told Ashley you planned to make me kidless as soon as you could."

"I didn't take Benjamin." The words wheeze out of me as I try and fail to drag Timofey's arms back down to where I can reach my phone.

"'What does him having a kid matter? Benjamin is adorable,' you wrote back." Timofey scrolls through the rest of the conversation. "Ashley says she never wanted to be a mom, and she would be jealous of all the time I spent with the kid. Quality human you chose as your friend, Piper. Jealous of a baby. She's a gem."

Now, I fight a little less hard. Maybe...maybe these texts will get through to Timofey in a way my words can't. Maybe they'll make a difference.

He keeps reading, shifting to my response—and an even worse impression of me. "*Timofey might be the most beautiful man I've ever met, but the most attractive thing about him is the way he treats Benjamin. That baby boy will grow up knowing he is loved. That's almost all a kid can ask for.*"

His voice fades as he speaks until it's barely a whisper by the end.

I wish I knew what to say, but the words don't touch my tongue. Some part of me knows that if he won't believe the texts I never planned on him reading, there's nothing I can say to his face. It's a distinctly heavy weariness that settles in my chest as I watch him.

I'm no longer afraid of him—I'm just tired of fighting.

"I sent that message after the shooting at the rehearsal dinner," I whisper. "We were hiding out at the penthouse in the city, and I was watching you hold Benjamin up to the glass windows. You were pointing out the different buildings and showing him the cars on the streets below. It was... it was really sweet."

He stares silently at the phone for a few seconds. Then he pockets it. "You will take the big bed. I'll sleep on the couch."

"Timofey—"

"Don't try to leave," he continues, moving into the sitting room. "It won't work and all it will do is ruin our sleep."

Without another word, he drops onto the sofa and closes his eyes.

With nothing left to say, I walk into the master bedroom.

More alone than ever.

12

PIPER

Timofey is on top of me, his weight on his hands on either side of my head. I turn and press a kiss to the velvet skin of his wrist.

"Tell me a secret."

He settles his hips over mine. I feel the hard length of his erection. "If we're playing truth or dare, I'd rather take a dare."

I want to know everything about him. His thoughts, his body, his dreams. I want it all.

"I dare you to tell me a secret." *I flick my tongue over the bone of his wrist.* "Then fuck me until I forget it."

His blue eyes glimmer with mischief. In one move, he hooks his arm around my waist and rolls sideways. Suddenly, I'm on top of his bare chest, straddling his waist. Warm and naked.

He cups his hands over my breasts and thinks for a moment. His lips are pursed, his chin dimpled. He looks adorable.

"Secret. Secret... Hmm... Oh, I got one." *He smiles up at me.*

Then his smile twists into the most vicious sneer I've ever seen. "I wish you were dead."

The words douse me like ice water. I frown and pull back, but Timofey grabs my wrists. "Where are you going?"

"What are you—What did you just say?" The gauzy warmth of the room from a minute ago is fading. The light is sharp now, casting half of his face in shadow. That sneer grows worse.

"I wish you were dead." The words have a heavy weight of their own. Drenched in fear and unvoiced violence.

He grabs my hips and drags my aching core over his length. My mind is stuck on what he said, but my body is eager to forget everything so long as he keeps touching me like this. I can't swallow my moan.

"Now," he murmurs, "let me fuck you until you forget."

His hands and fingers are in all the right places all at once, and I can't seem to pull away like I know I should. I arch my back and roll into his touch until I'm dripping wet and quivering with need.

I should run.

I should come.

I should flee.

I should surrender.

Just as that sweet release starts to crest, a baby cries out.

I freeze. "Did you hear that?"

"Shut the fuck up, Piper," Timofey hisses. His teeth are sharpening to fangs with every passing second. "You can't save him in time. You can't save any of them."

More screams join in with Benjamin's cries. Ashley. Gram.

Then Timofey is gone.

And I'm falling.

I yank the comforter off of my face and inhale sharply. My heart is racing and I'm covered in sweat. The nightmare clings to me like an uncomfortable second skin.

I drag a hand down my face and sit up slowly. I don't want to risk the nausea if I move too fast. What I do want is a shower and a bagel.

"Maybe some therapy, too," I mutter.

My throat is raw as if I've been yelling. Maybe I was talking in my sleep. Or screaming, for all I know.

A blush warms over me as I realize all of the things Timofey could have overheard.

I carefully clutch the blankets against my chest and creep to the end of the bed. I lean to the furthest corner and peek through the open double doors to see if Timofey is still asleep on the couch.

But it's empty.

I frown and scramble off the bed, dragging the comforter with me. The living room is vacant. So is the bathroom. I even check the linen closet because...well, safe to say we have history with closets.

But no—he's not hiding in there, either.

"Timofey?" I finally call.

There is no response. I'm alone in the suite.

I fold my hands over my stomach and take a deep breath. I'm nauseous, but I'm not sure if it's the pregnancy hormones, the fact I haven't eaten anything yet, the nightmare, or maybe just the fact that Timofey dragged me to another country and then disappeared.

Isn't he worried I'll run away?

When I pass by the sitting room the second time, I see the note.

I lunge for it. The air from my movements sends it fluttering to the floor and it drifts under the couch. I curse and slide my hand under the plush furniture until I feel the paper. I crush it in my palm and carefully get back up with some help.

The note is written on nice hotel stationery. The paper is thick with burgundy embossed trim around the edges in the same shade as the bellboy's uniform. But all I can see is the sharp, angled writing in the center.

Have breakfast and relax this morning. You've earned everything coming your way.

—Timofey.

I don't even hesitate; I drop the paper to the floor and run to the bedroom. The same jeans and shirt I wore on the airplane are crumpled next to the bed, but they're all I have. I throw them on, splash water on my face, and rush out of the hotel. I don't remember to grab a room key or my wallet until I'm in the stairwell, but the door is locked and it would be too late to go back, anyway.

I have to get to Ashley and Gram.

The bellboy from yesterday is in the lobby. I ask him to call me a car.

"You want that charged to your room?" he asks.

I want to kiss him for suggesting the idea, because my genius plan was just to get out a block ahead of my stop and run from the driver without paying. "That would be great. Thanks."

If he notices my ragged appearance and breathlessness, he doesn't say anything.

Timofey is paying him well enough not to notice anything, I'm sure.

The bellboy flags down a driver and asks me where I'm going. I don't want to tell him. I don't want to give anything away that I don't have to. But I don't know exactly where I'm going, and I can't speak Spanish, so I need him to translate for the driver.

"It's called Los Sueños Bed and Breakfast."

He smiles. "I know it. It's very nice. Not as nice as staying here, but still lovely."

I search his smiling face for any sign that he is going to betray me. Will he send the address to Timofey? Is the driver even going to take me where I ask?

A web of conspiracies and possibilities play out in my mind, but I shove them aside. I don't have another option. Timofey got a head start on me this morning, and I don't have time to waste.

The bellboy speaks to the driver in Spanish and then opens the back door for me. "It's only a few minutes away. Have a nice day."

I slide into the backseat and try to keep my legs from bouncing with nerves.

Traffic is light this morning, and I look out for any black cars following us. Any suspicious men lingering on the sidewalks. Any sign of a tall, dark-haired devil on my trail.

But there is nothing. Absolutely nothing.

I'm not sure if I should be relieved or even more worried.

Then the car stops.

The bed and breakfast looks just like it did online. It's an orange hacienda-style house with wrought iron gates around the exterior and colorful umbrellas hanging over the courtyard. The morning sun is shining through the vibrant cloth canopy, casting the ground below in every shade of the rainbow.

"Thank you," I tell the driver, sliding out.

The older man gives me a wave and then drives away just as I close the door. I'm not sure how I'll get back to the hotel without him. Then again, maybe I don't want to get back to the hotel.

I look for a doorbell or some kind of intercom system next to the gate, but there is nothing. When I try the gate, it swings open without resistance.

"Zero out of five for security," I mutter.

I turn and close the gate behind me. But no sooner do I get it latched than an ear-piercing scream slices through the morning air.

13

PIPER

I'm ducking and clamping my hands over my ears, thinking, *Gunfire! Gunfire!* when familiar arms wrap around me and squeeze the air from my lungs.

"Bagpipes, what the hell are you doing here?" Ashley jumps up and down, both hugging and strangling me. "When did you get here? Why didn't you say anything on the phone? Are you here alone?"

Ashley has always hugged like an octopus. As soon as she's excited, it's like she has six extra arms and suction cups.

"Hi, Ash." I pat her back, trying to pry her away. "I'll tell you everything; you just need to—"

"Gram!" Ashley shouts over her shoulder, still squeezing me. "Look who is here!"

I guess I should be relieved Timofey didn't beat me here. I still have a leg up on him. But I have a feeling my head start is fading fast.

"Ashley, you need to listen to me for a second."

"I can't listen!" She squeezes me tight, swaying us both back and forth. "I'm too excited! How long has it been?"

"Only a few weeks."

"Only?!" She pulls me back long enough to frown down at me. "That's too much. I've missed you. Even though, I mean… Look around—I've been in an island paradise."

"This isn't an island."

She squeezes me tight again. "Whatever. You get what I'm saying. This place is great."

Her rush of excitement is fading, and I see my opening. I duck down and slide out of her hold. "Can you listen to me, though? I have important—"

But Ashley spins around mid-sentence and jogs towards the intricately carved wooden door of the bed and breakfast. "Gram!"

"Ashley!" I yell after her. "Would you—for God's sake, stop for a second. Listen to me!"

She waves a hand over her shoulder. "I will, but Gram needs to know you're here. She has missed you like crazy, girl. I've basically been her granddaughter while we've been here, but I'm no substitute for the real thing."

Underneath all of the urgency, I really am glad to see Ashley. I know Timofey isn't fond of her, and she definitely has her problems, but she has a good heart.

Maybe it took Noelle's betrayal for me to see exactly how good.

"It might actually be better if I talk to you without my grandma first."

Ashley can handle whatever is coming. I'm not sure the same can be said about Gram. I don't want to stress her out if it isn't necessary.

But suddenly, Gram is standing on the porch.

Her fists are planted on wide-set hips, and she is beaming down at me with her mouth wide open. "You aren't doing a darn thing without me, Piper Quinn!"

For just a second, the panic ebbs. I didn't realize how much I've missed her until this very moment. Seeing her brings literal tears to my eyes.

I take the steps two at a time and throw my arms around her waist, doing a pretty good impression of Ashley when I first arrived.

"Are you okay?" I ask, pulling back a bit when she wobbles.

She hugs me tighter. "The harder you're squeezing, the better I am. What are you doing here?"

"She hasn't told me yet," Ashley chimes in.

"It's a long story."

"Well, we have all the time in the world." Gram kisses my cheek and grabs my arm. "Come inside. They have good coffee in the drawing room."

I want nothing more than to sink into this daydream for a minute. I want to sit at a table and drink coffee and talk to Ashley and Gram. I want to hear about their friends and what they've been doing. I want to make sure Gram has been taking her vitamins and doing her stretches. But...

"There isn't time." I'm speaking to myself as much as to them. "We have to go."

Gram frowns and glances at Ashley.

"Go where?" Ashley asks. "You just got here."

I take a deep breath. "I know. It's all—It's a mess. But you know why I sent you here in the first place."

"Not really." Gram shakes her head. "It was all a bit confusing. Some kind of trouble with you and Timofey?"

"But we're here on his dime, right?" Ashley asks. "He's paying for all of this?"

"What? No, he's not."

Her eyes go wide. "Are *you* paying for it?"

"Yes! I'm paying for—I'm the one who sent you here."

It all happened pretty fast—buying the tickets, getting Ashley and Gram on the flight, booking the bed and breakfast. I guess I didn't explain myself that well. But I assumed if they agreed to get out of the country that they understood what they were doing here.

"I thought you were coming with us," Gram says. "I thought we were going ahead and you were coming after."

"I had to stay behind to watch Timofey. To make sure..." *Nothing happened to Benjamin.*

Failure hits me square in the chest.

Benjamin is missing and it's all my fault.

Timofey is threatening my family and that's all the Albanians' fault. Maybe Noelle's, too. I don't know anymore.

Everything is a disaster, and I don't know how to fix it. I don't know how to fix any of it.

"How did everything get so messed up?" I whisper.

"Piper?" Gram asks. "Piper, honey?"

I feel her hand on my shoulder, but the world is already fading around me. I feel disconnected from my feet. The ground is slipping away, tilting dangerously.

The only reason I don't fall backwards down the stairs is because Ashley wraps an arm around my waist.

"I got you, girl," she says, lowering me to the steps. "Sit down. Deep breaths."

I try, but my lungs are tight. I drop down onto the stairs. The morning is already hot, but the adobe is cool under my legs. I grip the edge of the stairs for stability.

Someone is smoothing my hair down. Someone else is patting my back.

Gram and Ashley are on either side of me, propping me up like bookends. I close my eyes and lean into their strength.

After what could be an hour or mere minutes, Gram bundles my hair in her hand and drops it over my shoulder the way she used to when I was little. "Now, can you tell us what is going on?"

I open my mouth, not entirely sure what's going to come out. The last few weeks have been so complicated that I'm not sure where to begin.

But I don't have to.

Before I can utter a single word, the wrought iron gate squeaks open. I look up, and I'm glad I'm already sitting down. If I wasn't, I'd be face first on the concrete.

Timofey is standing in the courtyard like an avenging angel, his skin golden in the morning light. He's smiling, but his gaze is cutting.

"Well," he says, slamming the gate closed behind him with finality, "isn't this a sweet family reunion?"

14

PIPER

I lunge to my feet so suddenly that Ashley and Gram collapse in on each other. As they right themselves, I move down the steps, throwing myself as a barrier between Timofey and the only family I have left.

"What are you doing here?" I ask.

"You're both here?" Ashley balks. "That would've been nice to know, Pipe. What is happening? Is this some kind of wild west stand-off?"

Timofey pats his hip where I know he has a weapon concealed. "Am I supposed to say, 'This town ain't big enough for the both of us?'"

Ashley laughs a bit behind me, but it's only because she doesn't understand the very real threat behind the joke. She's right. I should have told them the moment I walked through the gates that Timofey was in the city. I should have told them they were in danger and forced them into a car.

"Timofey." I inject as much meaning into his name as I can.

He's looking down at me, a silhouette in the morning sun.

When I blink, I see him hovering over me in my dream. Smiling while telling me he wishes I was dead.

I hope that isn't true.

When I look into his eyes, I know it isn't. The eyes are the windows to the soul, right? And in the depths of Timofey's soul, I know there's a good man.

I just have to believe it isn't buried *too* deep.

"Can you talk to me?" I gesture to the far end of the courtyard. "Give me five minutes. Please?"

"We can all talk," Gram interjects. "Someone needs to explain to this old lady what is going on."

"And this young, hot lady!" Ashley waves her arm over her head obnoxiously.

Timofey fights an eye roll and then runs his tongue over his teeth. "Five minutes."

I look back to Ashley and Gram on the stairs. "Stay right here. We'll be back."

They start to argue, but I hurry after Timofey so I don't waste a single second. I have no doubt he is keeping time.

He comes to a stop under the umbrellas. Spots of red, yellow, and blue light dapple his shoulders and the ground at our feet. It's a remarkably cheerful place to have a conversation as serious as the one we're about to have.

"Don't hurt them." I stare at the broad expanse of his chest. It's easier than meeting his eyes. Because the longer I stare at his chest, the longer I can live with the denial that begging will do anything to soften Timofey's heart. "Please. They didn't do anything wrong. This is all my fault."

"So you admit it?"

I shake my head. "Not about Benjamin. I'm telling you the truth. I don't know where he is."

He takes a step towards me. He's close enough that his breath lifts my hair. "But you know who has him, Piper. Even if you don't know where he is, you know who has him."

I start to shake my head—to deny it—but I can't. Not fully.

Because I've never been good at lying.

"Five minutes," I say, finally looking into his eyes. "Give me five minutes to try and…to try and bring Benjamin home."

I expect to see vengeance itself. Instead, he looks tired. As tired as I feel.

"Five minutes is more than you deserve," he says at last. "But I'll give it to you."

He starts to walk away, but I grab his elbow. "Was it the bellboy?"

He arches a brow, confused.

"Did the bellboy tell you where to find me?" I elaborate. "Did you pay him off to keep tabs on me?"

"He didn't have to," he says. "I knew if I left you alone, you'd lead me right where I needed to go. You have no one but yourself to blame."

Of course. "What's new?" I mutter. "I always have myself to blame."

Timofey and I walk back to Gram and Ashley, who are watching us with curiosity. I want to stay here with them. Even though Timofey said I have five minutes, I can't help but feel like it's a trap. The moment I turn my back, he'll disappear with them.

But I don't have the luxury of time. I have to trust that he's a man of his word, even if he doesn't think I'm a woman of mine.

"Ash, can I borrow your phone?"

She frowns. "Who are you calling? I still don't know if my phone plan has international minutes."

"This is a little more important than paying by the minute, Ash. I'll fund the difference, I told you."

"Don't you have a phone?" she mumbles, pulling out her pink bedazzled phone and thrusting it into my hands.

I don't waste time explaining that my phone is probably tucked in Timofey's pocket right now since he stole it from me so I wouldn't be able to call and warn them. Instead, I thank her with a nod and head back to the corner of the courtyard under the umbrellas. It's as close to privacy as I'm going to get right now.

The number I need is second in Ashley's recents, just under mine. I tap the icon and wait.

Two rings later, Noelle's voice comes over the line. "Miss me already, bitch? We just talked last night."

"Noelle."

She goes quiet. I know she recognizes my voice the same way I recognize hers. There are too many years of late-night phone calls and video chats in our past. It's why the line on her end is nothing but dead air while Noelle figures out what she is going to do: hang up or wait to see what I want.

I'm banking on the second choice.

"Noelle," I say again, "you have to talk to me. Please. Help me make sense of this."

"Make sense of what?"

"You know what." Part of me still doesn't want to accuse her. I want it to all be a misunderstanding, a terrible dream I can wake up from. But the clock is ticking and Ashley and Gram need me to face the truth. "Noelle, where is Benjamin?"

"I don't know."

Hope unfurls inside of me. I hear it in her voice, in the very subtle way it cracks and wavers. *She knows something.*

"You don't know what?" I press.

She sighs. "I don't know where he is. I don't know where they took him…after I handed him off."

I stifle a groan. Her betrayal is a physical ache deep in my body. I want to double over and hurl, or curl into the fetal position and cry. Preferably both.

"You took him," I rasp. "You really… You did it. I didn't think it could have been you, but you actually did it."

"I didn't have a choice." Her voice is flat and emotionless. If she has regrets, I can't hear them. "I had to protect myself, Piper."

I've always known Noelle is different with Ashley than with me. Different people bring out different sides in you. It's only natural.

Noelle and I bake cookies and watch *60 Minutes* documentaries. Ashley and Noelle are a little... rougher around the edges. They curse and call each other names. When I head home after dinner, they usually hit up another club.

Now, I know Noelle has even more sides to her. Dark sides. Pieces of her personality that can lie and betray and kidnap a defenseless baby from his crib.

"We all have a choice. All of us. You chose wrong."

"I didn't get to 'choose wrong.' I didn't get a choice because *you* chose wrong," she snaps back. "You chose to get involved with Timofey fucking Viktorov. The only reason the Albanians came knocking on my door is because of you."

"And you are the reason the Albanians had something they could hold over your head as leverage. I didn't make you steal from your company."

"But I would have gotten away with it if it hadn't been for you," she hisses.

I feel like the Scooby gang at the end of an episode, watching the monster be unmasked. *I would've gotten away with it, too, if it hadn't been for you meddling kids.*

I shake my head. "How can someone I've known for so long be such a stranger? I don't even know who you are anymore."

"God, you're so dramatic." She lets out a weary sigh. "Well, this has been fun, Piper. But I've gotta run. These baby seals won't club themselves." Sarcasm is thick in her voice, but at this point, I wouldn't be surprised if she was swinging a bat at Sea World right now.

"Is he okay?" I ask, hoping she's still on the line. "Is... Is Benjamin okay, at least? Can you tell me if he's hurt?"

She's quiet for so long that I'm not sure she's going to answer. But just before the line goes dead, she whispers, "I don't know."

My breath catches. My heart is squeezing uncomfortably in my chest. Not only because a person I considered one of my best friends kidnapped a baby and handed him to criminals for her own selfish gain—but because that innocent, beautiful baby boy might be...

I can't even think it.

Tears well in my eyes, and I swipe them away. Crying won't help Benjamin.

The phone line clicks closed. Noelle—like our friendship—is gone.

I collect myself as much as I can and turn to head back to Ashley and Gram.

But Timofey is standing behind me. I don't have to wonder if he was close enough to hear my conversation. I can tell by the bone-shattering clench of his jaw that he was.

"Timofey, that wasn't what you—"

"Well?" he growls. "Share with the class. Is he okay?"

My heart is racing. I don't want to tell him the truth. *I don't know.* The words are so insufficient. They are heartbreaking and horrifying. I don't want to put him through that. Because I can see how much he cares about Benjamin. How much he *loves* Benjamin.

He moves towards me so quickly I jump. But I'm not fast enough.

He grabs my arm. "Well? What did your little sidekick say, Piper? Is my son still alive?"

"I don't have a sidekick. That was—"

He yanks Ashley's phone out of my hand. Noelle's name is still on the screen, the "Call Ended" message flashing at the top.

"Noelle," he spits. "I fucking knew it."

"No. Listen. I went to see Noelle, and she told me she was working for the Albanians. As soon as I heard, I—"

"I know what you did. You sent her to my fucking house and kidnapped my son."

"I didn't!" I clench my fists at my side, wishing more than anything that I could pound the truth into his thick head. "I would never do that. Ever."

He has a crushing hold on my bicep. My arm is tingling from lack of blood flow, but I stand tall and meet his eyes. "I tried to call you. As soon as I met with Noelle, I tried to call you so I could warn you. But you didn't fucking answer."

It's fleeting, but I see it: Timofey blinks as the new information clatters against the wall he has built.

"You remember that?" I press. "That day before Noelle came to your house, I called you." The fury starts to pour out and I don't want it to stop. It singes my words and I want him to feel the scalding heat. "I fucking called you to *warn you* and you *didn't. Fucking. Answer.*"

I can tell he knows what I'm talking about. And I know I should be relieved when I see horrified realization bloom across his face, or when I feel his grip start to ease.

But I'm not. I'm not relieved at all. What I am is tired. What I am is simply *done with his bullshit*. He holds just as much responsibility for this mess as I do, and now, he's finally seeing it.

"Kindly let go of my best friend." Ashley's voice cuts through the tense silence.

I look over Timofey's shoulder, and she is standing behind him with her arms folded.

I swallow back a groan. There has never been a worse time for her protective best friend routine.

"Oh, Timmy boy," Ashley says in the most condescending way she can. "Would you mind talking to me for a moment? In private?"

Slowly, finger by finger, Timofey releases my hand. Without another word, he turns and walks away.

15

TIMOFEY

She called me.

Piper called me the day Benjamin was kidnapped.

I can see it all so clearly: Benjamin in his fifth or sixth outfit of the day. A pile of dirty diapers exploding out of the diaper pail. My shirt covered in formula and spit-up. My hands were full, and I couldn't answer the phone when it rang.

But it *did* ring. She called.

Is she telling the truth?

The question tickles the back of my mind as Ashley marches confidently ahead of me. She walks past the porch where Piper's grandmother is sitting and leads me to a bench in the shaded corner of the courtyard. It's within sight of the porch, but well out of earshot.

She sits down in the center of the bench, arms spread wide, making it clear I'm not welcome to join her. "We need to talk."

"I'm not sure that's true," I tell her. "It's probably better for both of us if we never talk."

She shrugs. "You might be right. Every time we do, I want to stab you in the eyes for hurting my friend."

I raise my brows, and Ashley meets my surprise with a smile. "What? You didn't know I had it in me?"

"Actually, no. I didn't."

Until this very moment, I saw Ashley as a useless parasite in Piper's life. Someone who took and gave nothing in return.

Now... She hasn't entirely changed my mind, but maybe she isn't useless after all. She has Piper's back. Even now, part of me is still glad Piper has someone in her corner.

"Well, I do," Ashley snaps. She keeps her voice quiet, but it's laced with venom nonetheless. "I have a whole hell of a lot in me, Timofey Viktorov. And I'll unleash every batshit crazy ounce of it on you if you ever hurt my friend."

My mouth quirks up at the corner. She sounds so much like Emily.

"I'm very fucking serious about the stabbing. So no smirking. Take this seriously."

I ditch the half-smile and take Ashley in with new eyes. She's a lot more like my sister than I ever let myself see. Both are a bit of a mess. But loyal until the end.

In Emily's case, until the very end.

I begrudged Piper for taking care of Ashley, but isn't that what I did for Emily all those years? As much as I tried to convince myself that Emily had something to give back, she really didn't. Not monetarily, not in regard to the Bratva. But she was there, and she was family. That was enough.

Maybe Ashley is enough for Piper, too.

She snaps her fingers in front of my face. "Hello? Earth to gangster boy. Are you hearing me?"

Just so she doesn't get too comfortable, I snatch her hand out of the air and twist it back down to her side. "Snap your fingers again and see how long you keep them."

Her jaw sets. "Fine." She holds up her other hand in surrender until I release her wrist. "But count yourself lucky I'm not armed right now. That was a stabbable offense."

"Noted. And count yourself lucky that Piper sent you to Mexico when she did. Otherwise, you might not be alive to make your threats."

"What does that—?" She narrows her eyes, then laughs. "Funny. You're funny, Timofey. Be nice to my friend, and we might get along."

She thinks I'm kidding.

Before I have the chance to correct her assumption, Gram joins our huddle.

"Okay, Ash, it's my turn." She shoos Ashley back towards the porch. "Go talk to Piper. I need to have a chat with Timofey."

"I have a feeling this is going to be good. I've never heard you get upset, Gram. I want to hear." Ashley folds her arms with a conspiratorial grin.

Gram firmly shakes her head. "No. Just the two of us."

Ashley grumbles, but apparently, her rebellious streak ends with Gram. She trudges back to the porch and plops down next to Piper, who hasn't taken her eyes off of me once. I can feel that vibrant emerald stare on my back, warming me like the sun.

"Ashley already threatened to stab me," I muse, redirecting my attention to the old woman. "So let's hear it. Give me your worst."

Gram smiles. Her papery skin wrinkles around her eyes and mouth. Her neck sags. But she looks like Piper. They share the same round eyes and pert nose.

"Sit down." She lowers down onto the far side of the bench and pats the spot next to her.

I cross my arms. "I'll stand."

"And if I'd told you to stand, I'd bet you'd want to sit, wouldn't you?" She shakes her head. "Stubborn man. I'm not sure if I should bother telling you to take care of Piper after I'm gone or not. You're a mule at heart. You'll probably just be more resistant to the idea."

"After you're gone? Piper and I aren't going to be together long enough for that to matter. You'll be around for her longer than I will."

She looks up at me earnestly, brows furrowed. "Are you planning to be gone tomorrow?"

I try to make sense of what she's saying and can't. "Are you dying?"

"I might. I haven't decided." She smiles sadly. "This seems like a beautiful place to die, though, doesn't it? I've thought that ever since we arrived. If I have to go, might as well be in a place like this."

I frown. "Maybe I'll take that seat after all." I sink down onto the bench next to her. The wood groans under my weight, but it holds.

She turns and looks at me with a strange distance in her eyes. "I'm dropping a lot on you, but it's only because I know you can handle it. You're tough. And I don't mean strong or scary or whatever you probably think I mean." Gram inhales, and I hear it catch. Then she coughs—a wet, wrenching sound from deep in her lungs. She's out of breath when she finishes. "You know how to lose people."

I see my mother. Emily. Now, Benjamin.

But it hasn't made me tough. It's made me hollow. I've never felt weaker in all my life.

"Losing people doesn't make you tough," I murmur.

"It doesn't make you tough, but it reveals just how strong you actually are," she says. "You have to know how to pick up and move on after loss. It's something I've never been very good at, I'm afraid. When my husband died, I kept the house we shared for too long. Long enough that I couldn't afford it and the bank took it. I kept boxes of his old shirts and photographs in a storage unit paid for by Piper for... God, it was years. I clung to every little piece of him even though it was hurting who was left. Even though it hurt Piper."

I remember the stack of bills on Piper's desk at her old apartment. The way her father smiled as I gave him fifty-thousand dollars to never see her again.

"No one in your granddaughter's life seems to mind hurting her," I grind out.

"People are selfish that way." She nods. "I am. Or... I was. Actually, I still am. But I don't want to be. I want to be like Piper. She's a good one."

"She's a doormat." *Unless she's betraying me, apparently. If she did even betray me...* I'm honestly not sure anymore.

"Because Piper doesn't know how to let go." She snaps her fingers like we've just solved it. The great puzzle of life. "She doesn't let go of the dead or the living. She holds onto all of it...and I need you to help her let go of me."

"You're not going anywhere."

She shrugs. "I might be. Or I might not. I've never claimed to be brave, so I might not do the right thing."

"What is the right thing?" I ask.

She inhales to respond and coughs again. In my peripherals, I see Piper sit up straight and look over, worried.

"I'm not well." She glances up at me for a second and then sags wearily. "I've been sick most of Piper's life. When she came to me, I'd been smoking and drinking and living hard for too long. That kind of lifestyle catches up with you."

"But you took her in."

"I had to. Her mom and dad couldn't do right by her. I couldn't, either. But I tried. In the end, Piper is the one who did right by me. She took out loans for me. She did everything she could to make sure I got the care I needed when my lungs went to shit and I needed a new hip. But I'm tired of being a burden to her. Honestly, I'm just tired."

Suddenly, it clicks. What Gram has been saying this entire time shifts into place. "You're going to kill yourself."

She stares straight ahead at the ceiling of umbrellas across the courtyard. "Life will be easier for her if I'm gone."

Somewhere deep in the past, decades gone, I hear my mother's voice. "You'll be better off without me here, Timofey," she'd said. "I can't help you. I can't raise you."

The number of times I comforted my mother when she should have been the one comforting me... I remember begging her to stay alive and then splashing in puddles outside an hour later. That shouldn't have been on me as a kid. I know that now.

But dealing with losing her was worse than the struggle to keep her alive.

No matter what it cost me, I would have rather she lived.

"Losing you won't make anything easier for Piper."

She shakes her head. "You don't know that."

"Actually, I do. You're the only family she has. If you left, she'd be heartbroken. She'd never recover."

Gram sighs. "I think she would. Because she isn't alone."

I look over, eyebrow arched.

"She has you." She nudges me with her elbow. It's a familiar gesture, but it feels right. I like this wry old woman. I understand why Piper is close with her.

Piper and Ashley are whispering on the stairs. It looks serious. I wonder if Piper is finally telling Ashley what my plans are. So far, it seems she has kept my threats secret. And strangely, I'm glad for that. If Piper had told them everything, they'd despise me. They'd be terrified. I'm glad they're not.

It's nice getting to know two of the most important people in Piper's life, even in this short amount of time.

It's helping me understand why she'd do anything to protect them.

"I see the way you look at her," Gram says with a smile. "You love her."

I quickly look away and stare down at the ground. "No. Don't do that."

"Do what? Tell you the truth?"

Is it the truth? Do I love Piper?

It's been hard to feel anything beyond the betrayal. I was blinded by rage in a way I've never felt before. Is that because I care about her?

Because I love her?

What if I'd answered Piper's call that night in Benjamin's nursery? How different would things be now?

I run a hand over my face to muffle the groan of frustration and regret. It's a pressure growing inside my chest that I do not want and definitely do not need. Ruthless tyrants can't afford guilt and regret over their actions. It shows an inability to make wise decisions. It shows weakness.

But the longer I hunt down Benjamin alone, the more I'm discovering all my weaknesses and terrible decisions.

Gram slaps me on the back surprisingly hard. "You don't have to admit that you love her. But I do need you to take care of her. Someone has to."

"You can. You're not going anywhere."

"Is that an order?" She lofts a brow.

"I can make it one if I have to." I came here to kill Gram and now, I'm trying to save her life. The irony is not lost on me. "Because I don't make promises I can't keep. I'm not going to tell you I can take care of Piper because…I don't know if I can."

Her breaths are short and quick. Gram is such a big personality that I guess I never noticed how bad her health really is.

"She'll be devastated when you leave," she says finally.

I look towards the steps, and Piper is looking at me. There's a question in her eyes. I wonder if it's the same question flashing in my mind.

What comes next?

Gram lets me off the hook and asks me to escort her back to the porch. "I'm tired," she says when we get back to the stairs. "I'm going to lie down for a while."

Ashley jumps up, hands waving. "No, wait! Wait. This is a special occasion. I was going to get the bubbly from the fridge."

"I'm not thirsty," Piper mumbles.

Ashley snorts. "I'm not suggesting it because I'm thirsty. It's because we're all together again—except for Noelle."

Piper goes stiff at the mention of Noelle's name.

Apparently, there's a lot she isn't telling Ashley about what's going on. Is it because she's working with Noelle? Or is it because, even after Noelle has done something horrible, Piper can't stop trying to protect her?

"We can celebrate with hugs. Or a picture!" Piper suggests. "We'll take a picture to remember the moment."

Ashley groans. "That's miserable. I won't drink any, if that's what you're worried about. If anything, you'll be helping me. The bottle was in the mini fridge in our room when we arrived. You can take it off my hands."

I expect Piper to jump at the opportunity to help keep her friend sober. Instead, her hands flutter nervously over her stomach again. "I trust you, Ash. I really don't want any. Maybe give it to someone else in the bed and breakfast. Or save it for the next guests."

I remember back to the flight yesterday. We'd just boarded and the attendant offered us drinks. Piper refused a mimosa and asked for ginger ale instead. And last night at the mini bar in the room, she drank sparkling water.

When Piper sees me watching, she drops her hands to her side. Her movements are stiff and clumsy, like she wants to wrap her arms back around herself but can't. Or won't.

The realization dawns all at once—and punches me in the gut.

She passed out in the closet. She didn't touch any of the food on the flight. She's refusing alcohol.

I'm not sure how many secrets Piper is keeping from me, but I know one for sure: she's pregnant.

And the baby is mine.

16

PIPER

We're back in the hotel room. It's even more beautiful in the daytime. Gauzy curtains diffuse the light, filling the room with a warm glow. The place is almost beautiful enough to explain why I willingly came back here with Timofey.

"I'm going to meet a friend for lunch, but you can come with me," Ashley had said. She was clinging to my hand like she was afraid I'd disappear if she let go. "I'll introduce you. I'd love for you to see what my life has been like for the last couple weeks."

Gram had already gone up for a nap, and I was finding myself exhausted, too. Creating a human will do that to you, apparently.

I waved her away. "No, it's okay. I'll catch up with you later."

"Are you sure?"

I could feel Timofey standing behind me. I nodded. "I'm sure. Have fun."

But now that our hotel door is locked and he's sitting at one of the barstools, his legs crossed casually at the ankle, I'm not sure at all.

Timofey wraps his lips around the edge of his glass. His throat bobs with every drink. I never knew hydration could be so sexy.

He looks over at me, and I blush at having been caught staring. So I duck into the bathroom and grab the robe from behind the door. My clothes are in desperate need of washing, and since I can't be wrapped in the warm, strong arms I'd like, the embrace of a clean outfit will have to do.

"What did Gram say to you?" I ask through the open bathroom door. I can't see Timofey, but I know he can hear me.

"Huh?"

"Gram," I repeat, leaning through the doorway. Timofey's blue eyes trail down to my bare shoulders. I barely resist showing him the rest of me just to feel that zing of his appreciation again and again. "She wanted to talk to you alone. What did she say?"

He turns away, taking another long drink. "Seeing as how she wanted to talk alone, it seems like I ought to keep what we discussed private."

I slide my arms into the silk robe and walk back into the bedroom. The garment is shorter than I anticipated, coming only to my mid-thigh. The top, too, gapes open. I clutch the material in one hand, but the moment I let go, it falls open again.

I throw my arms wide, gesturing to my exposed skin. "I think we've moved beyond privacy, don't you think?"

Timofey takes me in one bit at a time. My arms. My chest. I can practically feel his gaze inching down the collar of the robe to where it gathers loosely under my ribs. When his eyes seem to pause at my stomach, a wild idea hits me.

He knows I'm pregnant.

But as fast as it appears, it fades. There's no way. Silly thought. I have enough to worry about without conjuring up new fears.

Timofey skims my legs up and then down. Finally, he meets my eyes. "Your grandmother wants me to take care of you."

My thoughts are so filthy that all I can imagine is my grandma telling Timofey that he should *take care of me. Wink. Wink.* Then, thankfully, I come to my senses. "Were you getting her blessing or something?"

"Of course not," Timofey grumbles a bit too quickly. "She just… She wanted to make sure you were taken care of when she's gone."

"Why would she be gone? Is she going somewhere?" I think back to her wet cough in the courtyard. Maybe Mexico hasn't been as good for her health as I hoped it would be. Maybe the humid air is bad for her lungs.

I can feel my thoughts spiraling, panic creeping in. Maybe I screwed up by sending her here. Maybe I shaved years off her life. Maybe I—

Then Timofey lays his hand on my shoulder.

I'm not even sure when he stood up and walked over to me. But here he is, broad enough to block out all of the light from the window behind him. He's ringed in a golden glow.

"She's fine, Piper. She was just being protective."

"Okay." I nod dumbly. "But why…?"

"Why me?" he asks, guessing where I was going. "I asked her the same question."

"What did she say?"

He fills his barrel chest with air and breathes out slowly. "She seems to think I care about you."

I can't stop myself from looking up at him. The hope in my eyes must be painfully obvious, but I'm too tired to try to hide it. "She said that?"

"She said that I look at you."

I frown. "That's all it takes for her to hand me over to someone? They just need to look at me? Glad to know the bar is so low it might as well be on the floor."

"Do a lot of men look at you?"

"What?" I ask, distracted.

"Do a lot of men look at you like this?" Timofey's pupils are blown wide, the black eating away the ocean blue. He hasn't moved any closer, but there is less air between us. It's like negative pressure. Like I'm being drawn into him.

"No one has ever looked at me the way you do." The words are out of my mouth before I can stop them. I don't care, though.

It's the truth.

He hooks his finger under my chin and tilts my face up to his. "Do you want me to take care of you, Piper?"

It's not just me being dirty-minded this time. He's saying exactly what I think he's saying.

"I—What do you—Do you even care about me?" Every question churning inside of me tries to get out at once.

"Well, you aren't dead. So that has to mean something." There's a hint of a smile tugging at the corners of his mouth, and I realize he might actually be teasing me.

"What, though?" I rasp. "What does it mean?"

Slowly, almost as if he's trying not to spook a wild animal, Timofey hooks his hands around my hips and pulls me against his body. He walks me back toward the bed, and I'm so stunned that I let him.

He sets me on the edge of the bed and my robe falls open. Timofey presses his thumb to the exposed skin between my breasts and drags it down, over my sternum and across my stomach.

I suck in quickly like he might realize I'm pregnant if he touches my stomach. But he doesn't seem to notice.

"Why *am* I still alive? What does that mean?"

"It means I haven't dealt with you the way a don should."

My brows pinch together. "Should I be dead? Do you...do you wish I was dead?"

My dream from this morning plays against the backs of my eyelids between every blink. Timofey making love to me even as he wished me dead. Worse yet, the echoes of him saying as much while we were both awake ring in my ears.

I want to say I'd never let that happen, but right now, my body is aching for him. I'd put up with a lot to have the gnawing, burning need inside of me soothed.

Instead of answering, he pushes my robe the rest of the way open. My breasts are swollen and tender—yet another pregnancy sign—and he bends forward and smooths the flat of his tongue over my nipple.

Goosebumps explode across my skin as he sucks it between his soft lips and kisses the pebbled skin.

Then he releases it with a warm tug and moves to the other.

I wrap my arms around his neck and thread my fingers through his soft hair, holding him close to me in case he changes his mind and tries to leave.

He fists a hand in my hair as his mouth explores my skin. It feels a bit like he's holding onto me, too. Even though it isn't necessary.

I'm not going anywhere.

"Timofey." I arch my back and he kisses down the center of my body. He loops an arm around me and drags me to the edge of the bed.

My legs part instinctively, and he settles between them.

"Timofey. What are we doing?"

He kisses lower and lower, around my hip and on the inside of my legs. His breath cools over the dampness gathering between my thighs.

He still doesn't answer my question. Not with words, anyway. But he does me one better: he dips between my legs and drives the question from my mind entirely.

He circles my clit with his tongue and teases my opening until I'm grinding against his mouth. Until he has to lay an arm across my hips to keep me on the mattress.

"T-Timofey…" I tug on his dark, silky hair as he devotes all of his energy to making sure I lose the power of speech. And when he sucks, that's exactly what I do. A garbled mess of vowels and consonants pour out of me in a breathless fog. My thighs clamp around his ears, and I jerk against his mouth until I melt into a useless puddle on the bed.

When Timofey climbs over me, his lips are shiny from my orgasm. I brush my thumb over them, seeing him through my lust-colored glasses. "What are we doing, Timofey?"

He glances down towards my waist. "If you don't know what that was, then I must not be doing it very well."

I smile, but it's hesitant. I'm waiting for him to flip the switch again.

I wish you were dead.

"You know what I mean," I whisper. "Does this mean you believe me? What does this mean for—"

His mouth whispers over mine, stealing the words from my lungs. He kisses me slow and steady until I forget the question. Until I forget anything except the way his body feels against mine.

When he does pull away, I don't even open my eyes. I want to stay in this bliss for as long as possible.

He moves his mouth to the shell of my ear. "We are forgetting for one second how unbelievably fucked everything is. Can you do that for me, Piper? Can you help me forget?"

Forget what? About Benjamin? About me? About us? Maybe this is his way of telling me goodbye. This is the goodbye tour of whatever the hell we have together.

Except, I'll never forget.

Not Timofey. Not the way he feels against me, and certainly not the way my life has been changed since meeting him and Benjamin.

I want Timofey to believe me, to know I had nothing to do with Benjamin's kidnapping. I want him to trust me and for things to go back to the way they briefly were—comfortable and easy.

But if I can't have that, then giving each other this one moment will have to be good enough.

I push on his chest until he's lying on the bed and I'm straddling his hips. I work his shirt up and over his head so I can trail my fingers across his abs.

"Yes," I whisper, delighting in the feel of his skin. "I can help you forget."

Timofey watches me move over him as if from a distance. His eyes are glazed over, his mouth tense. I kiss his chest and stroke my hands down his strong thighs.

It isn't until I sit up and let my robe fall down my arms that it feels like he is really looking at me again.

He grips my waist gently, his thumb brushing over my stomach.

Does he know his baby is in there? I dismiss the thought and slide away from his hold, moving downward.

He is hard and ready. That much is obvious before I even get his pants off. But I want this to be mind-scrambling good.

I wrap my hand around the base of him and take him into my mouth.

"Fuck." His groaned curse almost sounds involuntary. He tries to stifle it. But when I swirl my tongue around his head and plunge deeper, he can't. "Holy shit…Piper…"

God, how I love hearing him say my name like that.

I twine my fingers through his and bring his hand to the back of my head. It's my quiet way of telling him to control the depth and the pace. And he does.

With slow strokes, Timofey tenderly prepares me to take all of him. He tightens his hold on the back of my head and drags me down his length until my nose is buried in the soft hair of his stomach. Until I'm completely at his mercy. Until he's thrusting into my throat while letting out a string of incoherent curses.

"Fuck, Piper," he pants, pulling me off of him and throwing me down on the bed. "How am I supposed to—" He stops himself and kisses me. His tongue swirls into my mouth, teasing and tasting.

I want to know what he was going to ask, but then he is sliding into me.

I'm ready for him. So ready.

One stroke and he is as deep inside of me as he can be. He holds there for a second, savoring the sensation. Then he slides out slowly before thrusting in again.

"Like that." I claw at his shoulder blades and hook my ankles around his lower back. "It feels so good."

Timofey lowers his forehead to mine and looks into my eyes. Whatever distance was between us before is gone. Every wall has been demolished, every obstacle gone. "It's fucking perfect."

The sweetness mixed with the vulgarity feels right. I wrap my hand around the back of his neck and hold him there. He stares into my eyes as he drives into me again and again.

Finally, I can't hold back anymore.

"I'm coming," I cry out, bucking up to meet his movements. "I can't stop."

"Then don't. Come for me."

As soon as he gives me permission, a bone-melting orgasm rages through me. Heat pulses to my extremities. I can't see or speak, but I hear a primal kind of mewling coming from my mouth.

Then Timofey slows. His thrusts become more purposeful, his blue eyes determined as he nears the finish line.

I stroke the back of his neck. "Inside me. Please." My words are raspy whispers. That's all I can manage between my gasps of pleasure.

It's not as if it matters, anyway. He's already claimed me inside and out. This won't change anything.

Except, that's a lie, isn't it? Knowing that this is possible— that this kind of connection and passion could have been mine, if only this or that had gone a different way—will change everything.

He pumps into me with new ferocity and then groans his release. He gives me exactly what I asked for: all of him. We hold each other there, trembling and shuddering, as I feel him fill me. His hips continue to roll, working every last ounce of his release into me.

It's a gradual comedown from the peak. His hips slow. His body grows heavier on top of mine. The sweet, carnal, beautiful weight of him.

Finally, he pulls out and rolls over so we're both staring up at the ceiling.

The thoughts come rushing back in as soon as it's over. Once again, I want to ask what any of this means. What's going to happen now?

Before I can ask, Timofey speaks. "I bought tickets. You, Ashley, and Gram to go back to the United States. Tomorrow."

My vulnerable heart stutters. "Oh. Are you coming with—"

"I have business to finish here," he answers quickly. "You'll go back without me."

How long will I be without him? I want to ask.

But I think I know the answer to that, too.

Timofey wanted me to help him forget. And I have.

Now, it's time for me to try to forget, too.

17

PIPER

"I just don't understand what we're going back to," Ashley says for the third time.

We haven't even made it through security at the airport, and she is already driving me insane. It's not that I don't love her —I do—but I can't handle all of the questions. Not now. Not when I'm barely holding myself together.

"We're going back to our lives, Ash. We can't stay here in hiding forever."

What life is that, though? My new life as a homeless, single mother drowning below the poverty line?

Now that Timofey has removed himself from the picture, the reality of my situation is sinking in. I'm no longer his nanny, which means that huge paycheck is no longer going to be hitting my account every two weeks. I barely survived off the CPS income, and aside from now having a baby to care for, I'm not even sure I still have my job with them. I have enough to skate through the next few months, but nowhere near enough to support a newborn when the time comes.

Things are not exactly on the up and up.

"'Hiding'?" she snorts. "Is that what I was supposed to be doing here? Because I was *not* in hiding. I actually had a date tonight until your boyfriend rudely pulled the ripcord on my vacay. It's probably because I threatened to stab him in the eyes."

I turn to her, mouth hanging open. "You did *what*?"

She winks at me. "I want to make sure he takes care of you, girl. But I botched it, I guess. 'Cause now I'm going back to my rinky dink apartment without a tall, dark, handsome Mexican man on my arm. What a waste."

"You're not the only one," I mutter.

Ash frowns. "What?"

Before I have to answer, Gram comes huffing and puffing into our group, her rolling suitcase in front of her. "How much further?"

"Let me help you with that, Gram."

She swats my hands away. "I can take care of my own luggage, dear. I already told you that. Just point me in the direction. I'll get a headstart."

"We need to print off our tickets still. Why don't you sit down on that bench and I'll handle it?"

She wants to argue, but she also needs the break. So she relents and wheels her suitcase towards the wall. "Holler when we need to get rolling again."

I give her a thumbs up and try to find the email confirmation for the tickets. Timofey forwarded everything to me and explained what needed to happen right before he dropped us off at the airport, but I was too busy trying to come up with something—anything—to say to make him change his mind about sending me away, so I wasn't really listening to his instructions.

Out of habit more than anything, I tap on my photo gallery. The first picture fills the screen. It's a snap of Timofey sleeping on the couch at the penthouse with Benjamin snoozing on his chest. I've looked at it too many times to count in the last few days. I suspect I'll be looking at it a lot more in the days to come.

"Well, I don't think you're gonna find the tickets in your photo album," Ash says, peeking over my shoulder.

I swipe the photo away, but not fast enough.

"What's going on with you two?" she asks.

"Nothing."

"Yeah, right. I may not be as smart as Noelle, but I know something weird is going on." She snaps her fingers. "I know something weird is going on between you and Noelle, too. She basically hung up on me the last time I mentioned your name. And you go pale and clammy whenever I talk about her."

I stare straight down at my phone, pretending to be absorbed in finding our tickets, even though I already found them.

Ashley lays her hand over my phone screen. "Pipes. Seriously. What is going on? What aren't you telling me?"

Tears burn at the backs of my eyes. I'm not even sure why; I have nothing to cry over. Then again, I have everything to cry over.

I'm milliseconds away from throwing my arms around her and baring my soul when a suitcase rams into the back of my leg.

I yelp and fall into Ashley as a man grabs my arm to steady me. "I'm so sorry. I got distracted and wasn't paying attention to my suitcase. Are you okay?"

"Asshole," Ashley mutters under her breath.

The last thing I need is her making a scene in the airport. And she absolutely will if I don't diffuse this pronto.

The back of my ankle throbs, but I wave the man off with one hand as I swipe my hair out of my face with the other. "I'm fine. It's okay."

"I was distracted," he repeats. "I'm so sorry."

"I bet you are," Ashley mumbles.

"It's fine. I'm fine. Really." I step between her and the man and, for the first time, really look at him.

He's an older gentleman with graying hair and a softening jawline. But under the loose skin are the signs of former strength. A square jaw, a defined brow. Even the way he holds himself—shoulders wide and back straight—pings some sense of familiarity. Like I've seen him before.

But no. Not possible. I'm in an airport in Mexico. I don't know anyone here.

He smiles, revealing a mouth of perfectly straight, blindingly white teeth. "You're being kind, but I deserve worse. You can run over my ankle if you'd like. Fair is fair."

Ashley holds up her hand. "I'll do it."

I laugh like she's joking and toss a glare at her before addressing the man. "That's not necessary. Really."

He extends his leg out in offering. "It's only just. After all, I believe in an eye for an eye."

Speaking of eyes, something sinister sparkles deep in his. I've always tried to see the best in people, but a chill runs through me. Maybe Timofey's cynicism is rubbing off.

"Then the whole world would be blind." I force a smile onto my face.

The man shrugs. "Only the people who deserve it."

He leans in, and I feel like a rabbit being sniffed out by a wolf. Like, if I don't get out of here *right now*, I might not ever make it out.

Maybe Timofey *has* rubbed off on me, but I'm not sure it's all bad. If anything, he has taught me to trust my instincts. And my instincts are screaming at me to get as far away from this man as possible.

Ashley laughs. "Damn straight. I think it's fine to exact revenge."

"I guess I should be glad I didn't run over your ankle, then. Your friend is much more forgiving." He looks back at me, eyes narrowed. "I was actually thinking... Do we know one another?"

"I'm... I'm not sure." If he's thinking the same thing I am, then we must. But from where?

"Do I look familiar to you?" He lifts his chin and turns from side to side, giving me a better look at him. On anyone else, it would be silly and charming. On him, it feels like a facade.

"You do. But I'm not great with faces. Sorry. We actually need to get going so we can catch our—"

"Timofey Viktorov." The man snaps his fingers and points at me.

Ice floods my veins. I feel frozen to the floor.

"You're his girlfriend, aren't you?" the man asks.

Ashley snorts. "Depends what day it is."

The man ignores her, his eyes fixed on me. Now, I know there's a good reason I felt like prey: because I am.

"Timofey and I are... acquainted." My hands are shaking, so I hide them behind my back. "How do you know him?"

"We go way back, Timofey and I."

The conversation lulls. People are blurring past us, heading wherever they're going, but the man and I are in a standoff.

Who will make the next move? Who will play the next card?

Over his shoulder, Gram is standing up from the bench. She's frowning at me, questioning what is going on. I don't know why, but I don't want her over here. I glance in her direction and that is all it takes. Gram knows me well enough to know what I'm saying.

She sits back down.

"Interesting that you accidentally ran over the ankle of someone you know," I blurt. "In another country, no less. What are the odds?"

"Well, truth be told, I thought I recognized you before I clipped you with my suitcase. That's why I was distracted." He circles a finger in the air in the general direction of my face. "I was trying to figure out where I knew you from, and I wasn't watching where I was going."

"Where do you know me from?"

"A party." His words are as clipped as his smile.

The only party I attended with Timofey was the wedding rehearsal dinner at his mansion. The one Albanians crashed with AR-15s.

"Those parties can get pretty wild."

He chuckles. "Yeah. Timofey especially throws some exciting ones. People would kill to be there."

The hairs on the back of my neck stand on end.

"I'm actually hoping to see Timofey while I'm here." He looks from me to Ashley, widening his net. "I hear he's in the country. Have either of you seen him?"

"We've more than seen him," Ashley says before I can stop her. She hitches a thumb in my direction. "Piper came here with him."

I've never wanted to muzzle my friend more than at this very moment.

The man grins. Am I imagining it or is the light from the windows glinting off his front teeth? I half-expect to see neon green fog wafting around him like he's the villain in a children's cartoon.

"Amazing. Would you mind telling me where he's staying? I'd call him and ask myself, but my phone is dead. I left my charger Stateside, I'm afraid."

Ashley's chest hitches to respond, but I cut her off. "Timofey is actually leaving Mérida today for Mexico City. Apparently, he had some business there to deal with."

"Shame." His eyebrow arches, and I know he doesn't believe me. "Go ahead and tell me where he's staying. I'll see if I can't catch him before he leaves."

"He left this morning. He checked out when I did."

The man's smile falters. "I need a place to sleep, too. If a hotel is good enough for Timofey, it's good enough for me. If I happen to run into him, all the better."

"Then I'm sure you'll have no problem finding one to your liking." I keep the smile plastered on my face as I mentally scramble for ideas. I scan my brain for any hotel names I can remember from when I was booking Ashley and Gram's stay at the bed and breakfast. I say the first one that comes to my mind. "I know we enjoyed Flor de Mérida."

Ashley turns to me, and I pray she either doesn't know I'm lying or knows enough to keep quiet about it.

She doesn't say anything. Maybe I don't need to muzzle her after all.

"Flor de Mérida," the man repeats slowly. "Never heard of it. Is it nice?"

"Wonderful. You'll love it."

His eyes crinkle at the corners, and he really does look familiar. Maybe I did see him at Timofey's house the night of the wedding rehearsal. Maybe he's nothing more than an old friend.

But I'm not willing to take that risk.

"Well, thank you ladies very much." He bends in a slight bow. "Sorry again about your ankle."

I wave him off. "It could've been worse."

"Very true. It could've been your head."

The words steal my breath. I stare after him, watching as he navigates deftly through the crowd and out onto the sidewalk in front of the airport.

"Who in the hell was that?" Ashley asks.

"I have no idea."

Gram appears at my side. Her shaky hand grips my elbow. "Piper?"

Two choices unfurl in front of me. I can print out our tickets, go through security, and leave with Ashley and Gram. Or I can sprint out of this airport, hail a taxi on an absolute whim, and warn Timofey about an encounter that might be nothing.

"Piper?" Gram asks again. "Are you okay?"

"We need to go. If we don't get through security soon, we're going to be the last ones to board," Ashley says.

She's right. I need to go.

But where?

18

TIMOFEY

I haven't been in the bedroom since before we left for the airport this morning.

The sheets are still in the tangle we left them in last night. The scent of her clings to my skin. I should wash it away, but I'm not quite ready to be rid of the reminder.

I asked Piper to help me forget. But how do I walk away from the night we had? How do I forget the way she said my name while I filled her?

She claimed some deep, unseeable part of me while I claimed her. I'm not sure if that's something I can forget or get back.

But telling her to leave was the right call. Shit is complicated enough without sorting through the mess of my feelings for her. Without trying to figure out why she hasn't told me about the baby. Is she even having my baby? I haven't given much thought to her options, and it's just now sinking in that she might not want to carry my child to term. What ties the sickening knot low in my gut is knowing that I can't blame her.

As I wander around the empty hotel room, I talk myself into and out of believing Piper is pregnant with my child. That she'll keep our baby. That she'll *want* our baby.

"I should have fucking asked her," I grumble, pouring the first tiny liquor bottle I find into a shot glass.

Then again, if she wanted me to know, she would have told me. She wouldn't have left. She'd be here right now. She would have at least put up a fight to stay.

Three quick knocks on the door stop me from taking the shot I just poured.

It's probably the bellboy. I gave him a big tip the first night we were here, and he hasn't left me alone since.

"I don't need anything," I call. "Do not disturb. It's on the door."

There is no answer, just three more knocks.

"Fucking hell." I stomp to the door and throw it open. "What good is the door hanger if you don't read—Oh, for God's sake."

19

TIMOFEY

Piper raises a hand in both greeting and apology. "Sorry. I thought I might be an exception to the 'Do Not Disturb.'"

"What are you doing here?" I glance down at her stomach and quickly away. Hopefully, she can't hear my heart slamming against my ribcage.

She wastes no time in shoving past me into the room.. "Can I come in? We need to talk."

I step aside and let her through, purely on ceremony. I'm too curious and elated and perplexed to see her here to nitpick over being shouldered aside.

This is it. She's pregnant, and she's come back to tell me.

Piper leaves her suitcase by the door and turns to me suddenly. "Has anyone come here to see you?"

"I just dropped you off at the airport. I've only been back for half an hour."

"But are you expecting anyone?"

I stare at her, waiting for the line of questioning to make sense.

She winces in frustration. "Do you have plans to meet up with anyone? Is anyone supposed to be here in Mexico to see you?"

"Are you asking if I have a woman coming to see me?" I finally ask.

"No! That's not what I—Do you?" She shakes her head. "No. Never mind. Don't tell me. That's not what I meant."

Her cheeks and chest are flushed red, and she can't look me in the eyes.

"I don't have a woman coming to see me. I don't have anyone coming to see me. Except you, apparently."

She exhales in obvious relief. Then her brows pinch together. "That's what I figured. I knew that guy in the airport was weird. That's why I'm here, actually."

"What guy in the airport?"

"There was a... a guy." She shakes her head. "It probably sounds stupid, but I got this weird feeling from him. It was like I knew him. He ran into me."

Possessiveness flares in my chest. "He ran into you? Did someone attack you?"

"No. I'm fine." She holds out her arms to show me that fact. I can see exactly how fine she is. The tight fit of her jeans is not helping my comprehension of this conversation.

I grab her shoulder and steer her towards the sofa. She lets me, dropping down onto the cushions at the slightest push.

"Start at the beginning."

She takes a deep breath and launches into the story, leaving nothing out. She describes the man running into her ankle, the eerie feeling he gave her, and the strange comments he made as she left.

"I said, 'It could've been worse.' And he gave me this weird smile and said, 'Yeah, it could've been your head.' Who the hell says that? I don't know, Timofey. Maybe I should have just called you. But the way he was asking about where you were staying… I just felt like he was up to something weird." She slouches forward, looking exhausted. "I'm sorry. I tried to call, but you weren't picking up."

"I didn't get your calls."

I don't know why it's important for her to know I wasn't ignoring her, but it is. I had my phone on "Do Not Disturb." Stupid in hindsight, but I needed the quiet.

Because of it, Piper is standing in front of me. Is that failure or fate?

She nods. "I didn't want to leave without you knowing that something is going on. Do you know who he is?"

Piper recalled the story quickly, but she didn't skimp on details. She noticed everything from the streak of white in the man's hair to the freckle that isn't quite hidden by the stubble of his gray beard.

It's how I know Piper just brushed shoulders with Kreshnik Xhuvani, the leader of the Albanians.

A man who wants me dead.

20

TIMOFEY

If Kreshnik really is here, it's not hard to understand why. The death of a loved one is a good motivator for all kinds of chaos. If I'd known Sergey was responsible for Emily's death from the beginning, I would have destroyed him. There wouldn't have been anything left.

Kreshnik is coming after me because I saw to it that his son was murdered for his attack on my home.

The one thing I don't understand is, why didn't Piper recognize him? If she's working with the Albanians, surely she'd recognize their leader.

Instinct wants to accuse her of setting up a trap, but logic and the sight before my eyes shuts that theory up before it can fully form. She's taking deep breaths to remain calm, but she's shaken by the encounter. It's in the way her fingertips tremble, the half-formed words she uses to describe everything. And why would she abandon her grandmother and Ashley after coming all this way just to find them?

I flip the bolt on the door closed and move past Piper to the window. The street below is busy. It makes sense—my hotel is in the city center. But nothing looks out of the ordinary. No lingering cars. No suspicious men loitering.

"Were you followed?"

"Huh?" Piper crosses her arms lower over her ribs. I push aside thoughts of my baby inside of her womb and focus on the moment at hand.

"Did anyone follow you?" I grit out. "How did you get from the airport to here?"

"I-I took a taxi. Should I not have done that? I didn't have another way to get here." She blinks and her eyes go glassy. She's on the verge of tears.

"Where did the man go after he spoke with you?"

"He walked out of the airport," she says. "I watched him step out onto the sidewalk and wheel his luggage away. I don't know where he went after that. Do you think he followed me here?"

Piper walks over to the window where I am, but I throw my arm out to keep her back. "Stay away from the window."

"Why? Is someone after us?"

"Maybe."

Her face creases in desperation. "Talk to me, Timofey. Tell me what is going on."

"You tell me."

"I did!" She throws her arms wide. "That's what I'm doing here. I came to make sure you knew you might be in danger. The second that man walked away from me, I made my way back here to warn you. I got in a taxi and…" She trails off, looking past me to the window.

"And what?" I bark.

"I took a taxi." Her full lips tip up in a smile. "I took a taxi by myself. The windows weren't even down."

I'm about to snap at her to focus when I realize what she's saying. "You didn't have a panic attack."

Her green eyes are clear and bright when she meets my gaze. "No, I didn't. I was… I was so worried about you, Timofey. I guess I didn't have room for anything else."

I spin around and drag my hands through my hair. "Why are you here, Piper?"

"I told you. I'm here because—"

"No," I bark, turning back to face her. "Why are you here to warn me about a threat after I flew here specifically to murder your friends and family?"

Piper just shrugs, her mouth sealed shut. I can see her mind working, but she isn't responding.

"Why?" I demand. "I'm the monster, Piper. I'm the person you should be running from, not the man you run to. Don't you understand that?"

"No."

"No, as in, you don't understand?"

"No," she says again, "as in, you're not the monster. You're… You've done bad things, but you have your reasons. You aren't cruel. You're ruthless, sure. But you also make up for your mistakes, and you've shown your compassion and mercy more times than I can count.. Like after Ashley threatened to stab you in your eyes."

I scoff. "I haven't dealt with any of this the way I should have. If I acted like the don I'm supposed to be, all of you would be dead."

That's the key issue, isn't it? If I dealt with everything according to how a don "should be," I'd be acting in Sergey's design. He's the one who set the expectations, the demands, the standards.

And for a brief but dangerous moment, I was so close to becoming the beast he trained me to be.

I sigh and run a hand through my hair. I'm half-tempted to rip it out of my scalp. "If I'd been a man of my word, I would have believed you the first time. I never would have doubted you."

If I'd acted like the man Emily believed me to be, enough to leave her only child in my care...

I shake my head before the tears have a chance to sting my eyes.

Suddenly, Piper is in front of me. She has her fists in my shirt and tears in her eyes. She's looking up at me with as much sincerity as I've ever seen. "I have nothing to do with Benjamin's disappearance, Timofey. You have to believe me."

I take a deep breath. Hold it. "I do."

She stifles a gasp. "You...you do?"."

I let that breath out and nod. "I do. There's too much pointing in a different direction. I think I've wasted enough time chasing the wrong shadows."

Her suppressed giggle comes out in a very unattractive snort. I love it. Piper bites her lip for a moment, and I'm suddenly distracted by thoughts of biting that same lip myself. She breaks me from my reverie when she asks, "So does this mean you're finally going to hunt down the ones who really did it?"

I raise my brows. "I didn't know you were the vengeful type." But *goddamn*, is it hot.

"That was before they took Benjamin. Before..." She blows out a shaky breath. "That was before Noelle betrayed me. Before she threw a tiny baby under the bus to protect herself. She is the one working with the Albanians, Timofey. Noelle wanted me to kidnap Benjamin for her, but I wouldn't. So she took things into her own hands."

I stare down at her as seconds stretch and pass without either of us saying anything.

Finally, Piper sighs and releases my shirt. She backs away. "If you don't believe me, there isn't anything else I can do to change your mind. So you might as well—"

"Give me your phone."

I hold out my hand and she stares at it.

I wag my fingers. "Give me your phone. *Now.*"

Slowly, she obeys, sliding her phone into my palm. I unlock it and turn away. In her recent calls, I see Noelle's number just before mine. Piper hasn't called her from this phone once since before Benjamin disappeared.

I tap Noelle's name and put the phone to my ear. Each ring lasts a lifetime, waiting to see if Noelle will answer. It's the only thread of Piper's story I've refused to unravel because of how fucking unlikely it seems.

Instead, the voicemail beeps and that thread starts to fray.

"If you don't return my son to me immediately, you traitorous bitch, I will make you beg for a life in prison," I growl. "Return Benjamin to my house immediately. If you fail, I'll use all of my energy to make your life as excruciating as possible."

I hang up before I crush the phone in my hand and turn back to Piper. She's staring at me, her mouth hanging open.

When I hold her phone out, she takes it with trembling fingers. "Does this mean...we're good?"

I nod. "Yeah. We're good."

21

TIMOFEY

I peer through the curtain down at the street below. In the heat of the afternoon, most people are off the streets. The shop on the corner has a "Closed" sign in the front window. Even the man with the rickshaw who has been preying on the hotel's guests relentlessly since I arrived has his feet kicked up on the dash and a hat pulled down low over his eyes.

"I don't think you were followed."

I turn back to the room and glance around. Piper is sitting on the edge of the sofa. Her elbows are on her knees, her back hunched. The shaft of light from the window angles across her face. When she looks over at me, she squints.

"Really?" she asks.

I drop the curtain and take a second for my eyes to adjust in the sudden darkness. "I don't see anything on the street, at least. If Kreshnik was going to attack, he would have. If you were involved, I assume you would have done something by now, too."

She nods. "It's true. This has been very boring. Killing you would have livened things up."

"That's not as funny as you think it is."

"Yes, it is." She grins and, for a second, we're back at the penthouse in the city. We're lounging on the couch with Benjamin between us, music playing through the bookshelf speakers.

It's a flash of how things were. Of how I briefly hoped they'd be forever.

But life isn't a fairytale. Mine sure as fuck isn't, at least.

I pace over to the bar. The shot I poured before Piper arrived is still sitting there. I toss it back. It's lukewarm, but it still burns.

"How long are we going to stay here?" Piper sits down on the barstool next to me. Her long legs are crossed at the ankle. "If Kreshnik is wandering around, wouldn't it be better to head back?"

"Are you in a hurry?"

She shrugs. "Not really. I'm not even sure if I still have a job anymore. I haven't talked to anyone at work in… days. James texted me two days ago about a lunch for my…" Her voice drifts off as if she regretted saying anything at all.

"For your…?"

"My… my birthday." She grabs her phone and checks the date. Then she chuckles sadly. "Happy birthday to me. That's today."

"Today is your birthday? *Today* today?"

She circles a finger over her head in a half-hearted celebration. "The big three-oh. Welcome to my thirties, where I am homeless, jobless, and potentially being hunted by the leader of a criminal organization."

"That's only half right."

Fuck if I'll let her be homeless. What kind of monster does she think I am?

Oh. Right. The kind who'd accuse her of kidnapping and betrayal immediately after confessing his feelings for her. The kind who threatens her inside a closet, who hunts down her family in Mexico, who all but torments her with her own trauma.

I shake off that cold splash of reality and manage a smirk. "You're not potentially being hunted. You *are* being hunted."

"Hooray for me." She swivels her stool in my direction. "What do you usually do for your birthday?"

"Akim makes a ridiculously fancy cake."

"Naturally."

I nod. "Yeah. So, I eat cake and… I don't know. I'm not much of one for celebrating."

"What about Emily? I bet she was into it."

I smile sadly. "You're not wrong. She always dragged me out to some club and made sure I got all my drinks on the house."

"That's nice."

I nudge her with my elbow. "What about you? Before all this shit went down, you and your friends seemed close. Didn't they ever plan anything for your birthday?"

"Sure. We went to dinner. Noelle would usually buy me something. One year, she got me tickets to a play. Her company had a discount, so she got them real cheap. It was fun."

"Figures. Nosebleed seats, I'm sure. What about Ashley? She must have done something. Pitched in for her own bail?" I say.

"Har-de-har-har. Once again, you fail to see the complete picture, Timofey Viktorov. She's not a bad person."

"I know she's not," I murmur. "She actually reminds me a bit of Emily."

Piper does a double-take. "She does?"

"When I squint hard and don't look too close."

Piper laughs. "That makes sense. Ashley would usually show up on my doorstep with an armful of bad ideas, too. Most often, it was a few bottles of tequila. I usually ended up mopping her up off the floor and making sure she didn't choke on her own vomit in her sleep."

"Lovely."

"Not so much. But I'm not sure if that would have been better or worse than this year. At least all the other years, she remembered."

I pause. "No one has told you happy birthday yet?"

She shakes her head. "I can't really blame them. It's been a crazy day. Plus, I just remembered myself."

"Fuck that. It's your birthday." I stand up and pace back and forth across the floor. "When it's your birthday, someone should… I don't know. Someone should do something."

She smiles shyly. "It's fine. Really. It's not that big of a deal."

Usually, I'd agree with her. But right now, I can't. This feels like a big deal. *Piper* feels like a big deal.

"You're entering into your third decade of life. That's huge."

"Okay, relax," she says, narrowing her eyes playfully at me. "I feel old enough already. You're making it sound like I'm turning a jillion."

"Age is just a number. You look incredible." I eye the long stretch of her leg and try to ignore the memory of that leg wrapped around my waist barely twelve hours ago.

She tucks a strand of red hair behind her ear. "Thanks, Timofey."

"It's the truth. Aging is a gift. Some people don't get the luxury."

All at once, her smile falters.

I said the wrong thing. Go figure.

"The people in your life own you this much, at least," I say, papering over my blunder.

She waves me away. "No one owes me anything."

"Like hell they don't. Ashley would be in prison if it wasn't for you. Your grandmother would be in debt. Probably homeless."

This conversation is taking a turn. I can see it on Piper's face that she's uncomfortable. But I can't stop.

"You deserve so much more than the shit you've put up with, Piper."

Piper stares at me, eyes wide. I expect her to mumble some half-hearted thanks. Maybe blush and shyly turn away.

Instead, tears fill her eyes. "I don't deserve anything."

"Yes, you do," I growl. "You just can't see it because—"

"Because I've been so consumed with my own drama and problems for so long that I didn't realize my best friend was committing fraud." She drops her face into her hands, her shoulders shaking. When she looks back up, her eyes are puffy. "I didn't realize Noelle was in trouble with her company. I didn't even consider that she or Ashley might be in danger because of my connection to you. And when I found out, I didn't act fast enough to save Benjamin. I... I fucked everything up. So I'd like to let this birthday slide past without any fanfare because I'm not worth it. Everything is... It's all my fault."

She drops her face back into her hands. I can almost see the weight of her guilt pushing her down.

It's another jarring blow to my reality. Why didn't I see it before? All the times she tried to tell me the truth, I couldn't hear it.

No—I *wouldn't* hear it.

Now, though, it's as plain as day. Piper never betrayed me. She never put Benjamin in danger. She is just a woman who is out of her depth and surrounded by vultures and wolves.

Which one am I?

"Piper." I grab her hand and tug it away from her face. "Look at me."

She shakes her head. "No."

I pull her hands away and force her face up to mine. Tears streak down her cheeks. Her lower lip trembles as she meets my eyes.

"I feel guilty, too."

Whatever she was expecting me to say, it wasn't that. "What?"

"I feel guilty that I didn't protect Benjamin. I feel guilty that I didn't believe you. I feel guilty that I couldn't save Emily." I sigh. "But you have nothing to feel guilty for. You haven't done anything wrong."

"You're just saying that."

I brush her tears away with my thumbs. "I wouldn't lie to you, Piper. Maybe once upon a time, I would have. But not anymore."

She studies me for a moment. There's a shift in her posture. She arches into me slightly and her hands grip my arms. "Timofey... tell me a secret."

I think for a moment, screwing up my face in concentration until she giggles. Then I slide my finger over her full bottom lip and lean in close, whispering, "I'm about to give you the best birthday you've ever had."

Then I scoop her into my arms and carry her, laughing, to the bed.

22

TIMOFEY

The sheets are still tangled from last night. It's strange to think the two of us were just here less than twelve hours ago. Especially because this time feels so much different.

Everything has changed.

Piper picks up on the strangeness, too. When I lay her on the bed, she stretches a hand out over the mattress. "No one made the bed."

"I don't like maids in my space."

She smiles and her nose wrinkles. "You have maids at your house."

I lay down next to her and scoop her closer to me. "Yeah, but I trust those maids."

She places her palm on my chest and spreads her fingers wide. Her eyes are fixed there, like she's studying the size of it compared to me. "It's hard to earn your trust."

"And easy to lose."

Green eyes flick up to my face. "I'm sorry. I... I shouldn't have left that day. After I found out about my dad and the money, I mean. I should have—"

I lean forward and press my lips to hers. She goes still for a moment, the words still trying to escape. Then she gives into the kiss.

There will be a time later for all of that. Right now, I have other plans.

Her hand on my chest kneads and then fists in the material of my shirt. With a sudden burst of strength, Piper pulls me towards her. I let her move me, but I'm careful to give her space.

"You can relax." She tugs on my hips, forcing our lower bodies together so my erection is straining against my pants. Being so close to her always has that effect. "I like your weight on me. I've missed it."

"I'll crush you."

Piper takes a bite out of my neck and then whispers in my ear, "Then crush me, Timofey."

I claim her mouth again and curl my fingers in her hair. Her lithe body writhes under me, seeking and taking. She slides her hands under my shirt and plays my ribs with her fingers. Her hips rise up to meet me again and again.

I break away, panting. "You're overdressed."

Piper holds her arms up. "Help me out then."

I want to savor every exposed inch of her skin, but the fire in my belly is growing wild. If I linger too long, we'll both burn up.

I toss her shirt over my shoulder and tear down the cup of her bra. Her breast spills out, and I take her nipple into my mouth.

"Oh," she sighs, fisting her hands in my hair.

Her back arches and it could be a painting. This moment. This woman. Artists should capture the way she is bent in ecstasy.

I reluctantly tear my eyes away so I can shift down her body, swirling my tongue around her belly button, nipping at her hip bone. Then I slide to the end of the bed and pull her jeans down.

I stare up the length of her figure. "Fucking incredible."

"You're just saying that because I'm about to have sex with you." She smiles and rests a protective hand over her stomach.

No, I'm saying it because I've never wanted to claim someone as mine so much in my life.

Because you might be carrying my baby.

Because even after all the shit I've put you through, you're still here.

I massage my hands up her thighs and around her waist as I crawl back over her. "I don't waste words on empty flattery, Piper."

"Oh, no?" Her eyebrow arches.

I suck on her breast, depositing lazy kisses across her skin and up her neck until her jaw is between my teeth.

"No," I say. "I can make love without it."

I don't give her time to register what I just said—I slip a hand between our bodies and drag my finger through the pooling dampness between her thighs. Her breath hitches, and she bucks into my palm. When I slide two fingers into her and curl them against her insides, she lets out a low moan.

"I—I—" She babbles for a moment, then shakes her head and sighs. "I can't think when you're doing that."

Her muscles grip my fingers tightly as I pulse in and out, driving her closer to breathlessness and incoherence. When I pass my thumb over her clit, her mouth parts in a cry.

"How many noises can you make?" I whisper. "How many moans do you have? I want to hear them. I want to hear every last fucking one of them, no matter how long it takes."

She blushes pink, but she can't stop from crying out again when I slip another finger into her.

"Timofey. I'm going to—I want you inside of me." Her hips lift off the mattress, grinding down on my fingers.

I flick my tongue over her pebbled nipple, drawing another strangled sound out of her throat. "There will be time for that later. Right now, this is all for you."

She starts to argue, but I increase the pace, pulsing and rubbing and flicking until Piper can't hold back. She tosses her head to the side, burying her scream in a pillow as her body clamps down around my fingers.

My fingers are soaked as they work in and out of her thrashing body, escorting her down from the high until she's sweaty and limp in the already mussed sheets.

I kiss her hip bone and slide my fingers out of her. She shivers at the stimulation. Then she grabs my arms and yanks me up her body. Between kisses, she gives her review.

"Best. Birthday. Ever."

I smile. "And to think, it's not over yet."

The sleepy smile on her face sharpens. Her eyes brighten with mischief, and before I can comprehend what she's doing, she grabs my cock and presses it to her entrance.

"Take me," she whispers. "Don't make me wait. I want you now. Like this."

Piper is begging for me—for *me*—when she could demand anything, anything at all, and I'd bend over backwards to give it to her.

"You have ruined me."

But the words are lost in the moaning and sighing as I slide into the only thing in the entire fucking universe that makes sense to me.

She moves her hands down my arms, gripping my forearms as I drive into her. In a quick reversal, I pin her hands to the mattress.

Her back arches, her delicate neck long. I kiss the pulse in her throat and match the rhythm as I pulse between her legs.

"You're everywhere," she gasps, straining against my hold on her hands. "Don't stop."

I couldn't if I wanted to. I'm half-crazed, driving us both towards a pleasure I could never have even imagined was possible.

I've fucked plenty of women. It's always been fine. An acceptable way to spend an hour.

But being inside of Piper is *spiritual*.

"Let me touch you," she gasps. "Hold me, Timofey."

I release her hands, and she sits up. I slide her easily onto my lap. We move together like that, our gazes locked, our breath mingling between us in a way that is somehow more intimate than kissing ever could be.

"Like that." She arches back, grinding down on me as I drive upward. Meeting me thrust for thrust until the tight coil of need in me pleads to release.

I tighten my hold on her waist. "Piper…"

She nods, understanding immediately. "Come with me. Together. Please."

I slide her perfect body over me and let go. Pleasure pulses in me, bone-deep and all-consuming.

"Fuck, Piper." I bury my face in her auburn hair.

She whimpers, and I feel her insides clench. She tries to say something, but the words fall from her lips in panting, broken gasps as she shudders. "I—I—You—"

She doesn't finish her sentence, but she doesn't need to.

Her kiss says everything that needs to be said.

The orgasm lasts damn near forever. When it's finally over, I loop my arms around her waist and hold her there. I let our heart rates settle and our breathing slow. I hold her until she's half-asleep on my shoulder.

I'm not sure how I ever thought I could let her go.

But I know that it's never happening again.

23

PIPER

Timofey cleans me with a warmed washcloth from the bathroom, then curls me naked against his chest. I'm putty in his hands. He could put me here, there, anywhere he likes, and I'd let him.

"It's unbelievable," I sigh, arching into the curve of his body.

"The way you're about to coax another round out of me?" His hand encompasses my hip. "Scientists would have said it's impossible, but here you are, making me hard again."

I laugh. "*This* is unbelievable. You and me. Here. Now. If you'd told me two days ago that I'd be here with you like this, I never would have believed it."

He nuzzles his chin against my shoulder. His stubble scratches me, and I have the sudden dirty thought that I want to feel that between my thighs.

"I would have believed it," he murmurs.

I look up at him. "Really?"

"This is where I want to be. And I usually get what I want." He says it simply. As if his words aren't turning my world inside out. As if my entire future isn't being reshaped in this moment.

I gulp and plow into what I really want to say to him. "By the way, you cut me off earlier. Before we... well..."

"Suddenly shy, are we?"

"Okay. Before we sexually ravaged one another, I was telling you that I'm sorry." I swallow down the guilt threatening to rise up. I don't want anything to ruin this post-coital bliss, but I need to take advantage of the fact that he's actually listening to me. "I got so mad about you paying off my dad. I guess I...I don't know. I felt like you didn't trust me to make the right choice. I got mad and stormed out, and now, Benjamin is missing."

"That isn't your fault," he says firmly.

"Yeah, but in a way—"

Suddenly, he's hovering over me. He grips my chin, forcing my eyes to his. "What happened to Benjamin started long before you showed up. It isn't your fault, Piper." He pauses, then sighs and glances away. "It's my fault."

I want to believe him. Desperately. I want to get rid of the guilt gnawing at my insides. But this is new, coming from him. "What are you talking about?"

He sits back on his heels. "I guess I should tell you something. Since we're being honest."

I think of the baby growing inside me. *We're not being fully honest.*

"I know who killed Emily."

Every thought drops out of my head. "What?"

"The night Benjamin was taken. I was… I was distracted. Noelle gave me a note her FBI boyfriend had stolen. It was about Emily's murder. It turns out, Emily knew who Rodion's real dad was: Sergey."

I gasp. "Did Sergey know?"

Timofey nods. "Sergey knew, but Rodion didn't. Which is why Sergey killed Emily. So she wouldn't tell him."

For a second, the information slips past me. Then I double back, eyes widening with understanding. "Sergey killed Emily?"

Timofey's nostrils flare. His knuckles turn white as he fists his hands on his thighs. "Yes."

I reach out for him, offering cold comfort in the face of everything. "I'm so sorry."

"Yeah. Well, I shouldn't be surprised. He never liked Emily."

"Still… She was important to you. As your dad, I'd expect him to—"

"He wasn't my dad," he grits out. Then his expression softens. "Though maybe I should count myself lucky we weren't biologically related. It didn't turn out too well for Rodion."

"Wait. Rodion is dead, right? You killed—" As the words are leaving my mouth, I realize my mistake. The assumption I jumped to back at Noelle's apartment was wrong. "Sergey killed his own son?"

"He shot him in the head. All so no one could question my leadership."

The things Timofey kept saying are now making sense. How he wasn't acting like a don would; how he should have had me killed, had Gram and Ashley killed. Things that were taught to him by a man who murdered his own family.

Timofey isn't the monster I thought he was.

Sergey is.

He hangs his head, and I recognize exactly what he's feeling. I know it well. I curl my hand around his stubbled chin. "You have nothing to feel guilty about, Timofey."

"That's my line," he whispers in a haunted voice.

"It looks like we're both going to need to repeat it a lot."

He shakes his head sadly. "I should have seen it. I was so focused on Rodion being Emily's killer that I never even guessed it could be Sergey."

"Because you trusted him," I say gently.

He snorts. "That was my mistake, too."

"Trusting people isn't a mistake. If they lose your trust, that is *their* mistake. It's one I almost made," I whisper. "I can see now why you didn't trust me when you found me in Noelle's apartment."

"What were you doing there, anyway?" For the first time, his question doesn't sound accusatory. He's genuinely just curious.

Finally.

"Looking for evidence. It sounds stupid now, I know. I should have just called the police. But I wanted to make sure that I found enough evidence to lock her away for good. I wanted her to go to prison. At least in prison, she'd be safe."

Timofey's mouth twists to the side. "Safe from me, you mean."

I shrug. "Yeah. You didn't make a secret of the fact that you're willing to kill my friends."

"For you and Benjamin," he clarifies. "I would kill anyone for either of you."

I should be horrified, but my heart swells at the sincerity in his voice. "I know you would. But do you think…maybe we could not threaten my loved ones anymore? Like, Gram and Ashley—they're safe, right?"

Timofey grabs my hands and folds them up in his long fingers. "They're safe. You can trust that."

I press a kiss to his knuckles. "I know I can. I do trust you, Timofey. I trust you. And that's why I need to be honest."

His head tilts to the side almost imperceptibly. A strand of dark hair falls across his forehead. Timofey is a strong, intimidating man, but he is also remarkably beautiful. I focus on his ocean blue eyes as I find my courage.

"So when I was in the hospital… after passing out in Noelle's closet…"

He winces. "Sorry about that."

"It's fine," I say quickly. Truthfully, it was more than fine. I've thought back on it more than a few times in the last couple of days. "But when we got to the hospital, a nurse told me that I was dehydrated and had low iron. Apparently, anemia is really common…during pregnancy."

I tiptoe to the edge of the truth, but I can't quite make the plunge.

"Okay." He nods and then waits.

"And pregnancy is really common among pregnant women. Of which I am one. I mean, a woman, yeah, but also a—" I grimace at my graceless delivery. I tried for humor but it feels like I didn't stick the landing. "I'm pregnant."

He blinks slowly. "I know."

I expected Timofey to be stunned, but I'm the one gawking at him wordlessly, trying to process. "Come again?"

"I know," he repeats. "I figured it out yesterday."

"You—You figured it out yesterday. Okay. Well, uh, how did you figure it out?"

He rattles things off on his fingers. "You passed out in the closet, you didn't eat your pancakes on the plane, you didn't take the bottle of champagne from Ashley yesterday, and you keep touching your stomach."

I glance down at my hands folded over my stomach even now. I slide them away, but Timofey catches my wrists and places both of our hands back where they were. He leans forward, looking into my eyes.

"I'll raise this baby, Piper. With you. Without you, if that's what you choose. No matter what, I'm going to be here for this baby. And I'm here for whatever you want, too." He sighs. "I know this world isn't safe. If you want to leave, then I'll do this alone. I want—"

"I want to be here," I interrupt. "I want to be *there*. Here and there. God, I'm really bad at making speeches."

He laughs. "I think you're doing fine."

There was a time when I didn't know if I'd ever hear Timofey laugh. I didn't know if he was capable of it. There was a time when I wanted nothing more than to get a child away from him.

Now, despite how dangerous his world is, I know that he is a safe place in the storm.

He'll take care of me and our child with everything in him. What more could I possibly ask for?

"I want to raise this baby with you," I say clearly. "I want… I want you."

He smiles and opens his mouth. But before he can speak, a vibration cuts through the room.

Timofey grunts in annoyance and reaches around my back to pluck his phone off the nightstand. Then he goes rigid.

"What is it?"

He raises his eyes to mine. "Noelle."

24

PIPER

Timofey answers the phone and puts it on speaker.

"Hello?" I recognize Noelle's voice immediately. It's high-pitched and breathy, but I'd know it anywhere. "Hello? Is anyone there?"

"Unless you have my son, we have nothing to talk about," Timofey grinds out.

I have a lot to talk about with Noelle, but I bite my tongue. Now is neither the time nor the place. Getting Benjamin back is the most important thing.

"I don't—" Noelle's voice cracks. I can tell she's close to tears. "I don't know where he is. The numbers I had before are all disconnected. No one is answering me."

"Try harder."

She whimpers. "I did everything I could. When I asked where they were taking him, the boss guy told me it was dangerous for me to know anything."

Timofey and I look at one another. "Give me the name of the *boss guy.*"

"Um... Krenshaw or—"

"Kreshnik," I gasp.

"Piper? Is that you?"

I look at Timofey, and he nods. I wrap my hand around his wrist and lean in. "It's me, Noelle. Whatever you know, you need to tell us."

"I don't know anything! Really! Kreshnik told me not to call anymore. After I got Timofey's voicemail, I called every number I'd been using to stay in touch the last couple weeks, but they're all disconnected. They must have been burner phones or something."

Timofey bites the inside of his cheek, holding back what I know must be a string of curse words a mile long. "Did you meet with anyone face to face?"

"Everything was over the phone. *Shit.*"

I can hear traffic in the background like she's walking down the street. Even after everything, I'm worried for her. Will the Albanians come for her?

"Did they tell you what they had planned?" I ask. "Did they say what they were going to do to Benjamin?"

There's a long pause before Noelle speaks. When she does, her voice is soft. "Piper, you have to know that I had no idea what they had planned. I knew you wanted to get Benjamin away from Timofey, so I didn't think I was doing such a bad thing, you know?"

"Bullshit," Timofey growls. "You're just trying to rationalize your heartless choices."

"You don't have to believe me, but it's true," she insists. "I thought I was saving a baby and myself at the same time. Win-win. I didn't know they had other plans for him until I handed him over. Things got so out of control."

My stomach bottoms out, but it's nothing compared to the physical pain I see written on Timofey's face.

His son is in the hands of his enemies. I can't imagine a worse feeling.

"Noelle, what were they going to—"

"I don't know!" she blurts. "They really didn't give me any details. But... well, I think you're better off looking for remains, at this point. If I had to guess, Benjamin is dead."

The words knock the wind out of me. I double over, too sick to sit up straight. But Timofey doesn't move. He just closes out the call and sits there, staring straight ahead, his eyes unseeing.

"Timofey," I rasp. "I'm so sorry. I'm—I had no idea any of this would happen. I'm—"

"Pregnant. You're pregnant, Piper. Calm down before..." He swallows and stands up. "Calm down before I lose both of my children."

Then he walks into the bathroom and closes the door.

25

TIMOFEY

The flight is endless.

Piper spends most of it with her head against the window, pretending to sleep. I let her. It's easier than trying to make conversation.

How can we talk about anything else when Benjamin's fate is a dark cloud over our heads? No, not a dark cloud—a lightning storm. A hurricane.

Everything feels drenched in the hopelessness that he is gone.

That I failed him.

That I failed Emily.

The pilot announces our descent, and I turn off Airplane Mode. There are a few messages from Akim, but nothing important.

Piper stretches an arm over her head, feigning a yawn. She looks exhausted. "Are we there?"

"We'll land in a few minutes."

She nods and gives me a small smile. I don't return it.

I've never wasted time pretending in my life. I'm not going to start now.

When the plane lands, I'm the first on my feet. I move into the aisle and make space for Piper to go ahead of me. I want eyes on her the entire time we are going through the airport.

Akim suggested a private escort to meet us on the tarmac, but that would be even more ostentatious. I don't want to draw more attention to our arrival than necessary.

"Where are we going next?" Piper asks.

"Home."

She looks back over her shoulder. "Both of us?"

I don't answer. She won't like it, but she's too fragile now. I've already lost one child; I refuse to lose another before they're even born.

I look over her head towards the few passengers greeting the attendants and shaking hands with the pilot at the front of the plane. A vaguely familiar head of gray hair stops me in my tracks.

Instinctively, I grab the back of Piper's sweater.

"What?" she hisses. She understands immediately that something is wrong.

I shake my head. "I don't know yet."

"Did you see someone?"

I squeeze her hand. "Stay close to me."

The attendants wave Piper forward, and it's not as if we have a choice. Even if I broke out an emergency window, how would I lower her fifteen feet down to the ground? There's only one way in and one way out.

I send a quick text to Akim. **Something isn't right. Meet at gate.**

"Timofey?" Piper squeezes my hand. "Is everything okay?"

I'm on edge. Given everything going on right now, I have a right to be. Still, that doesn't mean I need to bring Piper along for that ride. Not when she needs to be focused on taking care of herself and our child.

"It's nothing. Just a precaution."

She looks back at me, exhaustion pressed into the skin under her eyes.

"It's fine," I tell her again just as we approach the flight attendants.

A blonde woman smiles and waves. "Welcome home, Mr. and Mrs. Viktorov. I hope you had a nice flight."

Piper chuckles. "Oh, we're not—"

"Thank you," I interrupt, ushering her into the walkway.

"They thought we were married." She laughs nervously. "And she knew your name. Is that normal for first class?"

"It's normal for me."

I'm aware of how much Piper still doesn't know about my life and this world. People recognize me all over for all kinds of reasons. My life is lived either in the spotlight or the underground. There is no in-between.

Suddenly, I'm not sure that's a good thing. Is it because Piper is pregnant? We started the whole dating charade, and I knew she'd be in the public eye. But there was always the opportunity for her to disappear. For better or worse, I've now roped her into a dangerous existence. One where her connection to me is permanent.

Thoughts of what the right thing to do is—what my next steps should be—swirl around my head. I bat them away to focus on getting Piper through the airport and back to my gated, secure mansion as quickly as possible. That's the nice part about my life—at least I have the resources to keep her safe.

When we step out of the jetway and into the airport, Piper pulls right, following the crowd. I grab her arm and steer her to the left.

"But baggage claim is that way," she protests.

"Someone else will collect my luggage. Or I'll leave it. I don't care. We're not wasting our time there."

She frowns. "You're going to leave your luggage? Why? Are we in danger here?"

"No."

"Then why can't we wait and get your suitcase?"

"Because," I bark, growing frustrated.

Another flight has just arrived. If the sounds of grumbling passengers are anything to go by, it was delayed. Now, both planes are disembarking at the same time and there are too many people clogging up the walkway.

Piper pulls back, trying to slow me down even more. "Timofey. What is going on? Should I be worried?"

"No."

That's my job. I'll be worried enough for the both of us.

She blows out a frustrated breath. "If something is going on, you need to tell me. Honesty, remember? We're going to be honest with each other. Is something going on?"

"I'm trying to navigate a busy airport and get you home."

"You looked like you've seen a ghost."

I'm scanning the crowd now, still looking for that same gray-haired ghost. Every face I see is a potential threat. "Real people are scarier than ghosts," I mutter.

"Timofey!" She says it loud enough that the people around us turn and look. Even more eyes are on us now. "Tell me right now: are we in danger? Do I need to be worried about—"

The rest of what she says is lost when a man passes closely by Piper's shoulder. He's wearing a suit and carrying a briefcase. It's the man from the plane. But this time, I have a much closer look.

I can see the streak of white hair over his forehead. There's a freckle on his jawline, hidden beneath a couple days of growth.

In one instant, I shove Piper aside and thrust my arm into the crowd. She yelps in surprise and people jostle and grumble. But I don't pay attention to any of that. I snatch the man up by his arm and spin him around to face me.

He doesn't even look surprised.

"Kreshnik," I growl.

The older man looks remarkably relaxed, given his position. He smirks up at me. "Always a pleasure, Timofey."

"Where is he?"

His eyebrows lift. "Who?"

"You know who!" I tower over him, completely ignoring the shocked cries of the people around me.

Somewhere, a woman calls for security.

"Timofey." Piper tugs at my elbow. "Timofey, you can't. Not here. We have to go."

Kreshnik looks at Piper. His eyes sharpen. He looks like a predator watching dinner scurry by. "Good to see you again so soon, Piper. Even if you weren't quite honest with me the last time we met. It looks like Timofey wasn't in Mexico City, after all."

I trust Piper, but it's still nice to hear her story confirmed. She tried to lead Kreshnik away. She tried to protect me.

But now, it's my turn to protect her.

I lift Kreshnik by his shirt collar until his toes are barely touching the floor. "Don't talk to her and don't fucking look at her. I'll rip your goddamn eyes out."

"Security!" A woman yells again. More voices join in with nervous agreement.

"Are you worried I'm going to hurt her?" Kreshnik asks. "You don't have to worry, Timofey. If I wanted to kill her, I could have."

"Shut your fucking mouth." I'm losing hold of my rage. If I'm not careful, I'll break his neck right here in this airport. I'll do it in front of a sea of witnesses and gladly spend the rest of my life in prison just for the pleasure.

"But like I told your little girlfriend," he continues, "I prefer an eye for an eye. Or, in this case, a son for a son."

Blood is pounding in my ears. I can't hear anything else. Can barely see. My vision is down to a pinprick, Kreshnik's smug face at the very center.

Piper lays a hand on my bicep. "Timofey. Security is coming. We have to go. We can't be here."

She can't be here. Not for this. Not for what I'm going to do to Kreshnik.

But I can't let go. My hand tugs on his shirt until I'm sure it will strangle him.

"That's right." Kreshnik nods and gives me a sick little smile. "You're angry, Timofey. You're angry like I was. Devastated, like I was. Welcome to the hell you sent me to. You stole my son from me. Now, yours has gone to join him."

The world is red.

Grief and adrenaline swell through me. I lift Kreshnik off his feet.

I'm going to slam him onto the ground and drive my knee into his throat. I'm going to watch his eyes pop out of their sockets, and then I'm going to make him choke on them.

Fuck the witnesses. This will feel good.

"Timofey!" Piper yells just before security rips Kreshnik out of my hands.

The security guard has five of his buddies with him. They pull me away from Kreshnik and lead the man I'm going to murder down the hallway.

"Calm down," the guard says. "Relax, man."

But I can't relax when the man who killed my son is being escorted to safety.

I look over and Piper is standing next to a guard. The man has his hand on her arm, holding her away from the chaos. Protecting her.

She meets my eyes, and I see a sudden flash of something new. Something vicious.

She nods. "Go get him."

God, I love this woman.

Without hesitating, I rip away from the security guard holding me, shove a second one back into the crowd, and run headlong through the crowd after Kreshnik.

26

PIPER

We need to get out of here.

It's the only thing I could think of as Timofey lifted Kreshnik off the ground. As the intensity of the moment swelled and shattered.

I need to get Timofey out of here.

But then the guards came. They whisked Kreshnik away. And Timofey looked at me.

In that one look, I saw all of the heartbreak. All of the pain and the torment. I saw the rage.

I knew instantly what he wanted. It's what I want, too.

The man who kidnapped and hurt Benjamin is not only still breathing; he's walking away. Being led away, actually. Protected by security guards who have no idea the kinds of atrocities he has committed.

If it hurts me to see, I know it's killing Timofey. Which is why when his eyes meet mine, I nod.

"Go get him."

As soon as I say it, Timofey is nothing more than a flash of movement. He tears out of the arms of the guard holding him, plows his shoulder into the man across from him, and then weaves nimbly through the gathered crowd of rubberneckers. A woman with a neck pillow has her phone held up to record the whole thing, but Timofey deftly knocks it out of her hand as he passes.

If things weren't so tense, I would be fanning myself from the sheer grace of it all.

"What the—" The guard holding me lunges forward and stops. He glances back, sees that I'm not going anywhere, and then takes off with his coworkers after Timofey.

An elderly woman grabs my wrist. "Are you okay, dear? What was all that about?"

The passengers still lingering are starting to whisper. Some are moving closer to see what I'm going to say. But all I can think about is that Timofey isn't here.

He's dealing with the man who killed his son... by himself.

I want to be there to support him, whether he rips Kreshnik limb from limb or not. But more than that—wherever he is, that's where I want to be.

"Sit down, honey." The older woman tries to lead me to a bench. "You're in shock."

"No, I'm not. I need to go."

She shakes her head. "Security will come back. We can sit with you if you want. Hank!" She barks over her shoulder to an elderly man with her. "Hank, get the girl some water."

He groans. "We're going to miss our connection."

I don't want to hurt these poor people's feelings, but every second that passes, Timofey is getting further away.

"I'm fine. You two go ahead. I need to go find my…" Timofey isn't my husband. My boyfriend, maybe?

"Nonsense. We'll stay right here with you. Those men will be taken to the security office, I'm sure. Hank," she barks again, "ask the gate agent to get one of those golf carts here."

The man grumbles again, but turns towards the desk.

"No!" I stand up, still trying to extricate myself from the woman's tight grip. "Thank you for the offer, but I need to go. I have to—"

"You're in shock," the woman repeats.

All I can hear is Timofey's voice in my head. *You don't owe them anything, Piper. You don't have to be so damn nice all the time.*

With his words ringing in my ears, I jerk my arm away from the woman. She stumbles forward a little bit, then catches herself and looks up at me in horror.

"She's as crazy as her husband!" the woman shouts to the crowd.

But I'm already running down the walkway, chasing after the security guards I can barely see weaving through the travelers ahead.

People are gathered on the edges of the hallway, looking towards the commotion. I know I'm headed in the right direction.

But I'm so focused on getting to Timofey, on helping him do whatever needs to happen next, that I don't see the man waiting behind the pillar until it's too late.

An arm shoots out and snatches me mid-run. Momentum twirls me around, and we collide chest to chest. The wind whooshes out of me. I have to force my lungs to expand so I can breathe.

"Piper."

I hear my name, and my first thought is the Albanians. Kreshnik confronted Timofey, separated us, and now, I'm being kidnapped, too.

This is it. I'm going to die.

But not without a fight.

27

PIPER

I fling a fist at the man's chest, but it's like my body is moving in slow motion. When I connect, pain shoots up my fingers and around my wrist.

"Piper!" The man grabs my fist and bends down to look into my face. "Piper! It's me!"

I blink through the pain and confusion. "Akim?"

He smirks. "I guess I should count myself lucky Timofey hasn't put you through training yet. Otherwise, that punch might have left a bruise."

"You shouldn't be here. You should be—Did you see Timofey run by? Kreshnik is here and—"

"I saw him." His smile fades, and he glances up and down the concourse. "But it's time for the two of us to go."

"Go? We can't go! Timofey is here *with Kreshnik Xhuvani*. We can't leave him alone."

He nods at a few curious passersby, but I can't care at all about the optics of any of this. I just want to be with Timofey.

Akim pats the back of my hand gently. "Piper, I know you want to help Timofey, but the best way you can help right now is to get to safety. That is all he wanted for you."

"But he—"

"Can take care of himself," he finishes. "That's the reason I'm here. Timofey wanted me to pick you up and get you home. He'll handle everything else."

I asked Timofey on the plane if we were both going home. He avoided the question. I should have known then what that meant.

"He shouldn't have to handle everything by himself! He's alone in everything! Don't you care?"

Akim's mouth presses into a firm line. His hold on my hand tightens like he's worried I'll sprint away.

He's right to be worried. I'm considering it.

"Listen to me. I've known Timofey for a long time. And this —" He gestures from himself to me and back again, "—this is how I get to help him. I can't fight and I'm shit at negotiating. But I can make sure the woman he loves makes it home safely."

The woman he loves.

I know that Timofey cares about me. He made that clear last night. Still, hearing…*the other word*…out loud stops me in my tracks.

"So can we go before Kreshnik calls for backup?" Akim smiles pleasantly at the people passing by, but I see the current of tension running underneath it. "Even if the Albanians don't show up, Timofey will kill me if I don't get you out of here."

I want nothing more than to run through this airport and find Timofey. I want to make sure he is safe and help him get revenge. But I don't want anything bad to happen to Akim, either from the Albanians or Timofey.

So I nod and let him lead me out of the airport.

"How about soup?" Akim pops his head out of the pantry, a bundle of kluski noodles in his hand. "It's not exactly soup season, but then again, any season is soup season if you're, you know...eating soup."

I shake my head. "No, thanks."

He lets the pantry door close and puts a pan on the stovetop to preheat. "You keep saying that, but I don't believe you."

"I'm really not hungry!" My nausea is out of control right now. I'm not sure if it's from anxiety or pregnancy hormones. Probably both. But Akim doesn't know about the baby yet, so I can't exactly explain myself.

"Everyone is hungry. It's just determining what you're hungry for." He taps his chin, thinking. "How about grilled cheese? Elevated, obviously. I use four different kinds of cheeses and can thaw out some of the tomato soup I made in bulk last month for a little soup-and-sandwich action."

We've been playing this back-and-forth game for half an hour, and I'm tired. So I nod. "Fine. That sounds fine."

He snorts and heads to the freezer. "It sounds *amazing*, is what I'm sure you meant to say. But you're stressed, so I'll ignore the omission."

I don't even hear him. My head is still back at the airport. I've been checking the news regularly to see if any stations are covering a disturbance at the airport.

Nothing.

Not a single peep.

Is that good or bad? If someone died, surely the news would report it. Then again, maybe it's a coverup. Timofey has friends in the police department. I'm sure Kreshnik does, too. Maybe at the papers and news stations, as well. Maybe one or both of them is covering up the extent of what happened, leaving me and everyone else in the dark.

"What do you think?"

I look up and Akim is standing across the island from me, a loaf of rye bread in one hand and a loaf of sourdough in the other.

"Huh?"

"Sourdough or rye?" he repeats. "What do you think?"

I look from one hand to the other, taking in the two loaves. Then I say the first thing that comes to mind. "I don't think Benjamin is dead."

Akim slowly lowers the loaves. His thin, happy mask crumples. His forehead creases, and he stares at me with forlorn eyes. "Piper…"

"No." I wave a hand in the air between us. "I've been thinking about it, and it doesn't make sense. Why would Kreshnik kill a baby?"

"Because he's a monster. Because—I don't want to talk about this." He tosses the bread on the table and spins to the fridge for the butter.

"Sure, he's terrible," I agree. "But it doesn't make sense for him to kill Benjamin."

"He wants revenge for Arber's death. I—Fuck!" Akim pinches his hand in the fridge. The stick of butter slides across the floor. He slams the door shut and turns to me. "I made a real artful arrangement out of Arber's death scene. I was proud of it, arranging his body on the porch like a scarecrow. I made him hold his own head."

I wince, and Akim just nods. "I know. Gruesome. Horrible. It seemed fair at the time. But now that Benjamin is... Well, I have some regrets."

"Not you, too. This guilt is tearing all of us apart." I walk around the island and squeeze Akim's arm. "None of this is your fault. You know that, right?"

He gives me a tight smile and then twists away to clean up the mess he made. "It doesn't really matter, does it? It doesn't change anything."

"But it could change something. What if Benjamin is still alive?"

"I don't want to imagine it," he says. "Because I'm barely holding it together, Piper. It hurts to think about him at all. I'm not going to live in a pretend world."

"I'm not living in a pretend world, either. Think about it: Benjamin is *leverage*. Alive, Benjamin is worth so much more to Kreshnik. Sure, he wanted revenge. But he's still a don. Kreshnik wouldn't miss the opportunity to take down Timofey's entire operation if he could, right?"

He cuts slabs of butter into the pan. They sizzle, swirling and bubbling in the heat. He lifts one shoulder. "Sure. If Kreshnik was thinking clearly, then maybe he'd keep Benjamin as collateral."

"See?"

"But he *wasn't* thinking clearly. He was wracked by grief. Because of what *I* did to his son." Akim throws a slice of sourdough bread into the pan. "I don't want it to be true, either. But Benjamin is—"

"No!"

I can't hear someone say it again. Kreshnik's words have been playing and replaying in my head since I first heard them.

You stole my son from me. Now, yours has gone to join him.

I squeeze my eyes closed, blocking out the possibility that Kreshnik was telling the truth. I take a deep breath. "I know you think I'm in denial."

"It's normal to feel that way. What we're dealing with is awful."

"I know you think I'm in denial," I repeat, "but I really think I'm making sense. Kreshnik knows if he kills Benjamin, Timofey will kill him. There is no world in which Kreshnik gets away with murdering Timofey's son."

"What else would he do with him?"

"I don't know. But I can find out."

I stand up, and Akim spins around, eyebrow arches. "What does that mean?"

"I need to go talk to Noelle. She knows more than she was telling us on the phone. She has to know something about what Kreshnik might want with Benjamin."

I make it to the doorway of the kitchen before Akim gets in front of me, cutting off my path.

"I have to do this, Akim."

He winces. "But you can't."

"I'm fine. I'm not in shock or injured. I'm completely fine."

"No, that's not what I—Where the fuck are you, Timofey?" he groans to the ceiling. He takes a breath and gives me a placating smile. "You can't leave. Because I'm not supposed to let you leave. I'm supposed to keep you here."

"Keep me here?" I repeat. "So I'm a prisoner. Is that what you're saying?"

"A prisoner who gets grilled cheese and soup." He tries to smile, but when he sees the look on my face, he drops the attempt. "I'm sorry, Piper. I don't have a choice."

I grit my teeth. "You always have a choice. We all do."

He holds up his hands, a spatula still held between his fingers. "Take it up with Timofey."

I throw my arms out wide to encompass the empty room. "He isn't exactly here for me to argue with."

"Then sit down and enjoy the food until he is."

Akim's eyes are creased at the corners. He's silently pleading with me not to make this harder on him.

"Fine," I say with a grimace. "But I won't like it."

"No," he agrees. "I don't suppose you will."

28

TIMOFEY

I pound my hand on the steering wheel and scream into the upholstered ceiling.

Kreshnik Xhuvani fucking escaped. I shouldn't be surprised. Rats have a way of wriggling themselves out of the jaws of a predator.

The airport security didn't pose any real threat, but they made tracking Kreshnik down much harder. I had to take circuitous paths and duck out of sight. By the time I scrambled them enough to get them off my tail, I was no longer on Kreshnik's.

Now, I have no clue where he is.

The only reason today isn't a total loss is because I know Piper is at the mansion with Akim. At least one thing went right.

I press my head back into the cushion and rub my aching eyes. I better get used to the pain. Sleep is unlikely.

When my phone rings, I fumble for it in the cupholder and answer. "What?"

"Is that your formal greeting now?"

The familiar voice sends goosebumps up and down my arms. I sit up straight, every drop of exhaustion in me subsumed in a rush of adrenaline. "What the fuck do you want, Sergey?"

"I want to talk. It's why I called instead of showing up on your doorstep. At least this way, you can't kill me on sight."

"Shame. Killing you on sight might improve my mood."

"But it wouldn't improve your claim on the Bratva."

"Fuck my claim," I snap. "And fuck you."

He sighs. "I know I upset you, Timofey. That's the trouble with being a parent: you don't always get to take the path of least resistance. Sometimes, you have to do the right thing— the hard thing—even when you know there will be consequences."

"Killing Emily was not the right thing to do. She was innocent."

"An innocent who knew too much," he says. "An innocent who was going to blab the truth to Rodion and see you knocked off your throne. Is that what you wish had happened?"

"If it meant Emily was still here? Then yes. But that wouldn't have happened, because I was always better suited to leadership than Rodion. That's why you abandoned your own son and adopted me instead. Why leave it to the genetic lottery when you can shop around a bit, right?"

"Amazing how you can turn me saving a poor, orphaned boy from the streets into a bad thing. Most people would call me a hero."

"Most people are sheep," I hiss. "Most people don't know you nearly as well as I do."

"We do know each other well, don't we? Maybe not the way fathers and sons usually do. But we understand each other. We work well together."

"It's hard to work well together when you take matters into your own hands, Otets. I would have handled Rodion. I would have handled any threat against my leadership. Emily didn't need to die because of your antiquated view on blood rights."

He sighs. "This is why you need me, Timofey. I see the bigger picture, and I will always put the end game above individual lives."

"Except your own," I growl. "You always manage to save yourself."

I should have killed him that night in the entryway. If Akim hadn't rushed in to tell me about Benjamin's disappearance, I would have. And I would have enjoyed every fucking second of it.

"I always manage to save you, too, Timofey. That's all I've ever done. Can't you see that?"

At one time, I thought Sergey was doing me a favor by taking me in. That opinion faded fast. I knew I was only as valuable to him as I was useful. I settled for that kind of love versus the alternative.

Sergey made sure I'd come to regret that choice.

"I see exactly what I need to see."

"Then you can forgive me." He says it like a point of fact rather than a question. It certainly isn't an apology. "If you see my true intentions, you'll be able to forgive me for what I did to save you. Now, we can both move forward together."

Maybe if Sergey had genuinely apologized, there is the smallest chance that I could try to forgive him.

But he isn't sorry. He is never sorry. I know, for a fact, that all it would take is the tiniest threat to his control and he would kill me.

He'd kill Piper. Our child. He'd kill Benjamin, too.

The loss of Benjamin is a knife in my side. One I can't forget or remove. It's a constant, aching loss I will have to learn to live with.

It's a loss I will use to fuel my desire to never lose someone so precious to me again.

That crusade starts with murdering my father.

"The only way forward for the two of us is for you to die," I tell him flatly. "I will do whatever it takes to make that happen."

Then I hang up the phone.

29

TIMOFEY

The entire time I'm driving, my phone is vibrating in the cupholder. I assume it is Sergey trying to contact me again. But when I park in the garage and grab my phone, it's not Sergey.

Reporters, journalists, and my own Vors have been texting and calling about a news story that broke thirty minutes ago.

CEO of Viktorov Industries Involved in Airport Brawl

"Shit."

I swatted a phone out of a woman's hand as I chased Kreshnik, but I knew she wasn't the only one recording. Everyone and their fucking dog has a camera permanently attached to their hand these days. I should have known this would make headlines. Especially since I was so busy chasing Kreshnik that I didn't pull any connections to try and get the story quashed.

I fire off a text to my publicist first. *Kreshnik had too much to drink on the flight, and I was defending Piper from his drunk attacks. I know I told you to pull the stories referencing her before, but release them now.*

The plan was always to capitalize on Piper's squeaky clean image. But after Arber's attack on the wedding rehearsal dinner, I didn't want to bring any more attention to her than necessary. I wanted to keep her safe.

Now, her connection to me will ensure people think twice before they fuck with her. It doesn't hurt that she'll make me look sympathetic in the papers.

The next message I send is for the chairman of the board for Viktorov Industries. *Meeting tonight to discuss damage control. Notify the board.*

I drop my phone in my lap as another reporter texts, desperate for an exclusive, and close my eyes.

What I wouldn't give to be back in that hotel room with Piper. Before Kreshnik resurfaced. Before I knew Benjamin was...

I shake my head. The words are too final. Too painful. Before my mind can dwell on the loss, I hop out of the car.

Keep moving. Just keep moving and you'll figure everything out. Don't slow down.

The house smells like browned butter and spices, and I realize all at once how hungry I am. I turn the corner into the kitchen, and immediately run into Piper.

She's standing in the doorway, hands on her hips, a frown pulling down the edges of her mouth.

"Hello!" Akim calls from the stove. "Good to see you. I made soup and sandwiches. Come on in. We're definitely going to let you eat and not attack you with accusations the moment you walk through the door. Right, Piper? Just like we disc—"

"Why are you holding me hostage here?" Piper snaps before Akim can even finish.

His shoulders sag, and he shakes his head. "I tried, man."

"And failed." I side-step Piper and walk to the island. I grab half of a grilled cheese sandwich and take a hulking bite out of the corner. "I would have sent someone else to pick her up at the airport if I knew you couldn't handle it."

Piper appears at my shoulder, her eyes now narrowed. "Don't talk about me like I'm not here!"

"Then don't ask stupid questions," I fire back.

"Asking why I'm being held hostage is not a stupid question!"

"It is when you aren't being held hostage." I finish the sandwich in two more bites and grab another one. "Hostages don't get Akim's cooking."

Akim spins around and nods. "It's true. I've tried, but Timofey thinks it sends the wrong message to our enemies. Too hospitable."

"Would you two shut up!" Piper explodes. She steps closer to me. "I want to talk to you, Timofey. Please."

This is the last thing I want to deal with right now. I'm tired and hungry. My chest feels scraped clean, hollowed out. I can barely find the energy to chew and swallow, let alone explain to Piper why I'm keeping her safe.

But there is a quiet pleading in her voice that reminds me of the vulnerability we found in that hotel room together in Mexico. Maybe, for a second, we can find that again.

"Akim." I dismiss him with a wave of my hand. "You can go now. I need to talk to my...Piper."

Piper's brow arches, noticing the way I stumbled over her title. I don't know what she is to me. There hasn't been time to puzzle that out quite yet.

To his credit, Akim slips out quietly, swiping a bowl of soup and a sandwich from the island on his way. Then Piper and I are alone.

"Well, you wanted to talk. So talk."

"Do I have your permission to speak?" she drawls. "Apparently, I need that nowadays to live my life."

"You don't need my permission to live. You need my *protection* to live. That is the difference."

"Protection from what? Getting assaulted at the airport? Too late!"

"I made sure Akim was there for you," I bark. "You're the one who told me to go after Kreshnik."

She crosses her arms, knowing full well I'm right. "Only because I knew you'd never forgive me if he got away! Did he, by the way? I assume if you'd caught him, you wouldn't be here right now."

I clench my teeth. "He slipped away, but it's only a matter of time before I catch up with him."

She nods. "Okay. Great. So what do I do until then? Should I live in the panic room just in case he attacks the house?"

"No, you should live in the panic room because you're driving me fucking insane."

Her green eyes flare in offense. I shouldn't have said that, but I'm tired. It's been a long, shitty day. "I didn't mean—"

"It's fine." The way she says it lets me know it absolutely is not fine. "You have a lot going on. I just want to help. Why don't you focus on dealing with Kreshnik, and I'll deal with everything else."

Everything else? What else is there?

"My focus is on protecting you and our unborn child," I tell her. "My focus is on protecting the family I have left. I'm not going to lose this baby the way I lost…"

The knife in my side twists painfully. I can't even say his name.

"Benjamin," Piper says softly.

I run my tongue over my teeth and turn away from her. "You and I are going to be in the headlines soon. Kreshnik got drunk on the flight, assaulted you as we disembarked, and I defended your honor. That's the story we're running with. It'll be safest for you if you lay low."

"I thought we already made headlines."

"We made our debut at that dinner. After the shooting, I quashed any press. I wanted to protect you."

"And suddenly splashing my name all over the internet is going to save me? Do you just make this stuff up as you go? Whatever it takes to keep me under your thumb, right?"

"Kreshnik knows who you are!" I stand up so fast my barstool tips over. It smacks into the tile floor, but all I can hear is the blood thrumming through my veins. "Before, I decided to fuck up my reputation to keep you safe. Keeping you anonymous was safest. Now that he knows who you are, making our connection public is a safeguard. You aren't just some nobody Kreshnik can wipe off the planet without—"

"A nobody?" Her brows knit together.

I groan. "You know what I mean."

"I thought I did." She takes a step back, shaking her head. "I thought we were on the same page, but now I don't know. Who am I to you, Timofey? Am I just some prop you can use for good publicity? Do you even care about—"

I grab her shoulders and push her back against the island. I'm gentle with her, but her eyes still go wide with surprise.

"You are you. I am me. That's what matters to me, okay? The two of us surviving this... That is all that matters to me." I glance down at her stomach. "We *all* are going to survive this. I've failed too many times before. I'm not taking any chances now."

Slowly, Piper reaches out and touches my elbow. Her fingers are hesitant. "Okay, Timofey. I hear you. I... I believe you. But you have to let me help."

"The way you can help is by staying out of sight. Lay low and let me handle this."

"But I need to go talk to Noelle."

I'm shaking my head before she can even finish. "No. You're not going anywhere near her. She's compromised."

"She has information. More than she told us on the phone. I know it. Benjamin is—"

"Piper," I warn her, "leave this. It's done. The only thing we can do now is not make the same mistakes again."

"But I think Benjamin is—"

"Piper!" The knife twists painfully. "Enough. I'm trying to move forward. I'm trying to—"

"Benjamin is still alive!" she shouts.

I stare at her, waiting for the punchline of that terrible joke. But one doesn't come.

"Don't say that."

"It's true," she says. "Or… I think it's true."

I drag a hand down my face. "Don't fucking do this, Piper. As if this isn't hard enough. Don't drag me into whatever denial fantasy you've created. I have real shit to deal with."

"That's why I'm asking you to let me deal with this." She reaches for my hand, but I pull away. I can tell it hurts her, but she stands tall and faces me. "I think Kreshnik is lying to you. Benjamin is worth more to him alive than dead. Maybe Noelle knows something. Let me talk to her."

"I'm not going to let you talk to that lying bitch."

"She only lied because—"

I fling an arm at her, wishing I could dismiss this entire conversation. "Are you defending her?"

She grits her teeth. "No. I'm not. But—"

"It sure as hell sounds like you are." I roll my eyes heavenward. "She is the person who took Benjamin from his crib. She handed him to the Albanians to protect herself. What excuse does she have?"

"Noelle is selfish and a coward, but she isn't evil. If she knows something now that can save him, I know she'll tell me."

"It's too fucking late." I kick the other stool over. It crashes against the island, taking a chunk out of the quartz countertop. I blow out a deep breath. "It's too late to save him, Piper. It's over. Thanks to you—your friend—my son is—"

"Me?" She blinks at me, her eyes suddenly glassy. "You just said… You think this is my fault?"

"This is Noelle's fault. This is Kreshnik's fault."

This is my fault.

"But you think I'm responsible, don't you?" she asks softly. "You're afraid that if I go talk to Noelle, I'll mess something else up. You don't want to keep me locked up for my safety; you want to keep me locked up for *yours*."

Her hair is limp from hours on the plane, but I can remember the way the auburn strands tickled my skin while we were in bed. I can perfectly recall the way her wide eyes looked up at me with wonder.

Now, that is all gone, stripped away.

Just like everything good in my life.

"You have to be able to see that everything I've done has been for you."

I hear Sergey in my words. And I hate it.

Because I know it's a fucking lie.

I want Piper to see that I'm just taking care of her, but I understand why she doesn't. Not after the hell I put her through.

She flips her hair over her shoulder and lifts her chin. "I appreciate everything you've done for me, Timofey. But that doesn't mean I'm going to become your prisoner."

With that, she swipes her phone off the island and turns to leave.

A slideshow flicks through my mind. Picture after picture of the people I've failed.

My mother committed suicide after her parental rights were stripped away.

Emily was killed after I let her withdraw from me and our bond.

And Benjamin… I left him unguarded with a strange woman in the house. Now, he is gone. Dead.

It's all my fault. All of it.

As Piper heads for the front door, the overwhelming urge inside of me is to stop her. To grab her by the hand and drag her back into my house. Back into my arms where I can protect her and the baby we've created.

I'm not thinking about how much she'll hate me for locking her up. I'm not thinking about anything.

Which is why I wrap my arms around her, pinning her hands at her sides, and carry her back to the nursery.

"What the hell are you doing?" she shrieks, flailing and kicking. But my grip is firm and she can't wiggle free.

I carry her into the nursery and head for Benjamin's closet. Piper gasps when she realizes what's happening. "Timofey! No! Don't put me in there! You can't—"

"I'll do whatever I have to do to keep you safe."

Then I put her in the panic room and close the door.

30

PIPER

The door closes as if in slow motion. The shaft of light grows smaller and smaller until I'm in total darkness.

The air feels stale. Already, my lungs burn.

I pound on the door with my fists and scream, even though I know it won't do any good. "Timofey!" I shriek. "Timofey!"

I try to convince myself I hear murmuring on the other side of the door, but this room is utterly soundproof. He can't hear me. I can't hear him.

I'm alone.

I stumble backward until my spine slams into the wall. Then I drop to the floor, my knees curling against my chest. If I pass out, I don't want to fall on my stomach. I should stay sitting.

Just as I start practicing slow inhales and exhales, trying to convince myself I'm not going to run out of oxygen in this cramped space, I hear the bolt on the door click.

"It's a mirage." I think mirages are visual, but that doesn't matter now.

My mind is tricking me.

Timofey wouldn't put me in here and then change his mind. He isn't coming back anytime soon. I better get cozy.

Then the door opens.

It's only been a couple minutes, but the light blinds me. My eyes burn, and I blink into the doorway, convinced this is all in my imagination.

It's not until Timofey grabs my arm and hauls me to my feet that I start to think this could be real.

"Is it you?" I pat his stubbled face, blinking repeatedly to try and clear the hallucination.

He arches a brow. "You were only in there for two minutes."

I stare at him as realization washes over me. As my mind catches up with my senses, and I realize this is Timofey. He's here. I'm free.

The first thing I do is haul back and slap him across the face.

My palm cracks across his cheek so hard it actually hurts my hand. But Timofey barely responds. His head shifts slightly. Then he looks back at me and nods. "I suppose I deserved that."

"You deserve worse, you…you…you jerk!"

"Harsh." He closes the panic room and pulls me after him. "Come on. I changed my mind."

"You changed your—Let go of me!" I rip my arm out of his hold, and I'm well aware that Timofey chose to let me go. If he wanted to still have a grip on me, he would.

"If you don't want to get locked in panic rooms, try not charging headfirst into disaster."

"So that was my fault?" I spit.

He shrugs. "Partially."

"You are such a—"

"A jerk, I know. Now, come on, we're going to be late."

I'm so busy thinking of the very long list of names I could call him that would make even a sailor blush that I don't process what he's saying right away. "Wait. Late for what?"

"I have a meeting. You're coming with me."

I frown. "You're taking me to a meeting with you? A Bratva meeting?"

"Fuck no," he snorts. "You aren't coming within a thousand feet of those brutes so long as I can help it. We've tried that once before. And once was enough."

I think back to the day I showed up at Timofey's house to work for him. He dragged me into a Bratva meeting. Rodion threatened me. The rest of them leered.

I felt like a ribeye being dangled in front of a den of lions.

"So then where are we going?"

He shuttles me towards the door and into the hallway. "Viktorov Industries."

"I've never even been to the building before; now, you are taking me to a meeting? Why?"

He sighs. "Do you always have to ask so many questions?"

"Excuse me, but something about being locked in a panic room and then whisked off to the board meeting of a billion-dollar company is a bit jarring. I just don't understand—"

"The board wants to talk to you," he growls.

And suddenly, it all makes sense.

"You don't even want to bring me, do you?" I turn to face him. "You would have left me in that panic room for the entire meeting."

He doesn't deny the accusation, and my hand itches to slap him again.

"You *were* actually going to leave me in there!" I gasp. "I cannot believe you would—"

Timofey turns, towering over me, his blue eyes vibrant. "Yes, you can. You can believe I would do that to you, Piper. You can believe a lot of terrible things about me. You just don't want to. Maybe it's time you stop wishing for the best in me and accept me for who I am."

No. This isn't who you are.

Maybe I'm being naïve, but I want to believe Timofey is better than this. That he could be.

"Why are you bringing me?" I ask, ignoring him. "What do they want from me?"

Timofey's eyes drift over me. Then he backs away slowly. Finally, he turns to keep walking. I follow along behind him.

"They want you to confirm my story," he says. "You are a major player in the damage control efforts. They want to hear your side of things."

I guess that makes sense. It doesn't mean I have to like it. "What *is* my story?"

"Exactly what I said earlier. Kreshnik was drunk on the flight, he assaulted you as we left the plane, and I defended your honor. I'm a hothead, but everyone knows that. It doesn't mean Kreshnik didn't deserve it."

After what Timofey just did to me, I'm not exactly in the mood to lie for him.

Then again, I know he's capable of better. Even if he doesn't believe it himself.

I don't want him to lose the reputation he's cultivated all because of Kreshnik taunting him. Because in reality, Kreshnik has done something so much worse than assault Timofey's "girlfriend".

He kidnapped his son. Maybe even killed him, though I still can't bring myself to believe Benjamin is dead.

If I have to choose sides in this war, I know exactly whose side I'm on.

"Okay," I say finally, quickening my pace so I'm walking next to Timofey. "Just let me fix my makeup first. My mascara is a mess."

Timofey glances over at the tear tracks on my cheeks and then quickly away. If he's surprised I'm agreeing to help him, he doesn't show it.

But I'm not surprised, either.

No matter what happens, I can't seem to quit Timofey Viktorov.

31

PIPER

The men watch me with cold, calculating eyes.

I feel like a bug in a code they're trying to fix. A glitch in a software that is causing all of their problems.

"You had an altercation with Mr. Xhuvani on the plane, correct?" a man with a bald head and a thick gray beard asks.

"Is that his last name?"

He purses his lips in frustration, but nods.

I've already answered this question three times, but this is the first time they've referred to him by his last name. Was that to trip me up? To try to trick me? Each time I repeat my answer, I'm worried I'm accidentally changing important details or forgetting something vital.

I take a deep breath and repeat my story as simply and clearly as I can. "I walked past his seat on the plane and he bumped into me." I decided on the drive here to merge my real life interaction with Kreshnik in Mexico and the story Timofey fed to me. I thought it would make it all sound more real. "He seemed nice enough, but he made me uneasy. Then he revealed he knew who I was."

"And who was that?" the bearded man probes.

I have to fight not to glance at Timofey. "Mr. Viktorov's girlfriend."

It was easier to claim that title when Timofey and I were only playing at having a relationship. Pretending is so much less complicated than this muddied gray space we are in now.

"Okay. What happened next?" A thin man in a suit is making notes on a laptop. The clicking of the keys echoes off the bare white walls. I feel like each tap is a needle being driven into my skin.

"I went to the bathroom and everything was fine for the rest of the flight."

"Did you see Mr. Xhuvani again once you were in the airport?" the bearded man asks.

This is where the details are fuzziest. Timofey didn't exactly give me a script. Actually, the drive from the mansion to Viktorov Industries was perfectly silent.

I wasn't in the mood to chit-chat after he tried to lock me in yet another closet.

Now, I wish I'd put my anger aside and focused more on the task at hand. I would have liked to know what Timofey would claim happened.

But I repeat what I've said each time so far.

"While we were disembarking, Mr. Xhuvani assaulted me."

The thin man in the suit looks up from his laptop. "In what way?"

I fold my hands in my lap. "I'd rather not say."

"It would help on our end if we had a full picture of what happened to you. Did Mr. Xhuvani hit you? Did he say something to you? Was the assault of a different nature? Maybe he touched you inappropriately?"

Timofey didn't give me details, so I decided not to elaborate. Now, I'm glad I didn't. The less details I have to make up, the better.

"What does it matter?" I snap. "Assault is assault. Why does it matter *how* he assaulted me? He treated me and my body in a way I did not like. Clearly, Timofey didn't like it, either. He reacted, and I don't blame him for it."

"Don't blame who for what?" the bearded man questions.

"Timofey! Of course I mean Timofey. I don't blame Timofey for what happened in the airport, but I blame that man for everything."

The list is endless, actually. I blame him for Benjamin being missing.

I blame him for Noelle betraying me.

I blame him for being yet another hurdle in the path forward for me and Timofey.

The men exchange a glance and the thin man closes his laptop. "That'll be all, Miss Quinn. Thank you for your time."

From the moment I walked into this room, all I've wanted is to get out. Even though these men aren't police or airport security, this has felt like an interrogation.

Now, I want to open his laptop and beg him to take more notes.

Wait, I can do better. Give me another chance!

"Is that all you want to know?" I ask.

He arches a brow. "Is there more you haven't told us?"

I swallow down my lies and shake my head. "No. Nothing else."

"Then you're dismissed."

I stand up on shaky legs, but Timofey doesn't move. Is he staying here? Should I go into the hallway alone? I'm about to find a discreet way to ask when I see the bearded man roll his eyes and scoff.

It's a subtle move. He didn't think I would see. But I did…and now I can't walk away.

"Actually, I do have something else to say," I blurt. There is no clear path forward. No plan. But I'm talking now and it's too late to turn back.

The men focus on me. I even chance a look at Timofey. His brow is furrowed. He shakes his head, silently telling me to be quiet.

But I can't.

"Timofey did the right thing," I announce. "Because he's loyal. Timofey is the most loyal person I've ever known. And he's honorable. He sensed that someone he cared about was in danger, and he acted. He did what he needed to do to defend me."

I see Benjamin's pink, chubby face in my mind. The way he fit so perfectly against Timofey's chest. I see his tiny fingers curled around Timofey's larger one.

And my heart breaks.

Kreshnik is lucky Timofey didn't catch up to him in that airport. Otherwise, he'd be dead right now, and I wouldn't be sorry at all.

The men are watching me, waiting. But I don't want to be talking to them. There is only one person in this room I want to talk to. So I look to him.

I meet Timofey's vibrant blue eyes. "Timofey Viktorov is a good man. No matter how anyone wants to paint him, I know in my heart that he is the best of us."

Timofey's face doesn't change. He meets my eyes, an intensity passing between us that I can't decipher or explain. It's broken only by the clearing of a throat.

The thin man in the suit nods. "Okay. Well, um…thanks for that, Miss Quinn. You've been quite helpful. You can—"

"Sit with me." Timofey pulls out one of the rolling chairs next to him and directs me into it.

The bearded man looks annoyed again, fighting another eye roll. But I don't care this time. I said what I needed to say. I did what I came here to do.

I settle next to him and Timofey turns to face the table. There are ten men sitting silently, hands folded in front of them, eyes searching for whoever will be the first to speak. I'm not surprised when it's the man with the beard.

"Timofey, we all sympathize with your situation," he says. "I had to push a drunk man off of my wife at a tiki bar on our anniversary last year. We've all been there. The difference is, the rest of us aren't the face of a corporation. Our actions don't control whether our stock prices rise or fall."

"Which means you don't have a single fucking clue the stress I'm under and you can't '*sympathize with my situation*,'" Timofey sneers. "You don't know what I deal with."

The bearded man's face turns red, and the thin man leans forward to cut through the tension. "You're right, Mr. Viktorov. None of us understand exactly what it is you endure as the CEO of this company. But we understand our own positions well. We know what things feel like when the company is operating smoothly."

"You mean you all get to lounge around in your offices, do nothing, and get sucked off by your assistants." Timofey nods to a red-haired man at the end of the table. "Isn't that right, Craig?"

Craig's face blushes the same shade of red as his hair. He ducks his head and stares down at his shoes.

The thin man clears his throat and continues. "We know what it feels like when the company is operating at peak efficiency, Mr. Viktorov, and it hasn't felt like that since your encounter with the doctor a few months ago."

That "encounter" was when Timofey fought—literally—to reclaim guardianship of Benjamin after he panicked and left him at the hospital. After Emily abandoned her baby on Timofey's doorstep. Right before she was murdered.

Now, Timofey is fighting with Kreshnik as retaliation for Benjamin's kidnapping.

If these suited men knew a single thing about what Timofey is dealing with, they wouldn't be nearly as critical. The fact Timofey hasn't killed someone is a miracle.

"Our stock prices were just starting to rebound from that crisis, and now, this…" The thin man pinches the bridge of his long nose. "If we want the company to continue on, we don't have another choice."

I frown, looking from face to face. What does that mean? What choice do they have?

I don't understand, but Timofey must. He stands up and leans across the table, jabbing a finger in the thin man's face.

"Oh, you mean the company I built from the ground up?" he barks. "The company I took from a single mechanic shop on the wrong side of town to a corporation that has operations worldwide? Is that the company that *you* need to take control of now? How convenient, showing up after I've busted my ass for over a decade."

The bearded man is calmer now. He takes over from the thin man. "No one is trying to diminish what you've done here, Timofey. And no one will forget your contributions. We just think it would be wise if we parted ways with you from this point on. We need to focus on stabilizing our image."

"Fuck you with the business speak, Manuel. You needed an excuse to use the power *I* gave you to boot me out so you could have more for yourself. I'd applaud you if I wasn't the one getting the shaft."

Timofey is scary angry right now. He's shaking, and I'm waiting for him to unleash the same kind of fury he unleashed on Kreshnik on this entire room.

I'm not sure I want to be here when he does.

"This has nothing to do with individual power," Manuel says. "We have the gala coming up soon, and we need to rally as much support as possible from the investors and government officials. That is easier to do when we can tell them that we are handling affairs within our own walls. I'm sorry that comes at your expense, but—"

"At least it isn't coming at yours, right?" Timofey snaps.

Slowly, I slip away from the table.

No one is paying any attention to me, which is just the way I like it. The interrogation alone drained me of energy. I can't handle the tempers in this room. When they explode, I'd like to be far, far away.

I step into the hallway as Timofey threatens the red-haired man. "I'll tell your wife why she couldn't tag along on that business trip you took last year. Or did you already tell her it's because there wouldn't be enough room in the bed for the two of you *and* your intern?"

I close the door to the conference room and wander down the hallway.

Viktorov Industries looks just like any office building I've ever been in. Modern, boring hallways with identical doors and silver nameplates. It's generic and the longer I walk around, the more I feel like I'm making circles, forever spiraling inward until this reality will collapse around me.

Then I see Timofey's name.

Timofey Viktorov, CEO

His office is at the end of a long hall. His doorway is wider than the others. There are windows set into the wall on both sides of the door, but the blinds are drawn.

I try the knob and am surprised to find it's unlocked. I push the door open and step inside.

The room smells like him, spiced and warm. Through the dark, I make my way to the wall of windows and pull back the blinds.

"Wow," I breathe. His view of the city is spectacular. I was so nervous about the board meeting that I didn't really register how high the elevator carried us.

It feels like I'm on top of the world. Timofey must feel like that every day.

Or, he did. When he was still the CEO.

The view turns stale, realizing it might belong to someone else in a matter of days. I drop the blinds and drop down onto the leather sofa.

Is it my fault? Maybe if I'd put on a better performance, the men would have kept Timofey as CEO. I considered crying. Should I have cried?

Or maybe I should have gone into detail about the assault. I should have made up something really egregious so they'd realize how depraved Kreshnik is. Then they could have excused any behavior from Timofey as completely and totally justified.

I drop my face into my hands and blow out a breath.

It's too late for all of that. Even if it wasn't, I'm too tired to stand in front of that emotional firing squad again.

After the late night in Mexico, not sleeping a wink on the plane, and now, pulling a second late night here, I feel dead on my feet.

It probably isn't good for the baby to be this exhausted and this stressed. Didn't Timofey tell me that was the most important thing? Making sure me and the baby are healthy?

I press a hand to my stomach and close my eyes. "No matter what, he'll take care of us. I know it."

Then I ball up my jacket as a pillow and lay down. "I'll lie down for just a few minutes. Then everything will be better."

I know that isn't true, but I fall asleep anyway.

32

TIMOFEY

The board meeting ends with a whimper.

The members, too afraid to even look me in the eye, scurry out of the room like roaches fleeing a nuclear bomb. I sit back in my chair and watch them.

They have no clue the mistake they are making. These men joined my board because they were wealthy. Because they had the kind of money and connections that I could manipulate. Without me, they have no idea how to pull the right strings.

They'll be back.

I just hope it isn't too late when they realize it.

The room is nearly empty, but a chair at the end of the table remains filled. "Go on, Ron," I say, gesturing to the door. "Flee with the rest of the vermin."

He crosses his legs, making it clear he isn't going anywhere. "I'm too old to flee. Craig was supposed to wheel me out, but you must have shamed him into amnesia."

Despite my black mood, the old man draws a laugh out of me. "He's probably going to make sure I haven't already called his wife."

Ron arches a brow. "Have you?"

"No. It wouldn't do any good. She knows he's cheating on her."

"And she doesn't care?"

"She doesn't exactly hold the moral high ground here. She's cheating on him with her trainer. They're both fucking clichés. They deserve each other."

Ron's mouth falls open for a second. Then he cackles. "Well, here I was feeling bad for you. Now, I feel bad for Craig."

"Fuck Craig. You should still feel worse for me," I tell him. Then I second-guess it. "Actually, save your pity. I don't need it."

He meets my eyes. "I know you don't."

I watch as he strokes his beard, deep in thought. "You must realize that these men are going to regret this decision," I say. "You know I'll be back at the helm shortly."

"They'll definitely regret it. But I'm not sure you'll be CEO again anytime soon." He props his soft chin on the palm of his hand, his mouth pulled to one side. "I've been around these kinds of men my entire life, Timofey. They don't admit when they're wrong and they don't apologize. We'll have a revolving door of failed CEOs in here before they even consider bringing you back. Men who can't hold a candle to you."

"Manuel wouldn't risk losing his investment for his pride's sake."

"Oh, no, he'll bring you back long before he's lost his money," Ron agrees. "But not a second sooner. You'll have to sit back and be patient, my friend."

I want to tell Ron he doesn't have a single fucking clue what he's talking about. I want him to be some delusional old man who isn't hip with the times. But I brought Ron onto the board because he always seemed to understand what was brewing under the surface.

Criminals, murderers, and gangsters? I know their motives like the back of my hand.

Weaselly fucking businessmen? They're like another species to me. Ron, however, speaks their language.

"Being patient doesn't suit me," I muse.

Ron slowly pushes himself to standing. He steadies himself on the table and looks at me. "You'll get used to it. As soon as you realize all is not lost."

I snort. "As far as I can tell, the board has stolen my reputation and my company. What else is there?"

"That woman of yours really thinks the world of you." Ron smiles. "Ask her what I mean."

He wobbles towards the door. By the time he reaches it, I realize I don't need to ask Piper.

I already know.

33

TIMOFEY

As I walk the halls, checking conference rooms and break rooms for Piper, I message my lieutenants and organize a Bratva meeting.

Hopefully, that one will go better than the board meeting just did.

Kreshnik needs to be neutralized. When all is said and done, I don't want to look back and realize I didn't use all of the power I had at my advantage. Perhaps my men will have an idea I haven't considered yet.

Affirmative messages start rolling in, but I pocket my phone and ignore them.

My office is up ahead. The door is cracked. I should have known that's where she'd go.

I open the door to see Piper curled up on the sofa. The muted city light casts the room in pale blues and yellows. Her head is pillowed on her jacket, a hand thrown protectively over her stomach even in sleep.

All is not lost.

How has Piper come to mean so much to me in such a short amount of time? And how did Ron see it so clearly before I did?

I shrug out of my jacket and creep towards the sofa. She needs the sleep, and I have other things to do. So I gently lay my jacket over her. But I can't help brushing a strand of auburn hair out of her face.

"You stood in front of those men, looked me in the eyes, and said I was the best of them." I snort quietly. "How in the fuck did I convince you of something like that?"

Her brow furrows in sleep for just a second. I pause until it smooths out once more.

Then I lower my voice and back away. "I'm not entirely sure, but I know that I don't want to ever give you a reason to doubt it ever again. You can count on that."

Then I slip out of the office and close and lock the door. I text the code to Akim and tell him to come watch Piper.

I have a Bratva meeting to attend.

I wait until I see Akim's car pull into the parking garage before I leave for the meeting. By the time I get back across town to the mansion, everyone else is already there. I make my way down the empty halls towards the muted sound of conversation and chatter seeping through the double doors.

I've stood in front of my lieutenants enough times to know this assembly will go better than the board meeting. Unlike the idiots of the Viktorov Industries board, my men know the full scope of what I have to offer.

That confidence wanes, however, when I walk into the room and hear an all-too familiar voice.

"I'm just glad you all gave me the opportunity to explain my side of things. It's been hard to be away from all of you."

I stop in the doorway, icy rage freezing me to the spot.

Sergey.

My adopted father is standing at the front of the room.

And *my* men, *my* soldiers… they're all watching and listening to every deceitful word out of that traitor's mouth.

"I would like us all to move forward together. It's good to clear the air and—"

"What the fuck are you doing here, Sergey?" My voice echoes across the room. All eyes, including Sergey's, turn to me.

He gives me a sad smile, playing for sympathy. "Am I no longer welcome in the home I gifted to my only son?"

"Which 'only son' could you be referring to? The one you adopted? Or the one you sired, abandoned, and murdered?"

Whispers percolate through the gathered men.

I should have told everyone what happened with Sergey the day it happened. The hour. The minute. I should have told them what I knew about Rodion's connection to Sergey and about Emily.

But Benjamin was missing and I thought Piper was to blame. I was busy.

Busy being an idiot. She'd tried to tell me, more than once, that I was wasting time pursuing her as if she had anything to do with the kidnapping. But I chose to ignore her.

I thought there would be more time.

Clearly, I was wrong.

"That is exactly what I came here to talk about with the men," Sergey says. "I wanted to clear up the rumors that have been floating around."

"There are no rumors. Only the truth," I spit.

"Oh. So is it true, then, that you killed Rodion out of jealousy?"

Sergey is fast. He's been in this world a long time, and he knows how to shift things to his advantage. I have to stay on top of him.

"That's the lie you created," I growl. "That's what you're saying to cover your own tracks."

Sergey smirks. "So now, you're saying there *are* some rumors? I can't keep up with your story, son."

Sleep. That's what I need. I need some fucking sleep.

It has been over twenty-four hours since I've closed my eyes. I'm regretting not curling up behind Piper on the sofa in my office and taking a nap with her. That might have been a more productive use of my time than this.

But I can't walk away now. I can't back down. Not when my men are expecting me to fight.

"I have no story to keep up with. I had no reason at all to kill Rodion."

"Except that you believed he murdered your little friend," Sergey suggests, not even bothering to say Emily's name. "You were open about your hatred of Rodion for months before he died."

"Rodion didn't die. You killed him," I correct.

Sergey continues on as though he didn't hear me. "There are also rumors that you loved her, but she didn't return the feelings. It must have burned you up when she started dating Rodion."

"I loved Emily as a sister. Everyone knows that."

"Because that is all you could get her to agree to?"

"Because that is all we ever were!" I should kill him here and now for the implication alone. But I don't. I need to be the calm head, the sane one between us. If he riles me up, he wins. "If I was upset about her dating Rodion, it's because he wasn't good enough for her."

"Would you have been good enough?" he asks.

"I wanted Emily to be my sister," I remind everyone. "I asked Sergey to adopt her, but he refused. Then he fucking killed her."

The room goes quiet. Sergey meets my eyes over the long table.

He thinks all of these witnesses will keep him safe. He's positive I won't try to execute him in front of men who were once loyal to him.

He shouldn't be so sure.

I'm certainly not.

"Now, Timofey," he chides softly. "Why would you say something like that?"

I turn to my men, meeting the eyes of each and every one of them. "I'm saying it because it's the truth. As your don, you can trust me."

"I was their don once, too. It was a position I inherited from my father," he says proudly. "Then I handed the mantle—willingly—to you. And this is how you repay me?"

I see the trap immediately.

Sergey handed the reins of leadership to me. If I call him a liar now, it will cast doubt on his choice in me as don. I'll become just another bad move in his long list of offenses.

Not to mention I don't have the blood connection he boasts.

But if I don't declare him a liar, then I cast doubt on my own story.

Either way, I'm watering the seeds of doubt Sergey has sown in my men. But silence is not an option.

"You have always been adept at playing this game, Sergey. You know how to manipulate the world to your liking. The trouble, though, is that you never could quite tame me. Not in the way you hoped. Isn't that right?"

He arches a brow. "Are you admitting to being a poor choice to succeed me?"

"I'm admitting to being my own man," I say. "I will always do what is right for the Bratva, even at my own expense. Unlike you, I'll tell these men that Rodion was your flesh and blood. Your *son*. By all measures, he should have been don over me. But you stole that from him when you refused to acknowledge your connection. You betrayed your own blood. Then you handed his birthright to me. Now, blood or not, I will protect this responsibility with everything I have left. I will honor Rodion and protect this Bratva from you and anyone who seeks to move against it."

I choose my words carefully. I have to play into the heart of the Bratva, the brotherhood and loyalty at its very core, if I'm going to get out of this alive.

Sergey laughs. "What a moving speech. If only it were true."

"If only I'd killed you when I had the chance," I growl.

A few of the older men shift closer to Sergey. They've followed him since they were young. They've known him longer than I've been alive. I can tell they are prepared to protect him.

His lies have already taken root.

I'm prepared to stand here until I've won the Bratva to my side. But then my phone rings.

I see Akim's name, and I know it's important. He knows where I am and what I'm doing. He wouldn't be calling now if it wasn't.

I turn and answer. "What?"

"See?" Sergey addresses the men behind me. "He is distracted."

"She's gone," Akim gasps into the phone.

My mind is split in half, partially listening to Sergey's sermon to my men, partially hearing Akim. "Who is gone?" I ask, only half understanding.

"Piper! Piper is gone."

I blink and turn my back fully to Sergey. "What? No. No, I left her in my office."

"And it's empty now," he insists. "I was waiting outside like you said, but there was no movement inside. I just entered the code and went in to check on her, but she's gone, man. Piper is gone."

"Well, son?" Sergey calls out, breaking through my panicked thoughts. "What will it be? What is so important now?"

For all I know, Sergey arranged this. For all I know, Piper is missing because of him.

What I do know is that she's missing because I brought her into this life. One way or another, this is my fault.

"Look for her," I order Akim. "I'll be there soon."

Sergey laughs. "Leaving so soon?"

I hang up and face him. "I have to go find Piper. There will be plenty of time to kill you later."

"That shows where your priorities are."

I ignore him and turn to Pavel. "Have my father escorted from the premises immediately. Anyone seen talking to him once I leave is fired."

34

PIPER

THIRTY MINUTES EARLIER

I hear Timofey come in.

I could open my eyes. I could turn to him and ask how the meeting went. But I already know the answer.

Everything is falling apart, and maybe he's right... Maybe it is all my fault.

The Albanians only cared about Noelle because of me. The only reason Timofey trusted her in his house is because I told him she was trustworthy.

I can't face all of that right now.

Suddenly, Timofey lays his jacket over me. It's still warm from his body, and I'm enveloped in the scent of him. I want to breathe in deep, but I resist the urge, continuing my ploy of slow, deep breaths.

His hand brushes gently across my forehead. Electricity sparks where we connect.

"You stood in front of those men, looked me in the eyes, and said I was among the best of them," he murmurs.

I'm dying to see his expression. To know what he's thinking right now. *Did I do a good job in the meeting? Is he proud?*

"How in the fuck did I convince you of something like that?" he asks.

I ache with the urge to open my eyes. I want to tell him that he is capable of so many great things. That he has already done so many great things. But I fight it.

His voice is softer when he speaks again. I can tell he's across the room, closer to the door. "I'm not entirely sure, but I know that I don't want to ever give you a reason to doubt it ever again. You can count on that."

Even after I hear the door click closed, I lie perfectly still on the sofa. I don't open my eyes until I'm sure he's gone. Until I know I'm alone.

Because as much as I want to cling to Timofey and assure him that everything will work out, I don't know if that's true. Which is why I'm going to fight like hell to try and *make* it true.

To a lot of people, Timofey is a monster. I know that. And monsters don't usually get happy endings.

But for his sake, I'm hoping to change that.

It's been years since I've been in this neighborhood.

When the cabbie deposits me along the curb, he leans through the window before pulling away. "Are you sure about this, sweetheart? A girl like you doesn't belong around here."

I wave him off. Even if I did want to leave, there's no way I can get back in that taxi. It took all of my energy to not have a panic attack on the drive here. Now, I need fresh air.

Besides, I've been here before. With Noelle, actually.

It was Christmas a few years back. Usually, Noelle's mom came to stay with her for the holidays, but she was sick and the elevator in Noelle's apartment was under construction. Since her mom was in a wheelchair, a visit was impossible. So we went to her instead.

"Now, you can see why I was so desperate to get out of here," Noelle said the moment we pulled up outside the rundown apartment building. "One day, I'll get my mom out of here, too."

The cracked sidewalk leading to the front doors is overgrown. Grass reclaims the pavement in large swaths. Soon, the sidewalk won't be visible at all. I wonder how Noelle's mom navigates her wheelchair up and down this path.

As soon as the thought enters my mind, I realize she probably doesn't.

I try all of the buzzers outside the front doors, but nothing happens. Based on the loose cords hanging out of the contraption, I'm guessing it doesn't work. Then I notice the door is propped open with a rock.

If I was involved with the Albanians and worried about my safety, I'm not sure this level of security would make me feel particularly secure. Then again, maybe Noelle is counting on no one caring about her enough to show up here.

The thought makes me sad.

I open the door and step into the corridor that passes as a lobby. A yellow bulb flickers near a wall of rusted metal mailboxes. A sign next to the elevator reads "400 LB WEIGHT LIMIT. DO NOT EXCEED."

I opt for the stairs.

Her mom's apartment is on the third floor. When I get there, I'm met with four identical doors. But I remember it's the one directly across from the stairs. I hurry forward and knock before I can lose my nerve.

I hear the muted sounds of a television coming from one apartment. As I'm waiting, a loud voice emanates from the one next door. It sounds like a man watching sports. Or someone getting in an argument.

I stare straight ahead and try not to listen. I'm here for one reason and one reason only.

I wait for so long that I knock again. Then I wait some more and finally shove my hands in my pockets to keep from knocking a third time. I'm glad for that, because a few seconds later, the door finally opens.

"What is it?" A squinted eye set in a well-creased cheek peeks out at me through the crack in the door.

I smile and then stop, deciding casual friendliness is not the order of the day. "Mrs. Levin? Hi. It's me, Piper. Noelle's friend."

The single eye looks me up and down, but the door doesn't open any wider. She repeats herself. "What is it?"

"I've been trying to get in touch with Noelle. She isn't at home, and I'm worried about her. I wanted to know if you've seen her."

I'm prepared for her to slam the door in my face. I expect her to shout at me to leave her and her daughter alone and mind my own business.

If she does, I'm not sure what I'll do. Breaking down her door and having the police called on me ranks incredibly low on the list of Things I'd Like To Do Today. Then again, I'm not sure the police would respond in time to catch me. This part of town in general doesn't rank high on law enforcement's list.

But the woman surprises me. She looks me up and down one more time, and then throws the door wide.

"Thank God someone is here." She wheels herself back into the house. "I'm not sure what to do."

"Is Noelle here?"

She waves me inside. "Close the door. Come in."

The door is swollen with humidity, and I have to lean into it with my shoulder to get it closed. I'm not sure how Mrs. Levin manages it on her own in a wheelchair.

"I'm sorry to show up like this. But Noelle isn't answering her phone. I haven't heard from her, and—"

"I have her phone." She points to Noelle's phone laying on the rickety kitchen table. "It stopped ringing yesterday. I think it died, but she didn't have a charger for it."

I frown. "Noelle was here?"

"She *is* here." She's whispering now, her eyes glancing nervously down the hallway. "She's asleep. Has been asleep for... for days."

"Is she sick? What's wrong with her?"

Mrs. Levin lays a trembling hand over her face. When she looks up at me, her eyes are glassy. "I don't know. Maybe I should have called someone sooner, but I don't have insurance. Or a car. I didn't know where to take her. And she won't walk on her own."

I came to Noelle's mom's house expecting almost nothing. If anything, I thought they'd slam the door in my face and I'd have to come up with some other way to smoke Noelle out.

But I have no idea what to make of this.

"Can I... Can I see her?" At this point, I'm not sure if I want to anymore. I don't understand what's happening.

The woman seems relieved. She points to the hallway. "She's in her bedroom. Go on in."

The linoleum flooring pops and crackles under my feet as I make my way down the hall. Possibilities run through my head. Maybe the Albanians attacked Noelle with some kind of chemical agent. A drug that can mess with her head or make her too weak to go after them.

I knock lightly at the door.

"She won't answer," Mrs. Levin says from the other room. "Just go on in. It's okay."

With a final deep breath, I turn the handle and open the door.

35

PIPER

The room is airless. The moment I walk in, I feel choked. It smells like sweat and dust, and I want to open the window.

But all of those thoughts fade when I see the lump in the middle of the bed.

Noelle is curled into a pitiful ball beneath the comforter. I can't imagine how she's surviving under there. I'm sweating, and I just walked in.

"Noelle?" I call softly.

She doesn't move, so I prod at the blankets.

Suddenly, the entire bed jolts.

The blankets are tossed back and Noelle is sitting bolt upright. Her cheeks are angry twin flames, her eyes wide and bloodshot. I've never seen her hair anything less than sleek and shiny, but it is an absolute rat's nest right now.

I jump back, hands up to protect myself in case she lunges.

But Noelle doesn't move. She stares straight ahead, catatonic and unresponsive. I'm not even sure she sees me.

I frown. "Noelle?"

She flinches at the sound of my voice, but still doesn't look at me.

"Noelle, it's me, Piper." I'm not sure that's going to be comforting to her in this state, but the truth is all I've got. "Your mom let me in. I came to check on you."

I actually came to pump her for information about Benjamin's possible whereabouts, but we can save that for a moment when she isn't having a psychotic episode.

"Stop following me," Noelle moans. Her voice sounds soft and far away, like she's not talking to me at all. "I can't be sorry forever. I can't. I'll die."

I inch towards the bed. "You aren't going to die. I'm not here to hurt you."

She closes her eyes and a full body shiver rips through her. "Everything hurts."

"Are you sick? I can take you to the hospital if you're hurting."

"Here." She presses a hand to her chest and tips her face back in silent agony. "What have I done?"

I stare at my friend, and I hardly recognize her. In every sense of the word, Noelle has fallen apart. The competent, put-together, rational woman I know is gone. The question now becomes: *Is this real?*

Is Noelle actually suffering through some kind of psychotic episode after the stress of the last few weeks? Or is she putting this on?

After everything she has been through, I wouldn't be surprised. Even the sanest person could crack under that type of pressure.

Then again, Noelle is smart. There's a reason she was able to pull one over on me and Timofey. And honestly, it wouldn't be a terrible idea to fake something like this. She could pretend to be in the throes of some psychotic episode to keep the Albanians off her back. Crazy people are as good as dead ones in terms of keeping a secret. Even if she does spout off about the truth, no one would believe her.

Slowly, I lower myself to the edge of the bed. "I'm not here to hurt you, Noelle—inside or out. I'm here to help."

"No one can help," she whispers.

"I can. If you let me."

I'm not sure it's true, but I do want to help. Noelle has messed up, and I'll never trust her again. But I don't want her to die. I don't want her to suffer.

I reach out and lay a hand on her shoulder.

Noelle jerks like I've electrocuted her. She flinches back and, finally, her eyes land on me.

They are wide, her pupils as vacuous black holes, eating away any color in her irises. "... Piper?"

"Yeah, it's me, Nono. I'm here."

She blinks, and I see a flicker of the woman I know. "What are you doing here?" She reaches up and pats down the mess of hair on top of her head, suddenly self-conscious.

That bit of self-consciousness tips the scales towards this all being real. Noelle doesn't want to be seen as weak, even now.

"I'm here to help you. Your mom is worried about you."

"She called you?" she gasps. "She told you I was here?"

"No. I came looking. She didn't tell anyone."

She blows out a relieved breath. "I'm supposed to be hiding, but... I guess it wasn't a good choice."

"No one else is looking for you, as far as I know."

"Timofey?" She swallows nervously.

I shake my head. "He's not looking for you. He's only looking for Kreshnik."

But if Timofey knew what I know—if he felt what I feel— he'd be talking to Noelle, too. If he thought for even a second Benjamin was still alive, he'd be here with me.

Since he can't have the hope I do, I'm here for the both of us.

Suddenly, Noelle drops her face into her hands and weeps. It's sudden and violent. For a second I can't even move. I just sit and watch.

Then I gently pat her back. She feels thinner than I remember. Her ribs visibly protrude through the thin t-shirt she's wearing.

"I swore to myself I'd never come back here," she sobs. "My whole life was about getting out of this apartment, making something of myself, and living a better life. I wanted that for me and my mom. But… look at me now."

"You did get out of here. You had an apartment and—"

"One I stole to get!" She looks up at me, fire in her eyes. "My whole life… Everything was a lie."

"Not… not everything."

I think back to all the girls' nights I had with Noelle and Ashley. All of the long lunches on hard days and the nights Noelle showed up at my place with a weeping Ashley and a pint of ice cream.

Was that a lie?

Noelle shakes her head. "All of it. I fucked up."

"Yeah, you did."

That catches her attention. She looks at me, her brows pinching together. "What are you doing here, Piper?"

"I told you, I came to check on—"

"But *why?*" Her voice breaks on the word. "Why do you care?"

I'm here for Benjamin. That's true.

But the moment I walked into this apartment and Noelle's mom told me she was worried, I couldn't quash the concern.

No matter what Noelle has done, all the hours and laughs and phone calls we've been through together still exist.

God help me, *I still care.*

"Because you're one of my best friends, Noelle. I'll always care about you."

Tears fill her eyes, and she flops forward onto the mattress. Her hand finds mine. Her fingers are dry and papery as they twine through mine. "I'm sorry. I'm really sorry. I'm so—"

Deep in the apartment, I hear a thud.

I turn my ear to the door, listening. Maybe it was Noelle's mom. Maybe it was her wheelchair moving around the apartment. Maybe—

"Where is she?" a deep voice growls.

Instinctively, I squeeze Noelle's hand as tight as I can.

Each footstep feels like an earthquake. The grimy windows rattle in their painted-over frames. My heart trembles.

Finally, Noelle hears it. She frowns. "What is—"

The door is thrown open so violently it bounces off the wall. The knob leaves a crack in the plaster.

Timofey takes up the entire doorway, his shoulders heaving with every breath. His nostrils flare. When his eyes land on me, heat races up my spine. I'm soldered to the spot.

Then he turns to Noelle, and he is murderous.

"Looks like you crawled back into the dank hole you came from, you conniving fucking bitch."

36

TIMOFEY

For Piper's sake, I was going to let Noelle live.

As it turns out, though, a vital part of that plan was never seeing Noelle ever again. Because the moment I lay eyes on her, huddled in bed like the sad, helpless victim she definitely isn't, I want to wring her traitorous neck.

"Piper!" I boom. "Get up. Now."

Piper stands up and shifts between me and Noelle, as if that bitch needs shielding. As if *I'm* the threat in this situation.

"Timofey, calm down. I came here on my own. Noelle didn't—"

"I'm not here because I thought you were kidnapped."

"Then why are you—"

"I'm here because you're a fucking fool."

Rage is boiling up inside of me. My hands are shaking with the sheer desire to crush Noelle's throat and drag Piper out of here.

The fact that she would walk out of my office—a safe place where she was guarded and secure—and walk into this pit with this... this *hyena...*

Why does she trust her more than me?

Piper's green eyes narrow to slits. "Don't talk to me like that."

"Then don't make the worst decisions imaginable at every fucking opportunity. I'll treat you like a rational, capable human when you act like one."

She gasps. "I don't need to run my decisions past you, Timofey. Despite what you apparently think, I'm not your prisoner. You don't get a say in what I do or who I see."

"So I should just let you get yourself killed?"

"Yes! If I choose that." She shrugs. "My freedom isn't dependent on anything."

I stare at her, a million arguments rising up inside of me. Then I look past her and see Noelle staring at me. Her wide eyes are ringed in dark circles. Her hair is a tangled mess around her gaunt face.

She looks like shit.

But appearances don't fool me so easily. There's understanding in her eyes. She's taking all of this in—the discontent brewing between Piper and me, the schism that *she* created.

I grab Piper's arm and haul her towards me.

"Hey!" She yanks on her arm, but she can't break my hold. "Timofey, no. Let me go!"

I grit my teeth. "I'd rather have this conversation in the hallway."

She glances over her shoulder at Noelle and then back to me. Only then does she nod reluctantly and follow me into the hall.

The hallway is narrow and grim. The light fixture is a mere inch above my head, and it doesn't have a cover or a bulb in it. I can barely see the outline of Piper's angled chin in the gloom.

"I know you don't have faith that Benjamin is alive, but—"

"It's not that I don't have faith. It's that I don't live in a fantasy world."

"It's not a fantasy! Noelle is—" Piper glances over her shoulder like Noelle might overhear her and then leans closer, voice low. I can smell the vanilla of her shampoo. "Noelle is confused right now. She's been through a lot. But I think, if I talk with her, she will start to remember some things. She might be able to help."

I rake my hands through my hair. "You're expecting the woman who threw you under the fucking bus to save herself to suddenly become chivalrous? She kidnapped a baby, Piper. My... *my* son. Benjamin. She did that."

"I know. I know what she did. But that doesn't mean—"

"Why the hell would you put your faith in her?"

"It's not like I'm going to put my life in her hands. But if she is the only way we are going to see Benjamin again, then I'm willing to try."

I grab Piper's shoulders and haul her off her feet. I hold her in front of me, looking directly into her eyes. "He's dead."

"Stop it." She wriggles, trying to get free. "Put me down. You can't just grab me and make me see things your way."

"Don't I know it!" I set her on her feet and force a deep breath in and out through my nose. "If that's all it took for you to see things my way, my life would be a whole hell of a lot less complicated. But you refuse to accept reality. In this life, people die. It happens. Good people. Innocent people. Babies…"

My voice cracks, and I clear my throat as quickly as possible to make it go away.

Piper tips her head to the side. Her eyes crinkle in sympathy. "Timofey, I know things are—"

"No." I shake my head. "Things are fucked because you are traipsing around the city with a traitorous kidnapper instead of letting me protect you. Now, instead of getting revenge on the people who did this, I'm here with you. Don't talk to me like I'm the problem."

Her jaw sets. "I'm not just going to sit in the high tower you've made for me and twiddle my thumbs while I could be doing something useful."

"How is this useful?" I fling my arms wide and my wrist smacks into the door frame. Pain ricochets up my arm, but I ignore it. In the other room, Noelle gasps at the thud.

Piper looks towards the sound and then back at me. "Just give me more time with her. If she can't tell me anything about Benjamin, then I'll… I'll let it go."

"Yeah, right," I snort.

"I will! You think I'm delusional, but I'm not. I'm only poking around here because I really believe she might be able to help us find Benjamin."

"I know you truly believe it. I just also happen to know you're wrong."

"Then let me be wrong!" she cries out. "Let me stay here. If you're right, I'll tell you. Actually, I won't even need to. You'll be chanting, 'I told you so' before I can get the words out."

"I'm not here because I want to be right. Of course I don't want to be—" I grab her arm. "Come on. This has gone on long enough. We're leaving."

She jerks away from me. This time, her arm slides free and she stumbles back a few steps. "I'm not leaving her."

Sirens blare outside, penetrating through the thin walls as if the ambulance is roaring down the hallway towards us. "And I'm not leaving you here," I fire back.

Piper stares at me and then shrugs, as if to say, *What now?*

The decision appears in my mind fully formed. I'll do whatever it takes to keep Piper safe. If that means bringing Noelle's comatose body with us... fine.

"So grab your friend," I grit out. "She's coming with us. She can stay at my house temporarily. But if she knows what's good for herself, she'll stay out of my fucking way."

Piper is shaking her head before I can even finish. "Noelle is scared. Being around you—in your house—is not going to help. I'll stay here with her and then—"

"Get kidnapped right along with her?" I lean forward, forcing her green eyes to gaze directly into mine. "That's what you're choosing right now, Piper. And what you choose for yourself is what you choose for my baby. It's what you choose for *me*, too. You're choosing for me to lose both of my children. Don't you fucking see that?"

I want her to argue. To get angry and fight back. But instead, her eyes go misty. She reaches out to touch my cheek, but I shift away.

"Timofey," she rasps, "I miss him, too. That's why I'm doing this. So you don't have to lose anyone else. I'm doing this so—"

My phone rings, and I don't even look before I answer it.

Anything to get out of this conversation. To give myself a minute to tuck these feelings into the box where they belong.

Benjamin is gone. There's nothing I can do about it. Revenge is the only path forward.

I press the phone to my ear. "What?"

"What on earth are you doing in the slums?"

I stiffen and look back over my shoulder. I'm surprised when I don't see Sergey standing behind me, a haughty scowl on his face. When will he stop being this shadow over my life?

"You followed me," I growl.

"Easy now," he croons. "Yes, I followed you from the meeting. But I'm just here to talk. Not judge your choice in... I presume you're here seeing a mistress?"

Of course that's what he thinks. Sergey had more than his fair share of women on the side. From time to time, I saw them leaving the mansion early in the morning, sneaking out of the guest room while his wife was asleep in the master.

"You couldn't have found a woman to fuck a little closer to home?" he snorts. "Then again, you probably didn't want me finding out about her. Don't worry, son—your secret is safe with me."

"Nothing is safe with you."

If he hears me, he chooses to ignore it. "Are you going to come down and talk to me or do I have to keep skulking around in your shadow?"

Piper is looking at me, her brow knit together in a question I don't want to answer.

I don't want her to pity me. I also don't want Sergey to know she's here with me. And I don't want to leave her here alone.

But life is full of hard choices. More than usual, lately.

I blink hard, once, enjoying the momentary rest. Then I open my eyes. "I'll give you five minutes."

He starts to respond, but I hang up.

"Who was that?" Piper asks. "Where are you going?"

I head down the hallway. I can see the woman in her wheelchair sitting by the rickety table. She's trying to pretend she isn't eavesdropping, but her head is tilted awkwardly towards our conversation.

Just before I reach for the door, I look back at Piper. "You only have five minutes, too. Then we're leaving. *All of us.*"

37

TIMOFEY

Unfortunately, Sergey is unarmed. Unfortunate in the sense that it doesn't give me an excuse to slaughter him immediately.

He's standing purposefully under a streetlight, his hands limp at his sides. He's ditched his coat to show that his silhouette is weapons-free. As the one who taught me to shoot first and ask questions later, he wanted to make sure I didn't have a question to ask.

"Are you done poisoning my men against me?" I ask when we're still far enough apart for my voice to echo off the line of rusted-out cars parked along the littered curb. "Decided to take a leisurely drive now that you've divided the Bratva I saved?"

He smirks. "You've always been grandiose. The Bratva existed before you, son."

"Don't call me that. And you know as well as I do that I saved your ragtag little ring of crooks and made it into something worthwhile."

"It didn't need saving."

Sergey is an easy liar. They say history is written by the winners, but Sergey rewrites his own history either way. He inflates his successes and papers over his own shortcomings and failures with an alternate reality. One that ignores how I streamlined his string of businesses into a corporation and once again made the Viktorov Bratva the most feared force in the city.

"If that's true, then why didn't you hand it over to your biological son?" I ask. "Afraid that one apple who fell a little too far from the tree could bring the whole thing tumbling down? Doesn't sound secure, if you ask me."

He arches a brow. "No one asked you."

Sergey and I have always been good at this back and forth. We've butted heads since the beginning, but I always curbed myself. I knew he could get rid of me if I caused too much trouble, so I mediated. I found the compromise. That's part of being a good leader, after all.

But now, being a good leader requires getting the Bratva as far from Sergey as possible.

"Tell me why you're here. You have three minutes."

"Has my time started already?" he sighs. "I should have known you'd try to waste it."

"You're wasting it now. Two minutes and thirty seconds."

His papery lips press into a thin line. "If the Bratva decides that you are the one who killed Rodion, they'll rise against you. Especially now that you've told them who Rodion truly was. His connection to me makes what you did that much more heinous. It almost seems like maybe you were nervous he'd claim your throne."

"I didn't kill anyone," I grit out. I'm stating the obvious, just in case Sergey is wearing a wire. I wouldn't put it past him.

"Maybe the men will believe you. Maybe they won't."

"I know you're not here to warn me since you're the one who set us down this path to begin with. You're lucky I don't kill you now for infiltrating a Bratva meeting against my direct orders."

His eyes flick down to my hip. To where he knows I have a weapon hidden. "I'm here to warn you that the men's anger might not be a clean shot. It could come with collateral damage."

He doesn't have to elaborate for me to understand what he's talking about.

Piper.

It wouldn't be the first time a girlfriend—or whatever the hell Piper is to me—was caught in the crosshairs of a mutiny. She may not have a ring on her finger, but she has a womb. Even the potential of an heir would need to be annihilated. Keeping the line of succession clean is the best way to avoid strife and division.

If they rise against me, they'll kill Piper, too.

And my unborn child along with her.

I hear Piper's voice in my head. *I miss him, too. That's why I'm doing this. So you don't have to lose anyone else.*

Griefs claws at my throat, but I fight through it. "I know the risks. And I know you aren't here to warn me about anything. You're far too selfish for that. Tell me why you are actually here. Two minutes."

Sergey talks a little faster now. "I'm here because I can get us both out of this tangle."

"You killed my sister, cast my leadership into doubt, and are threatening my family days after my son has been kidnapped and killed. These are things you can't untangle."

"I can make sure you stay in power long enough to do something about the Albanians," he says evenly. "They're the real enemy here, aren't they?"

I shake my head. "Don't tell me who my enemies are."

He holds up his hands in a casual surrender. "I'm just saying, I can tell the men that we were both wrong about who killed Rodion. Thanks to the Albanians' interference and deception, we were manipulated into fighting each other. It was a distraction technique, but we caught on just in time. Now, we will fight the Albanians together and take them down."

"You want me to help you destroy the Albanians so you can stab me in the back once the job is done? I'm not going to take out one of your enemies and make a takeover of the Bratva easier for you."

"*You* are not helping *me*, Timofey. I'm helping you," he says. "I'm helping you protect the loved ones you have left before it's too late. That's an offer worth considering, is it not?"

I want to reject this truce for the joke that it is. Sergey wouldn't be making this offer if he didn't benefit in some way. I know enough about him to know that for a fact.

But I can't quite tear my heart away from the hallway upstairs, from the woman with auburn hair and stubborn green eyes and the largest penchant for self-destruction I've ever seen.

I can't lose Piper and our baby.

The loss of Benjamin is proof enough that she is already in the Albanians' crosshairs. If I don't kill Kreshnik, he'll go after Piper next.

"How much time is left now?" Sergey asks. "Are you on the same countdown clock as I am? I think you only have a minute to decide."

"I have as much time as I want."

He clicks his tongue. "If only that were true. You've made a mess of things, Timofey. You need my help before it's too late."

"I don't *need* anything from you."

"This is your problem," he murmurs. "You want to be wholly independent, but a good *pakhan* knows how to rely on the people around him. He knows how to use their strengths to his advantage. I'm offering you my strength. You just have to be humble enough to take it."

I see my life with Sergey flash before my eyes. The years of striving to please him, trying to make myself useful so he wouldn't cast me aside. I'd seen him do it to more than enough soldiers and Vors over the years. The moment someone didn't serve his ambitions, he got rid of them.

He'd do the same to me right now if he thought there was any real chance that he could reclaim the Bratva from me by force. The fact that he's here means he is desperate.

"Come on, Timofey." Sergey tries to sound frustrated, but there is an edge of panic in his voice. "You and I have both lost sons this week. Let's not lose the Bratva, too."

"You killed Rodion, Sergey. You didn't *lose* him. But you did lose one son today," I tell him. "You lost me. Because I will never work with you or for you again."

"You're refusing me?"

"The only person who stands to lose anything here is you," I tell him. "And I'm fine with that. If you come near my family again, I'll kill you."

He splutters, struggling for words. I've never refused him like this before, so he isn't accustomed to the feeling.

"I won't need to come near your family. There won't be a family to come near," he spits. "Your pride is going to destroy the people you love. You're the reason Benjamin is dead and you're going to be the reason that Piper—"

The knife makes a satisfying whirr as it whips out of the sheath inside of my jacket.

Sergey makes an even more satisfying sound as I bury the blade in his stomach.

He doubles over, spit flowing out of his mouth, his body curved around the point of my blade. I twist the knife, and he groans. The warm spill of his blood covers my knuckles.

"If you survive this, then go ahead and try to take what is rightfully mine. If my men want to abandon me and follow you, that will be their mistake to make. Because I'll kill you and anyone else who threatens my Bratva. Do you understand?"

He releases a low groan. I take that as answer enough.

I slip my knife free, clean the bloody blade on Sergey's shirt, and then slide it into the sheath.

"Goodnight, Sergey."

He drops to his knees, and I turn around and return inside. I don't look back as my father dies behind me.

38

PIPER

As soon as Timofey steps out of the apartment, I spin around and go back to Noelle's room.

"We need to go," I tell her. "*Now.* You have two minutes to grab anything you might need. Can you do it?"

Noelle is shaking in the middle of the bed, staring down at her own folded up knees beneath the blankets. She looks like a helpless child.

I lean against the edge of the bed. "Can you hear me, Noelle? Do you understand what I'm saying? We need to go now."

If I can get Noelle away from Timofey and get her talking, maybe I can get more information about where Benjamin is. All I know is I won't get anything if I let Timofey drag me out of here and lock me up in his mansion.

"I can stay here. Mom said I can stay," Noelle says. "This is my room."

"I know this is your room, but we can't talk if we stay here. Timofey is coming back and—"

Her eyes go wide. "Timofey will hurt me."

"No, he won't. He won't do that. I promise."

She's trembling again, shaking her head gently back and forth.

I grab Noelle's hand and squeeze. "Please, Noelle. I'll take care of you. Just trust me."

Her eyes are glazed like when I first walked into the room. I'm worried we've lost whatever progress we made since I arrived.

But then she blinks and it's like someone has turned on a light. Her face is more flushed and her expressions are more animated.

She looks like Noelle.

"Piper?"

I'm so relieved I could cry. "It's me. I'm trying to help you, okay? Grab what you need. We have to leave."

"Because Timofey," she says, brows pinched together. "He's going to—"

"He'll be back, and we need to be gone before then. Can you hurry?"

Noelle doesn't respond, but she climbs out of the bed and places her feet on the floor. Like a newborn giraffe finding their legs, she takes a few tentative steps before she can move like normal. A pungent odor trails behind her. Cold sweat and panicked exhales.

"Grab what you need, okay?" I tell her. "It's chilly out. Get a jacket."

I glance down the hallway. Timofey still hasn't come back.

I walk into the living room and look through the least smudged of the glass panes to the ground below. I can see Timofey's broad shoulders standing in front of the building. His back is to me and he's talking to someone, but they are partially hidden behind the bare branches of a dead tree.

"Is he coming back inside?" Mrs. Levin asks.

I startle at the sound of her voice. I forgot she was here, actually.

"Oh, um…" I see the headphones sitting on the coffee table, and I grab them. "He will. When he does, you're going to tell him you don't know anything. Wear these."

She looks at the headphones questioningly, but I slip them on her ears.

"You're going to tell him you didn't see or hear anything. The less you know, the better."

None of this probably makes any sense to her, but hopefully she'll listen anyway.

"Are you running away from him?" she asks.

Guilt twists my insides. I know Timofey is only doing what he thinks is best, but he needs my help. Whether he knows it or not. The only way I can do what I have to do is to leave him.

I nod. "Yeah. We're running away."

She gives me a sad smile. "Take care of Noelle for me."

Mrs. Levin plugs the end of the headphones into the ancient stereo sitting on the desk next to her. After the press of a few buttons, music starts to play, soft and constant through her headphones.

I turn around and find Noelle standing in the doorway, holding a tote bag with a picture of an eggplant on the side. The sight of it makes me want to sob.

"It's my farmer's market tote," Noelle said a few months ago when Ashley and I first saw the bag. We immediately fell over each other laughing.

"Do you go to the market for the food or the farmers?" Ashley teased. "Because that bag is solely for letting everyone know you're there to fetch some dick."

"What? What do you mean? I took this with me to meet Wayne's parents."

Ashley and I howled until tears poured down our faces.

Noelle stared down at the bag for ten full seconds before she pressed her palm to the center of her forehead. "The eggplant stands for a… There's a reason it was on the clearance rack at the grocery store. I can never carry this again, can I?"

"No, you cannot," we told her.

Now, here she is, running into the night in her pajamas with the penis tote bag.

God, life changes fast.

"Do you have everything?" I ask.

Noelle nods, and that's all we have time for.

Timofey will be coming back any second. I don't want to run into him on the stairs.

So I hurry out of the apartment and Noelle stays close behind me.

I remember seeing a back door propped open once when a new tenant was moving into the studio apartment on the first floor. The man and his friend were yelling at each other through the opening, a couch with more rips than fabric wedged firmly inside the doorway.

The door is closed and couchless now, at the end of a dark hallway. I press my hands to the metal bar and hesitate for just a second.

Is this going to set off an alarm? Will Timofey be waiting on the other side for us, having anticipated my plan?

Do I have to run away or can I forget this whole idea and go find Timofey? Can we do this together?

Before the doubts can creep in, Noelle's hand falls over mine and she pushes the door open.

The alarm doesn't sound. When I look back, she isn't even looking at me. She's staring straight ahead.

"Yeah," I say softly, stepping out into the alley. "You're right. We have to keep moving."

We move down the alley to the right, take a left away from the building, and then another right. Timofey will look for me. I know he will. I don't want to be three blocks straight east when he does.

"I'm cold." Noelle wraps her arms around her thin pajama shirt. "Where are we going?"

"I don't know. It's late, so there isn't much open. I thought, maybe, we'd just... We could sit over there?" I point to a bench in front of a closed ice cream shop. The neon ice cream cone light has been shattered and the windows are boarded over with plywood covered in months, maybe years, of graffiti.

"Sit?" She says the word like she hardly knows what it means.

"Yeah. We'll take a load off and… and talk."

That's all I need. Twenty or thirty minutes to figure out what Noelle knows about Benjamin. Then she can be on her way, and I can be on mine.

Her thin wrist is in my hand, but she pulls away. She's shaking her head. "We can't sit. He'll find us."

"Not right away. We have time."

"He can't find us," she says. "*Ever.* That's why we're running away."

I sigh. "No, when I said that I didn't mean we were—We just need to get away for a few minutes to talk, okay? I need to come up with a plan before Timofey finds us."

"Before he finds us?" she splutters. "You said to trust you. You said nothing would happen!"

"Nothing will happen. I just need to figure out what my next move is."

"*Your* next… What about my next move?"

Noelle looks more like herself than she has this entire time. Her brows are knitted together, a line of worry folded between them. Beneath her wild hair, her eyes are wide and clear.

"Timofey said he won't kill you. I'll make sure he doesn't kill you, so—"

"I'm not just trying to survive," Noelle spits. "Not dying isn't quite enough to tempt me, Piper. I want to *thrive.*"

I blink. "Okay. Maybe you can still do that. I don't know. But I just need to talk to you about a few things."

"Maybe? Maybe isn't good enough. Are you going to help me hide from the people after me or not?"

I stare at her, realization beginning to dawn. "You're okay."

"Do I fucking look okay to you?" Noelle throws her arms wide. There's a hole in the armpit of her pajama shirt and the pants are rolled at the waist so many times there is a tube of fabric around her middle. "I'm eking out an existence while I wait for the Albanians or your boyfriend to hunt me down and kill me. I don't need to talk, I need to run. I need to escape. Where did you send Ashley? Send me there, too. I'll go with her."

"You're okay," I repeat in disbelief. "You were faking it before. You aren't having a psychotic episode. You're completely— You're fine! You lied to me!"

Noelle rolls her eyes, and I can't believe I didn't see it from the beginning. The way Timofey did.

He knew she was bullshitting from the moment he arrived.

He also knew I was too sympathetic to see her act for what it truly was.

"I didn't lie to you," she hisses. "I told you the truth: I'm being hunted by the Albanians and your deranged boyfriend. I'm in danger. I wouldn't call that 'completely fine.'"

"Before, when we were in your room, you apologized for Benjamin. Did you mean that?"

"Do I feel bad about what happened to him, you mean?"

"About what you did to him, yeah." I nod, already dreading the answer.

"I regret that it had to happen. I regret—"

"It *had* to happen? You make it sound inevitable."

"It was! Kreshnik was going to get him one way or another. Doing it meant that I could at least save myself. Isn't that better than me *and* the baby being collateral damage?"

I feel nauseous. I would assume it's pregnancy hormones, but Noelle's complete and utter lack of humanity is definitely the root cause.

"You could have gone down with dignity. Instead, you threw a tiny baby to the wolves. What the fuck is wrong with you?"

Noelle tosses up her hands. "Here we go. St. Piper is going to point out all of my sins. Just because you're prepared to throw yourself on the sword at a moment's notice doesn't mean the rest of us are. I have something called 'preservation instinct.' It's an evolutionary trait. You should try it."

Timofey has accused me of the same thing too many times to count. But this feels different.

Noelle is suggesting everyone outside of herself is dispensable. But Timofey is loyal. He looks out for himself *and* the people important to him. He'd rather die than let someone he counted as a friend suffer in his place.

He's a better person than she will ever be.

"Maybe I am too quick to help people who don't deserve it." I gesture to her. "Take yourself as the key example. You have been so busy kidnapping babies and hiding in your own filth that you never once stopped to consider that maybe you didn't have to do everything on your own. Do you realize that Timofey could have gotten your case at the FBI tossed out?"

At that, finally, Noelle seems to blanche.

"Timofey could have protected you, the same way I asked him to protect Ashley and Gram. He could have shielded you from the Albanians and kept you out of prison. All you had to do was ask."

Her mouth opens and closes in sheer shock. The realization seems to deflate her. "He wouldn't have done that for me."

"Yes, he would have. Because he wouldn't have been doing it for you. He would have done it for *me*."

There isn't a single lie in what I just said. No bending of the truth. No exaggeration.

I know Timofey would do anything to keep me safe, to make me happy. Including protecting a woman I thought was my friend.

"Then help me," Noelle begs, suddenly teary-eyed. The emotion looks real enough, but I've peeked behind the curtain now. I know who she really is behind it all.

I shake my head. "It's too late for that."

"The fuck it is!" she screams. "You're lying. You couldn't have done a damn thing to help me, and now you're trying to make me feel bad about helping myself."

"I'm not the liar, Noelle. You are. But you can make things right. You can tell me where Benjamin is."

She arches a brow. "I tell you where Benjamin is and then you'll help me escape?"

Again, nausea twists inside of me. How did I not see Noelle for who she truly is?

"The only way you'll tell me where they took the baby *you* kidnapped is if you get something out of it?"

"That's how the world works, Piper. Stop acting so fucking naive. It's not believable. I mean, you're shacking up with a Bratva don, for fuck's sake. Are you going to stand there and pretend he's some pillar of honesty and sacrifice? The only reason you can ignore his sins is because he's hot and flooded with cash."

Timofey has done bad things. I know that. But why?

That's the difference. Timofey does bad things to protect the people he loves. But he doesn't hurt good people. He doesn't kidnap babies.

I've always thought that to be a good person, I had to sacrifice myself. I had to give everything I had to protect the people in my life and take care of them. But Timofey is right: there's a way to do good and still take care of yourself.

I'm learning that now. I just hope it isn't too late.

"I'm with Timofey because I love him," I tell her. "The same way I was friends with you because I loved you. If you needed help, you could have asked me, Noelle. I would have done anything to help you. But now... now, that time is over. You deserve to be punished for what you've done."

39

TIMOFEY

The door to the apartment is cracked open ever so slightly, just the way I left it. The woman in the wheelchair is still sitting in front of the grimy window in the dining room. She is wearing headphones. I can hear the faint, tinny sound of something loud playing. I walk past her to Noelle's room.

I'm going to grab Piper, force her somewhere safe, and keep her there until this all boils over. Until Kreshnik is dead and Sergey has been neutralized.

Except when I push the door open, the nest of blankets where Noelle had been huddled are tossed to the end of the bed. The bed is empty. No one is in the room.

"Piper?" I spin around and then move down the hall to the next room. Then to the bathroom.

She isn't here.

I storm into the dining room. The woman in the wheelchair is facing me now. The headphones are in her lap and her mouth is set in a firm line.

"They left," she informs me. "They made me face the wall with these headphones on so I wouldn't see or hear anything. 'The less I know, the better.' That's what Noelle's friend said."

My fist clenches into a ball that might never come undone.

Piper was right. If this woman knew anything that could lead me to Piper, I'd torture it out of her.

Why is she always saving everyone else to the detriment of herself?

I run out of the apartment and stomp down the stairs. I know she didn't leave through the front door. She had enough sense not to do that. So I head to the back of the building and find a broken emergency exit door hanging open. I look up and down the alley, but it's empty.

Piper is gone.

40

PIPER

I reach into my pocket and pull out my phone. Timofey's number is the first one in my recent calls list. I tap his name.

Before the call can connect, Noelle slaps the phone out of my hand. "You're not calling anyone. You aren't turning me in."

"I'm calling Timofey. He'll decide where you belong."

I bend down to grab my phone and Noelle yanks my hair. "Fuck no."

My head snaps back, and I swing an arm towards her. My fist glances off of her cheek. Then Noelle takes a swing at me. Her knuckles connect solidly with my cheekbone, and I see stars.

"Stop fighting," she growls. "And stop looking for that baby. He's dead."

Maybe I would have laid down. But her words start a fire in my chest.

Noelle turns to run, and I grab the back of her pajama shirt. The material rips around the collar as she pulls.

"He is not dead! Tell me where—"

"No!" Noelle spins around, the oversized shirt twisting around her midsection. She shoves me back with both hands, and I lose hold of her.

I stumble back. My sense of balance is bad enough on its own, but made even worse by my pregnancy. I'm dizzy.

Noelle could turn and run, but she shoves me again. This time, I don't have any hope of staying on my feet. They're already out from under me.

Instinctively, I twist to try and catch myself on my arms, but I don't realize the bench is right behind me. The corner of the bench catches me hard in the side, and I slide to the ground with a breathless wheeze.

"Don't follow me," Noelle hisses.

Then she turns and runs.

But I'm not paying any attention to her. My hands are folded over my stomach as another wave of nausea rolls through me.

"You're okay," I tell myself, my breaths coming in ragged fits and starts.

Is my baby okay? Did I just sacrifice my child for Noelle? *How will I tell Timofey?*

"I c-can't breathe," I rasp to absolutely nobody. I've never hyperventilated before, but I think that's what is happening now.

My phone is on the sidewalk a few feet away, but I can't force myself to move. I'm afraid I'll cause even more damage. That I'll ruin everything.

I never should have run away. I never should have left Timofey.

I can't breathe.

I can't breathe.

I can't breathe.

41

PIPER

My lungs are collapsing.

My lungs are collapsing and my vision is going dark.

My lungs are collapsing, my vision is going dark, and I'm alone. Completely and utterly alone.

I'm going to die here.

Then a hand, strong and firm, wraps around my back. I'm hauled to my feet and pressed against a body as familiar to me as my own.

"Timofey," I sob, curling into him.

It's the only word I can manage before I have to draw in another shaky inhale. Though the tightness in my chest seems to be easing just with his presence alone.

"Don't talk. Save your breath. I'll take care of you."

His voice is deep and reassuring. I press my ear to his chest and listen to the constant thumping of his heart. In a way, it feels like my own heartbeat. So long as his keeps beating, mine will be okay.

Our baby will be okay, won't it?

"The baby will be fine," Timofey growls. "Just breathe, Piper."

I didn't realize I asked the question out loud. But I listen to his command and focus on inhaling and exhaling.

Time passes both too fast and too slow. It feels like a small eternity that I'm folded in his arms. But we arrive at his car faster than I would have thought possible.

"Watch your head," he says, settling me into the passenger seat.

It's as I watch him walk around the car that I remember Noelle.

"She ran away," I blurt as soon as he opens the driver's side door. "Noelle ran away. She was—"

He reaches out in a flash and brushes his thumb over my lower lip. "I don't give a fuck about her right now, Piper. I only care about you."

"I'm okay." I want to make him feel better. Timofey has lost so much already. Too much. I don't want him to worry about me, too.

He arches a brow. His icy blue eyes are dubious. "I just found you curled in the fetal position on the sidewalk. You aren't 'okay.'"

"Noelle pushed me and I—"

"Stop." His voice is quiet, but commanding. He revs the engine and peels away from the curb. "Don't talk about her right now. If you tell me what she did or where she is, I'll leave you at the emergency room and hunt her down. I'll kill her for this, Piper. So don't tell me. Not yet."

Noelle lied to me, but do I want her to die? It's scary to admit that the answer might not be "no." So I decide to stay quiet until I can see a doctor. Until I know whether my baby is safe or not.

Timofey soars through the sparse late night traffic. I lean back against the headrest and close my eyes.

I must fall asleep, because the next thing I know, Timofey is lifting me gently out of the passenger seat.

"I can walk," I mumble. Even though walking is the very last thing I want to do right now. My legs feel like limp noodles.

"You're exhausted. You haven't slept properly since we got back from Mexico. Let me carry you."

The emergency room is buzzing with people, but I'm taken straight back to a room. I suspect that has a lot to do with who Timofey is, but I don't ask.

"Do whatever tests you have," he tells the doctor as he lays me down on the exam table. "I want all of it. Everything."

I'm weighed and poked and examined. Then a blood pressure cuff squeezes my left arm as the doctor settles the probe of a doppler over my stomach.

The cuff releases and the doctor checks the results. "Good blood pressure."

I don't care about that, I think. *Is my baby okay?*

She continues with the probe, pushing the wand into one side of my stomach and then the other. Her face is twisting into concentration as a devastating silence fills the room.

Then, finally, a rhythm breaks through. But before I can even get excited, the doctor shakes her head.

"That's your heartbeat. Sometimes, when the baby is small, it's hard to latch onto their rhythm. I'll need to do an internal exam."

It's over. My baby is dead.

Hope sinks like a stone in me, but I nod and try a smile. "Okay."

"More," Timofey orders. "Every fucking test you have."

I can't look to see if Timofey is as hopeless as I am right now. Some small part of me is clinging to the fact that he's ordering more tests. He must have hope if he still wants tests.

I undress and don a blue checkered hospital gown. A machine is rolled in. Jelly is smeared.

Again, silence seems to press in on me from every direction. I've never had a claustrophobia attack like this one before, but the yawning silence seems to take up physical space. It's crushing down on me until I can't move. Can't breathe.

"There it is." I look over and the doctor is smiling now. She points to the screen and the small white orb in the center. "I see a little flicker. Let's zoom in on that and give a listen."

The screen shifts closer until the little orb is the size of a golf ball. I can see the flickering movement in the center, but I can't inhale until the sound fills the room. A constant *whoosh, whoosh* of life.

"Fuck yes," Timofey says softly. Then he sweeps forward and presses a kiss to my forehead. "The baby is fine. Perfect."

Tears stream down my cheeks, and suddenly, I can't breathe for the best reason in the world.

"I'll leave you two alone for a minute," the doctor says.

She skirts out of the room, and Timofey squeezes my hand. "This is good news."

"I know. I'm happy. I'm…" I shake my head, unable to find the right word to encompass exactly what I'm feeling. "I'm so sorry."

"For running off?"

"Yeah. And for not listening to you in the first place. You were right about Noelle." I squeeze my eyes closed. "I was so stupid. So fucking… I can't believe I didn't see it."

Timofey smooths my hair away from my face. His touch is surprisingly gentle. "It's okay."

I peek one eye open. "Aren't you going to agree with me? I wouldn't blame you if you did. You looked me in the face and told me exactly what was going on, but I refused to see it."

"Sometimes, love makes us stupid," he says simply. "And you still love Noelle."

I shake my head. "No, I don't. I don't know who she is anymore. I don't—"

"Some habits are hard to break. You love who she used to be. It will take time for you to figure out who she is now. Who she really is."

The weight on my chest eases. It's like, word by word, Timofey is stitching the broken pieces of me back together.

"She's so selfish." I swipe tears from my cheeks. "I don't even think she feels bad about what she did to Benjamin. She only cares about herself. I don't know how I never saw that in her before. How did I miss it?"

"The same way I missed that Sergey is the person who killed Emily."

I glance up, and Timofey's mouth is twisted to one side. It takes all of his willpower to stay calm and blow out a steadying breath.

"Even once I had all of the proof in my hand, I didn't really believe it until he looked in my face and admitted it." He shrugs. "Love and connection... it can blind you to the truth. It makes you see the world through rose-colored glasses."

I glide my thumb over the backs of his knuckles, slowly cresting and dipping between each of his fingers. "Having feelings for someone isn't all bad, though... is it?"

The anger in Timofey's face ebbs. His eyes brighten, and the way he is looking at me makes me flush from head to toe. I want to call the doctor back in and have her take my blood pressure now. It must be through the roof.

"No, it's not all bad. You care about me. It makes you have faith where I don't." He dips down and presses his nose to my cheekbone. I feel his breath warm against my skin. "If there is any chance at all that Benjamin is alive, no matter how slim, I have to look into it. I'm going to see this through to the bitter end with you, Piper."

"Really?"

He nods. "I have men combing through surveillance footage around the property and neighborhood from the night he was taken, including some of the common Xhuvani hangouts. There's also a contingent questioning Albanian allies and acquaintances. If anyone has seen or heard anything about Benjamin, we'll find out about it."

"But when did you—How? When did you change your mind?"

"The moment I went back into that hovel and you were gone." He unfurls my hand along the sharp line of his jawbone and tips his head into my palm. "If you believed that fiercely, then it was worth looking into."

"Do you believe me, then? You think Benjamin is alive?"

He sighs. "No. I don't." I start to frown, but he turns his face and kisses my palm. "I know you want me to have the kind of faith that you do, but I don't, Piper. I think Benjamin is… He's gone. Kreshnik isn't the kind to pull his punches. If he had the opportunity to strike, he would."

I chew on my bottom lip. "That's what Noelle thinks, too. She doesn't think there is any hope. I'm being stupid for—"

Suddenly, Timofey's mouth is on mine. His lips are firm and insistent. He curls his hand around my neck and holds me to him. He kisses me until the ache in my chest dissipates and my thoughts feel hazy and far away.

When he pulls back, he looks into my eyes. "I'm going to do everything I can to look for Benjamin. Then I'm going to do everything I can to track down Noelle. *No one* gets to make you feel stupid for caring, Piper. That's the best fucking thing about you. You care so damn much."

I blink away tears. "I care about you."

I confessed to Noelle that I loved Timofey, but I can't quite summon the words now. It's fine.

He knows.

42

TIMOFEY

Piper sleeps all day.

After we got home from the emergency room, I tucked her into my bed. She fell straight to sleep, and aside from one barely conscious bowl of soup and a bathroom break, she hasn't budged.

Late afternoon sun slants across my bedroom. Stripes of it warm the comforter. I'm lying next to Piper in bed, a book open on my lap that I haven't read a single sentence from in hours.

She's too fucking beautiful.

Her face is puffy and creased from sleeping. Her hair is a tangled mess. She is drooling slightly out of the corner of her pouty mouth. But she is the single most gorgeous creature I've ever laid eyes on.

I reach out and stroke a finger along the delicate hollow of her cheek. She stirs, her brows pinching together. "What time is it?"

"You've been sleeping for sixteen hours."

Her brows rise up cartoonishly, but she still doesn't open her eyes. "You let me waste so much time."

"My men are searching. We haven't wasted anything. You need the rest." I drag my hand lower, tracing her arm and her hip. I press the flat of my palm to her stomach. "The baby does, too."

She smiles sleepily. "Thanks for taking care of us."

"I'll always take care of you."

I'm staring at my hand on her stomach. But when I look back up, Piper's eyes are open. They are a vibrant shade of green, warmed by the golden afternoon light. The way they trail over my body warms me from the inside out, too.

"How are you feeling? Are you hurt or sore? Are you—"

"I'm fine."

She pulls her lower lip into her mouth, and she might as well have reached over and stroked my aching cock. I swallow down a groan.

"Good. Good."

I hold her gaze for another few seconds before I can't control myself. I tug down the blankets, revealing the long stretch of her smooth legs from beneath my t-shirt. She draws them up to her chest.

"I need a shower, Timofey."

"You will when I'm done with you."

Her cheeks turn a bright, bewitching pink. "I smell."

"You smell good to me." I prove that fact by lifting her shirt up and trailing kisses down her stomach and around her hip bones.

"I need to brush my teeth."

I playfully nip at the waistband of her panties. "I don't think I'll smell your morning breath where I'm going."

I press her knees apart and settle between her thighs, still warm from sleep and the blankets. Her panties are a simple blue cotton, and I can see the wet spot growing in the center.

"Fucking gorgeous," I murmur. Then I swipe my tongue over her center, and her thighs clamp down around my ears.

She moans, her back arching, as I suck her clit until she's bucking against my mouth, until she's crying out to the ceiling. By the time she's finished coming on my mouth, she isn't thinking about whether she smells or brushing her teeth. She just grabs me by the hair and pulls me up her body.

Nothing about her is satiated. She slides her hands down my body and reaches into my pants.

"You're so hard," she breathes, stroking me inside my suddenly very constricting pants. "Do you like making me come?"

I drop my forehead to her shoulder. "Fuck, Piper. Don't talk like that. I like it too much."

She giggles and licks my ear. "If you like it, then I'll let you do it again. Fuck me, Timofey."

I think I momentarily black out.

All of the blood rushing to the lower half of my body makes it impossible for me to think clearly. All I know is we are both naked, and I'm hovering over her.

She grips my hips and tugs me towards her. "Please, Timofey. I want you."

I want her, too. More than I've ever wanted anyone.

But I also want this to last.

One by one, I grab her hands and pin them to the mattress. Her body is stretched long, her swollen breasts laid bare before me. I lower my head and swirl her nipple into my mouth.

"Oh," she moans, her eyes fluttering closed. "I'm so... I'm so sensitive. The hormones, I think."

The fact that the baby I put in this woman is changing her body is more alluring than I ever would have imagined. Somewhere deep in my chest, I hear a primal echo.

She's mine.

I flick my tongue across the pebbled skin of her nipple until she's arching off the bed. Her wrists strain against my hold, but I don't let go.

"Please," she begs, squirming from side to side.

Slowly, I lower my hips until I'm pressed against the damp warmth of her opening.

"Yes." She lifts her hips, taking in the very tip of me with a groan. "Yes. Like that."

I'm tempted to sheath myself inside of her, to bury myself to the hilt and never come out.

Instead, I pull back.

Instantly, Piper frowns, ready to protest. But I inch in again. In and out, in and out. I tease her with a little more of my length on every pass until she is trembling.

"This is torture."

"I want to make it last." I kiss the soft skin between her breasts.

She growls in frustration as I tease into her opening again. "You don't need to make it last. We have all the time in the world to do this, Timofey."

Her words shouldn't be an epiphany, but they are.

We have all the time in the world.

She isn't going anywhere. Fuck knows I'm not. This thing between us isn't temporary, and I can make sure I make this woman come in every position known to man.

What a gift.

I look down, and Piper is flushed. She looks nervous.

"I didn't mean—I know we aren't, like, together. I just meant —" She stumbles over the words, feeling self-conscious over nothing.

So I silence her by finally burying myself inside of her.

Her lips part in an "O" of pleasure as I settle deep inside of her. And the primal echo in my chest claws its way up my throat.

"You are mine," I growl, grinding down into her. "You are mine, Piper Quinn."

She tugs against my hold on her wrist, and I let her go. Her hands slide over my shoulders to my neck. Then she's holding my face between her hands, sighing with every slap of our bodies.

"My don," she whimpers. "You're my don, Timofey. Mine."

And that's all it takes.

I grit my teeth and spill into her just as I feel her body clamp down around my length, milking my erection until I collapse on the bed next to her.

"Holy fuck," I rasp.

She laughs and tucks herself against my side, her head on my chest. "My sentiments exactly."

I tug on the ends of her hair and stare up at the ceiling. "We should just stay here forever. My men can handle the Bratva. Viktorov Industries obviously thinks they can operate without me. So I'll just stay here with you, endlessly searching for new ways to make you tremble in my arms."

She shivers. "Don't tempt me. It wouldn't take much to keep me in this bed forever."

"Good." I kiss her forehead. "Because that's the plan. Fuck work. Fuck galas. Fuck—"

Piper gasps and sits up. "The gala! The gala is tonight. The important one. Right? Isn't that what they said in the boardroom? It's a big deal for the company."

"The company that removed me as CEO," I remind her. "I'm not going to that party."

"But they'll come to their senses and reinstate you. I know they will. Once everything about Kreshnik comes out, then they'll—"

"They'll still be a bunch of *mudaks* who doubted me. They doubted my judgment and my leadership." I hold her chin between my thumb and forefinger. "But you never did, Piper. Not once. You always had faith in me."

She holds my wrist, resting her adorable chin in the palm of my head. "If you want to go, I'll be right by your side. Not like this," she says, gesturing to her sex hair and gloriously naked body. "I'll do my hair and get dressed. But you know what I mean. I'll be there for you and with you if you want to go."

I sit up and kiss her full lips. Then I slide off the bed and stretch. "I don't want to go. Viktorov Industries can burn for all I care."

"But Timofey—"

"I'm going to shower." I pad to the bathroom, but pause in the door frame to look back at her. "And to answer your question, I don't like making you come, Piper. I *love* it."

She flushes from head to toe. I know, because I can see every inch of her. I wink and step into the bathroom.

43

TIMOFEY

I meant what I said about Viktorov Industries. The place can fucking burn.

But as I climb out of the shower, I feel the gnawing urge to *do something.* I've never been good at sitting still, but that's all I've been doing for the last twenty-four hours.

I don't regret letting Piper rest. And I'll never regret a single second spent buried in her silky vanilla skin and warmth. Still, none of that eases the restlessness in my bones.

Maybe I could go to the gala. Making a scene in front of all those know-nothing suits might make me feel better.

Then I step into the bedroom and find Piper balled in on herself, softly sobbing in bed.

"Piper?" I'm across the room in an instant, my hand on her back. "What is it?"

She sits up and swipes at her eyes. It almost seems like she's surprised to see me. "It's nothing. I'm being silly."

"This doesn't look silly, Piper. It looks sad. What happened? What—"

Then I see it. The pink and blue striped blanket from the hospital.

After Benjamin's surgery, the hospital sent him home with us covered in that blanket. Piper swaddled him in it that night at the penthouse. She tucked him into his bassinet and cried happy tears over his tiny body.

"I can't believe he's going to be okay," is what she said. "It's a miracle."

Now, there are teardrops on the empty blanket.

And no Benjamin in sight.

"Piper... where did you find this?"

Her chin wobbles, and a fresh wave of tears roll down her cheeks. "It was in the bottom drawer of the dresser. I was looking for a shirt to wear, and I... It still smells like him."

She presses the blanket to her face and dissolves into a puddle.

My heart aches. I've never felt an emotion like this. It's a physical pain that wrenches me apart. The fact I know Piper feels it, too, and I can't do anything to help her only, makes it worse.

"He's *your* son," she sobs. "You're the one who should be upset. I'm sorry that I—"

I roll her onto her side and swallow her body with mine, wrapping her in my arms and tucking her against the curve of my legs until she stops shaking.

"You loved Benjamin as much as I did. You don't have to apologize for crying, Piper."

She nods, and I hold her until her breathing turns deep and even.

In the silence, the restlessness in my bones resurfaces. This time, it has direction.

My men are roving the streets looking for Benjamin. But Noelle is out there, too.

Piper may have been wrong about Noelle, but maybe she was right about one thing: Noelle might know a lot more than she has told us about my son.

If she does, I want to know what. Slowly, carefully, I peel myself away from Piper and tiptoe towards the door.

Once I'm in the hallway, I don't hesitate. I head for the garage and grab my keys.

It's time to do something.

44

TIMOFEY

I don't even need to pick Noelle's lock; the door has been poorly repaired from the last time I kicked it in. All it takes is a firm shoulder and the frame gives way with a groaning burst of dust and splinters.

The last time I was here, I thought Piper had betrayed me. Now, I'm here because she's the person I trust most in the world.

Funny how shit changes.

The room is dim and the air is stale. Clearly, no one has been here for some time.

Still, I call the traitor's name into the gloom. "Noelle."

I don't expect any response, and sure enough, there isn't one.

"Good," I snarl under my breath. If she'd answered, I'd have had to kill her.

I turn towards the desk where I found Piper hiding before. She thought I was the Albanians coming to slaughter whoever was behind the door, but it doesn't quite wipe away the guilt I carry that she was shaking and afraid because of me.

I shove the thought aside and shuffle through Noelle's desk drawers. Beyond bills, a stack of blank envelopes, and a half-used roll of stamps, I don't find anything worthwhile.

Her laptop is in the center of the desk. I grab it and toss it onto the couch. I'll take it with me and let the tech guys have a look at it. I doubt Kreshnik would be stupid enough to email Noelle about his kidnapping plot, but it's always worth checking out.

Smarter people than him have made worse mistakes.

As soon as the thought crosses my mind, I hear the floor creak, and I realize—*I just made a mistake of my own.*

I manage just a single step towards the exit before a shadowy figure appears in the doorway. "Don't move or I'll shoot."

Noelle is holding a gun with both hands as she emerges from the darkness. Her finger is hovering over the trigger.

"Didn't you hear me before? I asked if there were any traitorous bitches around," I *tsk*. "You didn't reveal yourself."

"I make it a point not to throw out the welcome mat for people who break into my apartment." She nods towards the door. "I found that hanging off the hinges when I got here. Was that you or should I be expecting Kreshnik to show up at any moment, too?"

"It was me both times. But don't flatter yourself: I was here to find Piper the first time."

She frowns. "Piper came here?"

"The night you kidnapped Benjamin. She was looking for evidence to get you thrown into prison."

"What a friend," she snorts.

"She thought prison would be a safer option for you, considering all the enemies you'd made. Though she didn't even know you'd kidnapped Benjamin, at the time. When I told her, she couldn't believe it. She didn't think you were capable of something so horrendous."

Even in the dark, I can tell Noelle is flustered. She isn't comfortable with her role as the villain in this tale. "Desperate times and all that. My back was against the wall."

"You walked into that corner with eyes wide open," I growl. "You fucked up, you stole from your company, and then you handed a child over to his death to save what was left of your pathetic life."

Noelle actually laughs. "You don't understand what I've been through. You have no idea what I've had to do. You know what's funny? Piper told me that I should have come to *you* for help. Can you believe that?"

I actually can't. I've hated Noelle since before I even met her. It was clear as day to me that everyone in Piper's life was a parasitic leech, sucking her dry. I would have happily cut every single one of them loose.

"Piper has always been an optimist."

"That's what I told her. But she seems to think you'd do anything to make her happy. Including helping me."

If Noelle had come to me, I would have slammed the door in her face. But Piper... If she'd come to me, worried about her friend, and begged me to help, would I have done it?

I know the answer instantly. *Without hesitation.*

My mouth quirks into a half-smile. "Piper is an optimist, but she is also far too smart for her own good. She's right. I would have done whatever she asked of me."

Noelle's mouth drops open for a second. Clearly, she didn't believe Piper. But hearing the words from my mouth has changed her mind.

She blinks, her hold on the gun going slack. The muzzle shifts off-target, pointing over my right shoulder now. "You would help me?"

"What were you guilty of before you added kidnapping to your rap sheet? A little white collar crime?"

She nods. "I stole some—a lot—of money. Over a long period of time."

I wave a dismissive hand. "Shit like that gets swept under the rug all the time. Pay off the right people and it all goes away. You would have been free and clear."

She is pale now. Her face glows like a full moon in the dark, cratered with regret and disbelief. "Well, could you—"

"Careful, Noelle. If you ask me to help you right now, I'll be sick."

Her mouth twists into a scowl. "You and Piper are the same, dangling hope in front of someone just to wrench it away. I was right from the beginning. You never would have helped me."

I hear Sergey's words again. *This is your problem. You want to be wholly independent, but a good don knows how to rely on the people around him. He knows how to use their strengths to his advantage.*

Noelle doesn't know how to depend on other people. She had the best friend she ever could have hoped for in Piper, and she tossed her aside for a life of forever running from her sins.

"I never would have helped you," I confirm. "But Piper would. She still will right now, actually. That's why I'm here."

Noelle looks past me like she expects to see Piper in the doorway. "What?"

"You ran off the other night, and I found Piper laying on the ground, hurt."

"I didn't hurt her!" she blurts. "I was trying to get away, but she grabbed me and—"

I hold up a hand to silence her. I'm not sure I'll be able to see my plan through to the end if I have to listen to her speak more than necessary.

"I told Piper I was going to hunt you down and kill you. But she begged me not to. She pleaded with me to give you another chance to make things right."

Noelle was right before. I am dangling hope in front of her now. And I can plainly see that she is ready to bite.

"She asked about Benjamin. She wanted to know more about where he was taken." The question lurks beneath the statement. She already knows what I want to know.

"Like I said, Piper is an optimist. She thinks Benjamin could still be alive."

Noelle looks down at the floor. "I told her what I thought."

"I don't care what you think," I retort. "I care about what you know. If you tell me everything that happened between when you took Benjamin from his crib and the last time you saw him, then…"

She stares at me, waiting for me to finish the sentence. But I don't know how to. Every fantasy I've had of this moment ends in Noelle lifeless on the floor. I'm not sure how to even pretend there is another possibility.

"Then what?" she snaps. "What will happen to me? Or maybe you haven't gotten that far yet. Maybe your plan doesn't extend beyond pumping me for information."

She's holding the gun more confidently now, once again aiming at my chest. I wonder how good of a shot she is.

When I don't answer, she grimaces. "I knew it. You're fucking lying," she says, shaking her head at her own gullibility. "You were never going to help me. Piper never asked you to spare me, did she?"

Her upper lip curls. I've seen this same expression on the faces of too many men to mistake it for anything else now.

Noelle is ready to kill.

45

PIPER

I fall asleep with Timofey's warmth blanketing me, his heart beating against my back.

The next time I open my eyes, I'm alone.

I know immediately that he isn't behind me. But I know he isn't in the room, either. It's the way animals know a storm is coming. Some mechanism deep inside of me that registers the difference in the air. The lack of him.

I roll over, arm stretched across the cold mattress. He's been gone for a while, then. Long enough for his body heat to fade from the blankets.

I wipe sleep from my eyes and sit up. His phone isn't on the bedside table and his wallet isn't in the cup on the dresser.

Would he have gone to the gala without me?

"No." I shake my head and lay back on the pillows. Wherever he is, I'm sure he'll be back soon.

I haven't had much to eat the last twenty-four hours. I consider padding down to the kitchen. Maybe Akim is there and can make me something. Though when I try to think about what I'd ask him for, nothing comes to mind.

I pat my stomach. "You're going to starve your mom if you don't quit making me nauseous."

Mom.

It's the first time I've really considered the title. It's the first time I've ever applied it to myself, that's for sure.

I smile. "I'm going to be a mom. *Your* mom."

Timofey will be a dad.

The thought sends an immediate shiver down my spine. I feel a quiver low in my core that tells me it wouldn't take much at all for me to have an entire brood of kids with this man.

I can see it, a little movie in my head. Timofey and I, surrounded by dark-haired, blue-eyed little angels.

"He's going to be such a good dad to you," I whisper, curling my arm over my midsection. "He will always protect you and take care of you. You'll be so loved."

I close my eyes and settle back into the pillows just as the door creaks open.

My smile splits my face wide. "I was just talking about you."

There's an unfamiliar chuckle. "Hopefully, all good things."

The hairs on the back of my neck stand on end, and I bolt upright in bed. Sergey is standing in my bedroom.

46

TIMOFEY

I dodge to the right a millisecond before she pulls the trigger.

Sound explodes in the small space. I smell gunpowder and see smoke in the air as I charge at her.

Noelle flails, trying to readjust her aim. Luckily for me, she hasn't had any formal training. She doesn't know what she's doing.

A second shot goes off. The blast rings in my ears, so I know it was close. But I'm still standing. I'm okay.

A moment later, Noelle can't say the same.

I drive into her midsection with my shoulder. The wind rushes out of her in a grunt, and she releases the gun. It clatters to the floor, but doesn't go off. Another stroke of luck.

By the time she recovers and tries to fight back, my hand is around her neck. "Tell me what happened to Benjamin."

"You'll kill me either way," she splutters.

Her face is turning red from the press of my palm against her throat. I press down further, though not as far as I'd like. What I wouldn't give to crush the life out of this snake here and now.

"Maybe I will," I admit. "But if you tell me what you know, at least you'll die with honor."

She tries to laugh, but it comes out choked. "Piper blabbed about honor, too. Funny, since she's dating you. There's no honor in a life of crime. I should know."

"You don't understand shit. Not about me or Piper."

"Look at yourself," she says. "You're choking a woman on the floor. What kind of honor is—"

I lean forward until I'm in her face, teeth gritted. "I'm here for Benjamin. And for Piper. I do what I do to take care of the people I love. I do it to make sure the men I employ can feed their families and take care of themselves. In the process, I hurt as few people as possible. There is honor in loyalty. There's honor in thinking about a single other human beyond yourself. Though you wouldn't know much about that."

She stares up at me, and for the first time, I look back. *Really* look back.

What I thought were exhausted dark circles under her eyes are actually bruises poorly covered with makeup. Her nose sits slightly crooked, the bridge holding onto a hint of swelling. A shadow along her jaw doesn't match the dim light source of the bedroom window behind her.

"Who beat the shit out of you?" I ask.

Her expression hardens. "Who the fuck do you think?"

"Kreshnik is not the kind of man people go into business with on a whim. You were stupid not to come to me for help."

She twists her head away, staring at the wall. "Yeah, well, it's too late for regrets now."

"It's never too late to make things right, though. Tell me what happened to Benjamin."

She sets her jaw. "You wouldn't believe me if I told you."

"Try me." She doesn't move, but I loosen my hold on her neck. "What else have you got to lose?"

I think Noelle might be stubborn until her last breath, but then she turns to face me. "I had Benjamin with me at first. I kept him for a couple days after I... after I got him from your house. Kreshnik was worried about me being followed or captured by the police. If I went directly to him with the child, it could be dangerous for him."

"Where did you take him?"

"A safehouse Kreshnik gave me the key to. It was some studio apartment uptown. I stayed there for a couple days. He didn't get the place ready at all. There weren't any diapers or other supplies, so I had to buy everything with my own money. Diapers, formula, a bassinet. It was expensive."

"If you're asking for a reimbursement, you can go to hell," I growl.

She swallows, her throat bobbing against my palm. "I'm just telling you that I... I took care of him. I took care of him, and doing that for someone changes things. He was so helpless. So tiny. I didn't—I couldn't—"

Her voice cracks, and I think it's real. Piper said Noelle didn't regret anything, but I see the hint of it now. I repeat her own words back to her. "It's too late for regrets."

She clears her throat and gathers herself. "I tried to get away. I know you think I'm some monster, but I had doubts about what I was doing. I wanted to bring Benjamin back to you, but Kreshnik was watching the safehouse. The moment I left, he tracked me down. He—he ripped Benjamin from my arms."

My hands are shaking with the desire to clench into fists. I let go of Noelle's throat so I don't accidentally strangle her. "Why didn't he kill you?"

"I told him it was a misunderstanding. I told him I wasn't trying to escape. And he believed me."

I arch a brow. "I don't know if you've looked in a mirror, but it doesn't look like he believed you. He broke your face."

She brings a hand to the bridge of her nose and touches it gingerly. "Yeah. Well, he wanted to make sure I understood what would happen if I did ever betray him. The black eyes and broken nose were just a taste, apparently."

I shake my head. "Again, why not kill you?"

"I didn't feel the need to question my good fortune. I was just happy to be alive."

"Did he tell you what he was going to do with Benjamin?"

"No. And I didn't ask. I didn't want to know."

"But you think he's dead?" I ask.

She looks up at me with wide eyes. "Don't you?"

I do. Or, I did.

Suddenly, I'm not sure.

Kreshnik should have killed Noelle. That's what I would have expected. But he kept her alive.

Why?

I seriously consider the question for a few seconds before the answer slaps me in the face.

"You're the distraction." I pound my fist on the floor next to Noelle's head. She shrinks away from my fury. "He left you alive to distract me. To divide my focus. Fucking—Fuck!"

"Let me live, and I won't be a distraction anymore," she blurts. "Let me live, and I'll... I'll tell you what I know!"

I narrow my eyes. "We just played that game. Were you telling me the truth or—?"

"I was! I was telling the truth, but I know more. While I was at the safehouse, I met one of the guards. He and I—well, we became close. I wanted a second source of information, so I—"

"You fucked him." I circle my hand in the air to encourage her to spit it out already. "I get it. What about him?"

Her face is flushed with embarrassment. "Well, he told me that Kreshnik was going to embarrass you in every way imaginable. The airport was one stunt, but he wants you to be left with nothing. No heir, no Bratva, and no company. He said Kreshnik was planning to crash a party you were throwing with your—"

"The gala."

I grab the gun from the floor and stand up. Noelle scrambles into a seated position. "Are you going to kill me?"

The gun is in my hand. It would be simple. One shot and she'd be done.

But when I look down at Noelle, all I see is Piper.

I curse under my breath and jab a finger in her direction. "I don't want to see you again. Ever. Don't darken my doorstep, don't speak to Piper. I don't even want to hear your name for as long as I live. You disappear and you stay the fuck away from my family. Do you understand?"

She nods frantically. "I understand. I'll never—"

I don't stay to listen. There isn't time.

My son needs me.

47

PIPER

I'm so shocked that I can't actually process what I'm seeing. My tongue is three times its usual size, and I can't form the words.

Sergey fills the silence. "Were you really talking about me or were you expecting someone else?" He smiles mischievously. His eyes roam over me, taking in my mostly bare legs peeking out from under Timofey's t-shirt. "Did the don leave you all alone?"

"What are you doing here?" I finally manage.

"Can't a father visit his son at home?"

"Timofey will kill you if he finds you here. You should leave before he gets back."

I'm shaking all over, but I do my best to put power behind my words. One day, maybe, I'll be a Bratva wife. I'll have to learn how to command a room the way Timofey does.

Clearly, I'm not there yet. Sergey doesn't flinch at all. In fact, he takes a step closer to the bed.

"I appreciate your concern, but Timofey won't find me here. I designed it that way. He's all the way on the other side of town right now."

I could scream. But the only person who might hear is one of the maids. Sergey will kill them dead before they can do anything useful.

I could fight, but I'm pregnant. And nearly naked. Sergey is old, but I don't think that's enough of an advantage.

Then I glance at my phone laying on the dresser at the end of the bed. I haven't even looked at it since Timofey brought me home from the hospital yesterday. It might even be dead.

But it also might be my only hope of escape.

"Do you have someone following him?" I ask, tucking my legs underneath me and sitting on my heels. It will be easier to lunge forward from this position.

"A good magician never reveals his secrets," Sergey says with a grin.

He wants me to think he has Timofey held hostage or something. It's a possibility, I know. But I dismiss it. Timofey would never go quietly. Besides, I'd feel it if he wasn't okay. I'd sense it in the marrow of my bones.

"Do good magicians reveal why the fuck they're in my bedroom? Because that's what I want to know."

"Oh my, someone has a mouth on her. Does my son like that about you or are you a work in progress?"

I frown. "Timofey likes me for who I am. I don't need to change for him."

He rolls his eyes. "Of course. I spent the last fifteen years molding Timofey into an alpha, and one good pussy is going to undo it all. Now, he's a weak beta, handing over his crown for the likes of you. That's the way it works, isn't it? Smart men wither to idiots over love. It's why I never bothered with love at all. Too much hassle."

"I doubt you're even capable of it. You have to have a heart to experience love."

"You think I'm heartless? I should be offended, but oddly, I feel nothing." He chuckles. "Maybe you're right after all."

"You have to be heartless. Or stupid. It's the only way you could be so blind to the fact that your 'son' is the most amazing man I've ever met. He is a better leader than you could ever be. But all you want is for him to be your foot soldier."

"Now," he tuts, "that is just not true. Timofey has always been obstinate, but he had a natural eye for business and a talent for leadership. I fostered those abilities and helped them grow into the great don he became. I always supported him. But Timofey didn't like everything I had to do to get there."

"You killed his best friend!"

Sergey shrugs. "I don't regret it. If that girl—"

"Emily," I spit. "Her name was Emily."

"If *Emily* really cared about Timofey, she never would have tried to tell Rodion who his father was. That girl was putting Timofey's leadership at risk. I did what needed to be done to secure it."

I scoot forward, hoping it looks like I'm shifting from the passion of the moment rather than with a destination in mind. If I get another foot or two closer, I'll be able to lunge off the bed, grab the phone, and hopefully call Timofey before Sergey can wrest the phone away from me.

"That's the difference between you and Timofey," I say. "He doesn't need to lie and cheat and murder to trick people into following him. He's charismatic and bold. He earned the respect of his men. You're probably just jealous of him."

I toss out the accusation as more of a distraction than anything, but it lands harder than I expect.

Sergey's face flushes. "How can I be jealous of a man that I built? I created the man you think is so wonderful. Timofey would be dead without me."

"That must make it even worse," I say. "You adopted him because you thought he'd be your puppet to control. But you couldn't even do *that* right. He outshined you in every way. Now, you're struggling to hold onto the reins."

His nostrils flare and his smile uncovers a new edge to it that wasn't there before. "I didn't come here to hear your amateur theories."

"Why did you come here?"

"To pick you up, my dear," he says as though I should have known it all along. "We have a gala to attend."

"I'm not going anywhere with you. If you don't leave, then I'll—"

"Die."

I blink at him, shocked. But Sergey only shrugs.

"You'll die," he repeats. "You are not a crucial part of the plan, to be honest. More of the icing on top. If you don't cooperate, I'll kill you."

"But if you—You can't. If you do, Timofey will never forgive you. He'll kill you."

Sergey grins, and I feel like there's ice water in my veins. "Come on, Piper. It's time to go."

He takes a step towards the bed, and this is my moment. There's no time for subtlety.

I lunge for the end of the bed, scramble onto the floor, and grab my phone. The moment I get my hand around it, Sergey swats it out of my hand.

The man has a surprisingly powerful hit. My hand stings. But I barely have time to register the pain before he has me pinned to his chest with the iron band of his arm. His free hand skates down over my hip, teasing the hem of Timofey's t-shirt.

His breath is heavy on the back of my neck. "It would be rude to take a call in the middle of a conversation, Piper. You have company."

"You are not welcome here," I spit.

"Oh?" He slips his hand down my thigh, curling his fingers dangerously close to the edge of my panties. "Am I imposing? I hate to intrude. I prefer a warm welcome. Then again, sometimes you have to do what needs to be done. If someone doesn't give you what you want, you have to take it."

My heart is thundering in my chest. Sergey's words are too plain to be misunderstood.

He sighs in disappointment. "Unfortunately, we don't have time to linger. As I said, we have an event to get to. Are you ready?"

"Fuck you."

He chuckles and slaps my ass hard enough to bruise. "Don't tempt me."

Then he leads me out of the room, down the hall, and out to a waiting car.

I don't see a single other soul the entire way.

48

PIPER

The front of Viktorov Industries is lit up. Garden lights lining flower beds and the manicured lawn. White and blue colored beams streaking up the white stone face of the building. The Viktorov Industries logo is projected on the water flowing from a stone fountain in the middle of the entryway.

People in their finest evening wear are mounting the stairs and making their way inside. Staff hired to work the event hold the doors open, ushering everyone into the warm glow of the lobby.

Sergey drives past all of this and wraps around the back of the building to the loading bay.

A single flickering white light hangs above a large garage door. The rest of the lights in the alley are burnt out. Or, more likely, shot out.

"What's the matter? You didn't get an invite to the big party?" I ask. "You have to sneak in the back like a commoner?"

Sergey's hands tighten on the steering wheel. "Shut your fucking whore mouth."

I jolt at the venom in his voice. I'm used to Sergey being the sly, smiling conman. The kind of snake charmer who will shake your hand as he empties your pockets.

But he is rigid now, his expression bleak as his eyes search the dark alley.

It hits me all at once: *he's nervous.*

"Are we here to meet someone?" I look out the windshield, seeing monsters in every shadow.

Suddenly, at the end of the alley, a light flickers on and off.

Sergey hits the gas and drives down to the end of the alley. As soon as he stops the car, a door opens.

I'm staring into the black mouth of the door, trying to make out anything about what's beyond it. About what is waiting for me.

Then I feel a gun pressed to my spine. "Get out and walk to that door. If you run, I'll shoot."

I hold up my hands on instinct. They tremble in the air. "Do you really need a gun to handle me, Sergey? I thought you were tougher than this."

"The plan is delicate now," he admits, his voice low. "I can't have you fucking it up. Now, move."

I'm barefoot and wearing nothing but a t-shirt. I won't make it far like this. Running isn't an option.

So I climb out of the car and walk towards the door. I hear Sergey moving behind me, his footsteps careful as he matches my pace.

"Who turned on the light? It flickered. Someone told you where to go. Who was it?"

"Shut up and keep moving," Sergey barks. "We don't have time for your—"

"Hello again, Piper." The man in front of me is doused in shadow, but I don't need to see his face to recognize his voice.

Kreshnik.

I try to scramble back, but Sergey's damned gun jabs into my spine. "I thought we were going to make the reveal once she was inside... and gagged."

Kreshnik Xhuvani smiles at me, a sick kind of amusement in his gaze. "I just couldn't wait. There's something about this one, isn't there?" He reaches out and strokes my cheek. "I like to see her scared."

"If we don't move quickly, lots of people are going to *see* her. This plan doesn't work if he—"

"This plan is going to work perfectly because I'm the one executing it," Kreshnik snaps. "You came to me, Sergey, remember? Trust that I know what I'm doing."

I turn back to Sergey, doing my best to ignore the gun aimed at me. "Be a good dog, Sergey. Do what Master says."

Sergey's face turns beet red. He raises his free hand like he's going to slap me, but Kreshnik claps his hands together loudly. The sound echoes down the alley.

"Save it for our audience, Sergey."

"What audience?" I ask.

Kreshnik shakes his head at Sergey, and the two men lead me silently into the hotel.

We walk down cinderblock halls with exposed pipes running along the ceiling, far from anywhere a guest might wander. We turn into a kind of storage room. Metal shelves line the walls. An artificial Christmas tree broken down into three massive sections hulks in the corner, covered in a large drop cloth. Two chairs sit in the middle of the space.

Sergey pushes me towards them. "Sit."

"Who else is coming?" I ask.

Kreshnik jerks his arm towards the chair, growing impatient. "Don't ask questions you know the answer to. Sit down and do as you're told."

"And what? You'll spare me?" I snort. "Don't pretend I'll get a gold star for following orders. You're going to kill me either way."

Kreshnik stalks towards me slowly. "You're right. I am going to kill you."

I stand as tall as I can. It's hard to feel powerful in a thin t-shirt and nothing else, but I refuse to die as a coward. "Then fuck you."

"Ah-ah," he warns with a wag of his finger. "You're being selfish, dear. Your behavior won't just reflect on you. It will be a reflection of the entire class. Everyone will suffer."

I look around the obviously empty room. "No one else is here."

"Not yet. But they will be."

My heart is in my throat. I have to clear it twice before I can voice the question. "Who?"

His smirk is lethal. "As I said, don't ask questions you already know the answer to."

"Timofey won't fall into your trap." I'm saying it mostly to convince myself. To ease the panic clawing at my insides.

"You don't think so?"

"No, I don't. He's smarter than you. He won't fall for it."

Kreshnik pushes me down into the chair and leans in until his cruel face is all I can see. "He already has."

I shake my head, even as his words drip like cold water down my spine. "If you think Timofey will throw away his entire Bratva for me, you're wrong. I won't let him."

"Don't underestimate your appeal." Kreshnik steps back and eyes me from head to toe. "Men have thrown away everything for less. But I'm also not the type to put all of my eggs in one basket. I have a back-up plan."

I'm about to ask what he means when I hear a sound. A soft whimper coming from the corner near the Christmas tree.

Is Timofey tied up beneath the drop cloth?

I search the tree, looking for signs of movement. All of my senses are heightened, my body in tune to every movement and sound.

Then I see it.

A basket on the floor. It's wicker, so it blends into the shadows. The blanket inside matches the drop cloth, a pale cream color. But it's... moving.

"What is—"

"Men will do a lot to avoid seeing their family murdered before their eyes," Kreshnik says, strolling over to the basket. He reaches down and plucks a bundle out, taking it into his arms.

I feel like I'm going to be sick.

He turns to me, and I can see Benjamin. Swaddled and perfect.

He's alive.

My hope wasn't misplaced. He's alive and breathing. Benjamin is alive.

"Unfortunately," Kreshnik says, pressing a kiss to the baby's pink cheek, "you, the baby, and Timofey will all die either way."

The hope turns to dust in my hands. Benjamin is alive.

The question now is: *for how much longer?*

49

TIMOFEY

The entrance to the building is lit up like a gaudy beacon. A signal fire screaming, "Invest in us so we can waste more money on fancy parties."

The fountain was brought in specifically for the event, driven in on an oversized truck and filled with water dyed a special shade of blue. It took eight men all day to set it up. Not to mention the valets, the servers, the women who are paid by the hour to make the important guests feel "welcomed."

They won't write "escorts" on the cost breakdown, of course. It will be lumped in with some other line item to make sure no one can accuse the board of bribing investors with prostitutes.

If it had been up to me, this event would have been an email. But the board, in all of their wisdom, insisted. I've made the company more than enough money that I relented. If they needed to burn some cash to blow off steam, then so be it.

Apparently, I should have kept them on a shorter leash.

But this party isn't a symbol; it's a target. And the only person who could have defended them from attack isn't even on the guest list.

I have a feeling that by the end of tonight, they'll all be forced to face their regrets.

I slam my car into park and climb out at the curb. A valet scrambles over. "Keys, sir? We can park—"

"Leave it. I'll be back."

"But, sir… You can't—I have to park—"

"Leave it," I repeat in a growl.

The kid is barely twenty, if that. He slinks back to the valet stand, and I cut through the crowd of guests mounting the stairs.

Women in gowns and jewels cling to the arms of their rich husbands. All of them have a scowl reserved for me.

They probably don't recognize me out of a suit.

The chairman of the board has no trouble recognizing me, however. Manuel is standing next to the fountain with an investor he's been trying to bag for months. I tasked him with talking to the man, despite the fact I have enough blackmail on the banker to demand not only his investment, but the keys to his house and the cut he makes laundering cartel drug money. I'll never tell Manuel that little secret now. His loss.

The moment he sees me, Manuel separates from the conversation and sidles up next to me.

"What are you doing here?" he hisses, a smile still on his face.

I don't break pace, forcing Manuel to jog to keep up. "I heard there's an open bar."

"Seriously, Timofey."

"Seriously," I say. "I could use a drink. By the looks of it, you could too. Maybe a few drinks would soften up your favorite investor over there enough that he'll forget you're an insufferable blowhard."

I can practically hear his teeth grinding together. "You aren't dressed for the event."

"Really? What do you think is the appropriate look for a former CEO? A suit felt too formal."

As we walk, my eyes scan the crowd. I don't see Kreshnik anywhere, but I'm not surprised. He'll reveal himself only when he is good and ready.

Unless I find him first.

"Timofey, I don't want to call security, but—"

"Fuck you. Of course you want to call security on me. It's the only way you would ever be able to personally escort me from the premises. You sure as hell aren't capable of doing it yourself. You couldn't move me an inch to the left if your miserable fucking life depended on it."

Manuel adjusts the cuff of his shirt. "I don't want to call security, but if you are here to fuck up this event, then—"

"Then what?" I snap, turning to tower over Manuel. "I'll no longer be CEO? You saw to that already. And you'll live to regret it. You'll live to regret interrupting me now, too. Because one day, I'll be back on top, and you'll still be a barnacle clinging to the underside of my boat for dear fucking life. If you're not careful, I'll scrape you off and let you float into the abyss."

Before Manuel can say anything else, I walk through the front doors into the lobby.

The main party is in the convention hall to the left, but the lobby is clogged with people. They are gathered around the coat check and taking pictures in front of the photo booth set up next to the receptionist's desk.

What's the point in attending a party full of rich men looking to get richer if you can't brag about it online while wearing a feather boa?

I weed through the slush in search of the only person who matters. I have no idea what Kreshnik has planned, but if he's willing to show up at this gala to unveil it, it can't be good.

I'm almost to the back of the lobby, ready to shift into the convention center to continue my search, when I hear my name.

"Timofey."

It takes me a second to spot the open door. It's the same wood paneling as the rest of the wall, clearly a come and go for the building's employees.

And standing in the crack is my father.

I walk towards him, hoping not to draw much attention. The last thing I need on top of Kreshnik crashing the party is Sergey showing up.

"You survived," I growl. His midsection looks lumpy. Probably bandages under his shirt.

"What have I always told you? Be decisive. Stabbing me in the stomach was a wishy-washy attempt."

"Noted. Next time, I'll go for the heart."

He shifts back further into the shadows. "'Next time' will have to wait. I have something to talk to you about."

"Not now. I'm busy."

"Looking for Kreshnik?" I stare at him, eyes narrowed, but he only shrugs. "I may not run the Bratva, but I still hear the rumors. He is here tonight."

"Tell me where."

"If I knew where he was, would I be lurking in a butler's closet?" He looks past me, eyes sweeping over the room. "But I am here to help you. If you'll let me."

"I'm not going to sell my soul to the devil to—"

"We've all sold our souls to something," he interrupts. "But this isn't about the partnership. I'm smart enough to know a lost cause when I see one. This is about avoiding a second knife to the stomach."

"Since when are you afraid of a fight?"

"Since I realized I'm not in fighting shape anymore." He gingerly pats his abdomen. "My value lies in my wisdom now. And I think you're going to want to hear what I have to say."

I have no interest in doing any business with Sergey, but I have no clue where Kreshnik is or what he has planned. If Sergey knows something, then I'd be stupid to refuse the information.

Plus, I can always kill him if the information doesn't pan out.

I nod, and he shifts aside to let me through. I step into the passageway and the door closes behind me.

"These secondary hallways were installed for the janitorial staff to travel through the building without being detected," he says.

Sergey trained me in this building—I was CEO for years— but I never knew these hallways existed. I'm sure Sergey did that on purpose.

"God forbid anyone catch sight of a mop and think the building gets cleaned."

"You laugh, but so much in life is about appearances. People want things to *be* clean, they don't want to see them be cleaned. It's the same way people want to be secure, but they don't want to see what it takes to make that happen."

I clench my teeth. "If you try to justify killing Emily for my good again, I'll kill you here and now. It'll make it easier for the janitor to sweep you away."

"I'm not saying anything," he says. "Just chit-chatting."

"Save your breath. Say what you need to say or—"

"In here." He points to the next doorway. "Sound carries down these hallways. I don't want any eavesdroppers."

I follow him into the room, keeping my hand on the gun I stole from Noelle's apartment.

It's a generic office. A desk and a whiteboard on one wall, an empty bookshelf on the other. There's no window, but a painting of a bear standing in a stream with a salmon in his mouth has the word "PATIENCE" written underneath it.

I'm sure that's the takeaway from the bear's perspective. I wonder what the salmon would have to say about it.

"I'm not going to waste your time explaining that I can help you secure your position as don and legitimize your claim to my throne."

"Good. I'd hate to stab you twice for the same offense."

He swallows, running his tongue over his teeth. "But you know as well as I do that allies don't need to be friends. They don't need to like each other at all. They simply need to have a shared set of interests."

"As far as I can see, your only interest is in saving your own skin." I shrug. "In that regard, our interests are diametrically opposed."

"No, my interest is in peace."

I bite back a bitter laugh. "Is that what you call murdering your own son in cold blood? Not to mention his girlfriend, too. Was it peace, Sergey, when you murdered Emily for learning about your secret bastard child?"

"I told you: people want to feel secure, but they don't want to see what it takes to get there."

I clench my fists. "I told you not to compare that to—"

"I'm only saying that I had my reasons. The status quo is a dangerous thing to upset. The Viktorov Bratva being in power—that is the status quo. It provides stability and peace. But Kreshnik Xhuvani has other ideas."

"Ideas I'll crush the moment I bash his skull in," I grit out. "He isn't a threat to me."

"If you truly believe that, you're a bigger fool than I thought."

He realizes the danger of his words the moment he says them. His jaw shifts back and forth, nervous under the intensity of my glare.

"What do you need to say to me, Sergey?"

"I need to tell you that I am an asset. More than you realize."

"How?"

"The men trust me."

I open my mouth to respond. Then I notice the look on his face. The smug smirk pulling up one corner of his mouth.

"What the fuck did you do?" I growl.

"It was easy to get inside your mansion, Timofey. A man loyal to me convinced a younger guard to allow me inside for a visit. No one stopped me on my way up to your bedroom. They never even saw Piper in the backseat as I exited through the front gates."

I'm across the room in an instant, my forearm pressed against his doughy neck. "Forget stabbing you. I'll fucking gut you if you hurt a single hair on her head."

Sergey has to stretch onto his toes to suck in a wobbly breath. "She's fine... for now."

"Is that it, then? You're going to blackmail me into working with you?" I growl. "What happens when Piper is back with me, Sergey? What happens when your leverage is gone? How long do you think you'll live, then?"

"I'll secure a deal with you. You're a man of your word."

"I was," I admit. "That has been the status quo. But I'm not as scared of change as you are. Maybe I'm ready to shake things up."

Sergey swallows. I feel the desperate gulp against my arm. He's nervous.

And it hits me then—all at once. Sergey is not some all-powerful leader. He isn't special.

He is a man. A selfish, prideful, foolish man.

And, worst of all, he's desperate.

Otherwise, he wouldn't be standing here in front of me. If he had any other option available to him, he never would have come to see me. Especially after I stabbed him in the gut. But he is pressed into a corner, and he doesn't see another way out.

"If the Bratva is as unsteady as you seem to think, you wouldn't need to secure a deal with me to survive," I tell him. "Would you?"

Sergey doesn't answer. His eyes are wide, and he keeps looking at the door like he expects someone to burst in and save him.

"Would you?" I repeat, squeezing the air out of him.

"I have allies that would surprise even you," he rasps. "Work with me, and you can keep your Bratva. You can even become CEO of Viktorov Industries again."

I lean closer, my teeth bared. "Fuck the Bratva and fuck Viktorov Industries."

"Some loyal don you are," he spits.

"Nothing is more important to me than my family. Nothing matters more than Piper and Benjamin." *And my unborn child.* "Do you have her?"

"No."

"Don't fucking lie to me."

"I'm not," he says. "*I* don't have her. But like I said, I have a lot of allies."

I'm torn between the urge to grab my phone and call to check on Piper and to keep interrogating Sergey. I should have stayed home with her. I shouldn't have left her alone. Piper's face floods my mind, and I have to wade through the images to focus on the task at hand.

"I have allies, too. Detective Rooney has proven to be well worth the money. He'll bury you so deep that no one will remember your fucking name."

He blinks, realizing I'm serious. "I'll tell you where Piper is if you let me go. I'll flee. You'll never see me again."

I wrinkle my nose. "Desperation does not look good on you. You are a rat fleeing a sinking ship. There's nowhere to go, but you keep scurrying in search of a lifeboat."

"You don't understand. Piper is in danger… right now. If you don't listen to me, she'll die. Benjamin, too."

I freeze, turning on him with full intensity. "What?"

"Kreshnik has them both. He's holding them as ransom to secure the Bratva from you. But if you listen to me, I'll help you keep the Bratva and—"

"I don't give a fuck about the Bratva," I growl. "And I don't give a fuck about you. There is nothing in the world that would make me trust you after everything you've done. You deserve to die, and I'll see that it happens. Either with my own hands or in prison. Either way, there is no happy ending for you."

Sergey shakes his head. "I took you from a nobody—a *nobody* —and gave you the fucking world. And this is how you repay me? By tossing me aside for some dead weight whore who can't give you a fucking thing?"

"Piper has given me more than you could ever imagine. She has given me everything I could ever need."

There's not a single cell of my body that doesn't believe that statement.

He snorts. "And when she dies, you'll be broken. Your enemies know that. They'll never stop going after her."

"I can keep her safe."

"No one is that powerful. She will die, Timofey. It's just a matter of when."

"Is that a fucking threat?" I hiss.

"It's a warning. Without me, you'll never find her in time."

Just as Sergey finishes speaking, I hear something. It's a distant sound. A muffled cry or a scream. I tip my ear towards the doorway. "You said these hallways echoed."

When I look back at Sergey, his face is pale. "There are hundreds of people in this hotel. It could be anyone."

"But it's not, is it?" I ask, studying his pained expression. "It's her. She's here in these tunnels."

His nostrils flare. "You can't beat Kreshnik on your own. You can't beat him without me."

All of the pieces start to fit together. "You brought Piper here so you could... You're working with Kreshnik to bring me to my knees, just so you can be the one to help me back up. You're trying to make amends."

"You don't know his plan," he continues, ignoring my accusations. "I can help you defeat him. I have—"

"Nothing," I finish for him. "You have nothing, Sergey. You chose to work with Kreshnik even though you know as well as I do that he'll kill you when he's finished with you. And your only other choice was to appeal to my sense of mercy. Unless you really think I'm a fool, in which case you hoped I would fall into your trap."

"It's not a trap. It's a—"

Another cry echoes down the hallway. It's Piper. I know it is.

Sergey knows it, too. He just lost his leverage.

His lips are pressed into a tense line. When he looks back at me, his eyes are wide and childlike. "You wouldn't kill your father."

"My father died when I was a kid. My mother, too." I shake my head. "I don't have any family left. You made sure of that when you killed Rodion and Emily."

He switches tactics. "You wouldn't kill me here. There are too many witnesses. Someone saw you come back here with me."

"I doubt it. Even if they did, they won't find you when I'm finished."

He's sweating. Fat beads of it rolling down his forehead. "I can help you! I can be… I can be useful! Whatever you need, I can—"

"I spent most of my life trying to be useful, Sergey. That's what you taught me: a person is only worth what they can do for you. But life is about more than that. Relationships are about more than that. They are about love."

I let go of Sergey just as I hear another muffled cry echoing down the hallway.

Sergey inhales deeply, assuming I'm sparing him. "I love you, son. I—"

Lightning fast, I grab each side of his face and twist with all my strength. His neck cracks in two, and Sergey's words dissolve into a strangled whimper.

And then there is silence.

50

PIPER

"Put Benjamin down."

My voice cracks with the plea. I'm scraping myself across the emotional coals, doing anything to apply to the still-beating heart I hope exists beneath Kreshnik's evil facade.

He stares back at me blankly. His arms are curled around Benjamin, but there's nothing gentle in his hold. Nothing loving. It's the careful way someone holds a bomb they've rigged to explode.

"He's fine here. Aren't you, my little friend?" He smiles down at Benjamin. "He's a great baby, you know? Hardly cries. Very obedient. It's a shame what's going to happen to him."

The last few days, while we searched for him, I wanted so badly for Benjamin to be alive. Now, I'm not sure that was the right wish. I should have hoped for a peaceful end for him. Wouldn't that be better than this?

"He's just a baby. He won't remember any of this. He can't tell anyone what happened here. You don't have to kill him. You can… You can adopt him off! Give him to someone who will love him."

Anyone but yourself, I think.

"Sure, I'll send him off to live in some nice suburb somewhere. Then he takes a DNA test and discovers his bloodline. Things will end exactly the same if he learns who he is and comes back for what is mine." Kreshnik shakes his head. "Absolutely not. I'm going to claim the Viktorov Bratva as my own, and I can't have any irritating loose ends coming to ruin that for me later. Even Sergey has to die, whenever he finally comes back."

"But you two were working together."

"The man is a means to an end," he says carelessly. "They all have to die, Piper. If you don't pull them up by the roots, the weeds grow back."

I can't even summon the words to argue. I stare at Kreshnik. He doesn't look human to me. He is cold and vacuous. The kind of energy that drains you. Was he like this before Arber died? Or is this all from grief?

"You may think I'm a monster, Piper. But I'm protecting my family. I'm building a legacy."

"A legacy of waste and bloodshed. Of broken families and dead children. How could you want to sit on that kind of throne?"

He shrugs, a sick smile on his face. "Human flesh adds a nice cushion."

My stomach turns, but I can't dissolve into despair yet. I can't give myself over to hopelessness. Not while Benjamin is still breathing. Not while I still have fight left in me.

"You lost your son, and it was…" I shake my head. "It was horrible. I'm sorry it had to happen."

Kreshnik's smile vanishes in an instant. "You make it sound inevitable."

"He stormed Timofey's house armed to the teeth. He shot into a crowd of innocent people. How would you have handled something like that?"

"Arber was always… impulsive. I would have punished him for what he did. Timofey didn't give me a chance."

"I know you're grieving. I feel bad for you, truly. No parent should ever have to lose their child."

"I didn't lose him!" His voice ricochets off the stone walls. Benjamin jolts in his arms. "Timofey Viktorov *stole* him from me. You talk about my path of destruction, but my son was beheaded and left on my doorstep like the morning paper. What about the rot Timofey leaves in his wake?"

"Then be better than him," I say. "If you think what Timofey did is so egregious, then be better. Killing an infant makes you just as bad as he is."

Having been at the party Arber shot up, I don't have any qualms with how he died. The man was deranged. He only would have gotten worse with more time and power to wield. But I can sympathize with Kreshnik all the same.

"Once you exact revenge, your son will still be dead. You won't have an heir to sit on your throne. So… what's the point?"

For a second, Kreshnik stops. He blinks and looks down at the baby in his arms.

It's like he's awakening from a bad dream. I'm sure he's seeing everything around him in a new light.

And it gives me hope. I'm going to save Benjamin and myself… and I'm going to do it without violence.

Then Kreshnik laughs.

He tips his head back and cackles. The sound fills the room like a toxic cloud. It makes it hard to breathe.

"You're so right, Piper," he says, sarcasm thick in his voice. He holds Benjamin out as if he's going to hand him to me. "Here's the baby back. My mistake. Now, we can all be friends, right?"

I know he's being facetious, but I nod anyway. "We could try."

"Timofey is going to try to kill me whether I apologize or not. I don't even blame him; I'd do the same thing. That's what this world is. It is death and vengeance. If you can't stomach it, I suggest you leave." He scoffs. "Well, I would suggest that. But it's too late for you. I hope your time playing House was worth it. Because the game ends today."

He glances towards the door and then down at his watch. Sergey has been gone for ten minutes. They wouldn't say where he was going, but I think I already know.

"If you hand Benjamin to me now, I can try to make Timofey spare you," I say in one last desperate attempt to change the tide. "If anyone could convince him, it would be me. I'll fight for you."

He arches a brow and assesses me. Once again, I'm reminded of how few clothes I have on.

"Is that all you have in your arsenal? You'll *try* to change Timofey's mind?" He clicks his tongue in disappointment. "I think we both know you can do better than that. I mean, fuck, forget Timofey. Save yourself."

I have no intention of forgetting Timofey, but as long as Kreshnik is talking, he isn't killing me. "How?"

His smile twists into a sickening mask. I'm instantly covered in goosebumps from head to toe.

"You pointed out that I'm lacking an heir." He runs his tongue over his lower lip. "Offer to give me one."

I gawk at him. "You want…"

He nods before I can find the words. "As I said, men have thrown away plenty more for less than you. You're not bad to look at and your fire is intriguing. I could be swayed to change my plans."

I want to refuse him outright. I mean, how could anyone accept an offer like this? It's repulsive. I'd rather die.

But… Timofey. Benjamin.

Would I rather they die, too?

"So if I—" I swallow hard. "If I went with you instead, you'd let Timofey live."

He laughs. "Fuck no. Timofey is dying. What, do you think he'd let me live if he knew I was fucking his girlfriend for the next twenty years? That wouldn't exactly encourage neighborly affection."

Twenty years? I feel faint.

My entire life, gone. It doesn't matter if I'll technically be alive. Living with someone like Kreshnik would be worse than death.

"What about Benjamin?" I ask.

"Afraid he has to die, too. He has the wrong blood pumping in his little veins. Can't have that." He looks down at Benjamin with a smile, no sign at all on his face that he plans to murder him in the next few minutes. "But you could save yourself, Piper. If you submit to me, I'll let you live."

The room is spinning. How long has it been since I've eaten anything substantial? My feet tingle. I can't even be sure they are connected to the ground.

Kreshnik moves towards me, and I'm so out of it that I don't even try to back away. "I could give you everything Timofey has offered and more. Luxury and finery. Fucking like you wouldn't believe."

I shake my head. "I can't—"

"You can," he purrs, suddenly persuasive. Was this his goal all along? Or maybe another in a long line of backup plans. "Timofey plucked you out of the sewer and polished you up. You don't want all of that to be for nothing, do you? You'll die if you refuse me."

I search his face for any sign of mercy or concern. Is he making me this offer because he doesn't want to kill me?

But the longer I hesitate over my answer, the more the amusement in his eyes becomes apparent.

"You're... you're fucking sick," I hiss. "You're doing all of this just so you can hurt Timofey."

"Of course I am. I want to kill him, so—"

"But you want to hurt him as much as you can before you do. And you realized the only thing better than killing me in front of Timofey would be revealing that I've turned my back on him. You want to parade me around as your new toy before you kill him. Well, sorry to steal your fun, but I'd rather choke on my own blood than even pretend to be interested in you."

His nostrils flare, and he pushes a rough hand through his gray-streaked hair. "That can be arranged."

He backs away slowly, moving towards the makeshift bassinet where Benjamin was sleeping. "Actually, maybe my plans should shift a little. You know what would be worse than Timofey watching you die? Him walking in and finding you already dead. No hope to be found in a corpse. No second chances. No emotional goodbyes. Just a quick, brutal end to your pathetic life. What do you say?"

Before I can respond, the door to the storage room slams open. We both turn to look.

"Sergey! Finally," Kreshnik crows. "I was starting to think you weren't—"

But it isn't Sergey.

"Timofey," I breathe.

He's here.

51

PIPER

When Kreshnik sees Timofey standing in the doorway, his face goes pale.

"Weren't still alive?" Timofey finishes for him. The gun in his hand is aimed directly at Kreshnik's head. "Then you'd be right. I killed your little pawn."

Kreshnik works his jaw back and forth, nervous energy oozing out of him. "You killed your own father? I guess I shouldn't be surprised."

"He was never my father. Not that you'd recognize that. If you'd been a father to your own son, maybe he wouldn't have grown up to be a reckless psychopath. Maybe he'd still be alive."

Kreshnik's arms tighten around Benjamin, and my heart is beating out a steady vibration in my chest. "Timofey..." I murmur.

He glances at me and then pins his blue eyes on Kreshnik. "My father was going to turn his back on you and side with me. Even if I hadn't killed him, your plan would have fallen apart. Now, you're going to die."

Timofey's hand tightens on the gun, and I scream. "Don't shoot! He's holding Benjamin!"

On cue, the bundle in Kreshnik's arms squirms. Timofey blinks. For a fleeting second, I see the shock and awe on his face. Then he schools his expression.

"Hand over my family and you live."

Kreshnik laughs. "Don't lie to me, Timofey. It's beneath you."

"I'll spare you if you spare them," he says. "My word."

"Your word is shit!" Kreshnik spits. "We were supposed to be allies, yet you butchered my son."

"Don't pretend we were friends now, Kreshnik. The only reason you didn't attack me is because you knew you wouldn't survive the attempt. Unfortunately, your son didn't have your survival instincts. It cost him his life."

"And unfortunately," he fires back, "you're too late to save your little orphan. I'm going to kill your son the way you killed mine."

"No, please," I rasp. "Please. I'll do—"

"I'll kill you next, bitch!"

Timofey takes a cautious step closer to me. Kreshnik responds by untucking Benjamin from his blankets. He holds his frail body against his shoulder.

"Don't get upset with her for rejecting you, Kreshnik."

I glare at him, shaking my head. *Now is not the time to taunt the man holding our baby.*

As soon as the thought enters my mind, tears well in my eyes. Benjamin is *our* baby. In every way that counts, we are the only people in the world he has to depend on.

And we've failed him.

"You've brainwashed her the way you have everyone else," Kreshnik growls. "Timofey Viktorov might as well be another name for the boogeyman the way people whisper it in fear. They think you are unbeatable. But I've proven them wrong."

Timofey shrugs far too casually. "It depends on what you consider beating me to look like."

"It looks like this!" Kreshnik holds up Benjamin. "I am going to destroy the future of your family. There will be no one with Viktorov blood left in existence."

"Except for me," Timofey says. Kreshnik frowns at him, so he continues. "Because the moment you move to touch my son, I'll kill you, Kreshnik. You won't live long enough to see my grief. And after your death, I'll scrap your empire for parts. Your legacy will be scattered to the wind."

Kreshnik looks from Timofey to me and back again. I see the moment he realizes Timofey is right.

"How noble of you, Timofey. Standing there while your son dies. I took you for a braver man than that."

Timofey roils with tension. "Sacrificing myself won't save anyone. You'll kill me and then go after Piper and Benjamin all the same. The only satisfaction I can take from this is to be the one to put the bullet in your head."

The two men stare at each other, the understanding of their mutually assured destruction pulsing between them.

But I think there might be another path yet.

Before I can talk myself out of it, I stumble sideways and crash into the metal shelf to my left. The metal bites into my ribs, and I wince in pain. My arm sprawls across the mostly empty shelf.

"Stand up!" Kreshnik barks.

As Timofey asks, "Piper?"

"I'm okay." I give Timofey a weak smile, trying to communicate my plan to him with nothing but my eyes. I really do feel faint, so I'm not sure it's working. "I'm just sick... because of the pregnancy."

Timofey's face pales as Kreshnik's lights up. "You're pregnant."

I turn to him, fake shock on my face. "No. I didn't—I'm not. That's not what I—"

"You're pregnant with a Viktorov spawn," he hisses. "And here you were, offering yourself up as a womb for me. As if I wouldn't recognize the baby wasn't mine."

As I clench my fists, I grab the sturdy metal rod in my hand, tucking it carefully behind my forearm. "I didn't offer anything to you! I'd rather die than let you touch me."

"We'll see how history remembers this moment when you're gone."

"I know how they'll remember it," Timofey says. "Since I'll be the one alive to tell the tale. You died like a dog, Kreshnik. After begging my woman to bed you. Don't worry, you'll be a sympathetic character. A cautionary tale, rife with pity..."

"I'm holding your son in my arms. Careful how you talk to me," he barks.

"If I beg for his life, it will only give you more satisfaction in killing him. I won't give you the pleasure," Timofey says.

I throw myself between the two men. "Then I will. Please don't hurt Benjamin. Let him live."

Kreshnik sighs as if he's bored. "We talked about this. If I don't rip the Viktorov line out by the root, they'll keep coming back."

"And you'll be dead, so what will you care? What good is any of this if you die?"

"Piper," Timofey whispers behind me. "What are you doing?"

The truth is, I have no fucking clue.

"I'm saving your life," I tell him. Then I turn back to Kreshnik. "And I'm saving yours. Because you'll die here today unless you change your plan. You know that, don't you?"

He doesn't respond, but he doesn't need to. I press on.

"I'm pregnant with Timofey's flesh and blood child." I swallow, blinking back tears. "If you want revenge on him... take me."

"No!" Timofey roars.

Whether he's trying to entice Kreshnik further or it's his genuine reaction, I don't know. But it's working.

Kreshnik smirks. "I thought you'd rather die than touch me."

"I would. I'm asking you to kill me instead of Benjamin."

"You want me to kill you?"

"Of course not," I hiss. "But if someone here has to die, I'd rather it be me."

"Kill me and save them!" Timofey says, apparently changing his tune on begging Kreshnik for anything. "Let them go. I'll put down my gun and—"

"I don't want you," Kreshnik grits out. "I want everyone around you. I want to pick apart your life like a vulture, leaving so little even the maggots wouldn't want it. I want you to suffer the way you've made me—"

His voice cuts off. Emotion I didn't think he was capable of clogging his throat.

I step forward, speaking softly. "Then take me. I was ready to spend the rest of my life with Timofey. I was going to give my entire self to him and our family. I... I love him."

Is that a soft inhale behind me or am I imagining it? I'm not sure, but I can't turn around to see. If I do, I won't be able to stop myself from running to Timofey.

I keep my eyes on Kreshnik. "I love him, and if you take me... it will as good as kill him."

Timofey's voice is thunder and the rage of the ocean. It's a wail of anger and pain I've never heard before. "No! Take me instead! Don't—"

"Done." Kreshnik nods once. "But you need to come with me now; otherwise, Timofey won't let me leave this room."

Timofey moves towards me, but Kreshnik wraps a hand around Benjamin's tiny neck. "Don't forget I still have the little one. Make any sudden movements, and he's gone."

Timofey is fuming behind me, his breath coming in fits and starts.

"Put him in the basket," I tell Kreshnik. "I'll follow you over there. You can transfer from him to me. Timofey won't be able to kill you while I'm standing in front of you."

I can hear Timofey growl in frustration, and I hope he can forgive me someday.

Kreshnik carefully backs towards the bassinet, his eyes never shifting away from where Timofey stands near the doorway. I follow him.

Anytime I get too close to him and Benjamin, Kreshnik warns me away.

"Move here," he says, pointing to the cement floor a foot in front of him. "Don't move while I drop the baby."

"While you place him carefully, you mean?"

He rolls his eyes. "Worry about your part and let me worry about mine. The baby will be fine."

I intend to do just that.

I hold my breath as Kreshnik lowers Benjamin into the basket. He's watching Timofey, making sure the gun is still pointed at the floor.

He isn't paying attention to me at all.

Which is why as soon as Benjamin is out of his hands, I lunge.

I've been holding onto the metal rod so tightly for so long that it is sweaty against my palm. But I let it slide down into my hand, draw my arm back, and drive it as hard as I can into Kreshnik's neck.

Blood sprays, warm and sticky. But I can't tell where he's been hit or how deep. The world is twisting and turning before my eyes.

Benjamin wails while Kreshnik yells a garbled mess of curses. He swipes at me. I feel a blow to my side and another to my chest, but I can't worry about that now. Not when the lives of everyone I love lay in the balance.

"Bitch!" he growls. He ducks behind his arm and leans forward.

I'm not sure what he's doing until I see the sharp point of a blade coming my way.

I scream and dodge to the side, swinging the rod at him as I fall back. I miss and the rod goes flying out of my hand from the force of my swing. It clatters against the cement as I fall flat onto my back.

I try to inhale, but the wind has been knocked out of me. All I can do is gasp for oxygen with failing lungs. Kreshnik stalks over me, a knife in his hand. He doesn't say a word as he lifts the blade over his head, but he doesn't need to. There is murder in his eyes and in the curl of his upper lip.

This is the end for me.

Then the shots ring out.

One, two, three. *Bang, bang, bang.*

Kreshnik rocks with each bullet that passes through his body. The final one cuts straight through his head—in one temple and out the other.

Blood showers over me. I taste the metallic bite of it coating my tongue.

Then Kreshnik drops to the floor, his mouth slack. An ocean of blood pouring out of him.

52

TIMOFEY

Benjamin is screaming.

The sound makes it almost impossible to focus on anything else. But there is so much to focus on.

Kreshnik Xhuvani dead or dying on the floor. And Piper…

"Piper!"

I jump over the metal pipe she used to attack Kreshnik and drop to my knees next to her. Kreshnik's blood soaks into my pants. It's still hot.

"Piper." I sweep my hand over her face. My thumb smears the fine mist of blood on her skin into a kind of war paint under her eye. "Are you okay?"

There is blood on her lips and her teeth. She's covered in it, and I have no idea how much is Kreshnik's and how much is hers.

"Piper, fucking talk to me before I go insane."

"I'm fine." She is trembling from head to toe. She's in shock.

"No, you're not." I haul her up. The moment she's on her feet, she runs for the corner. I try to grab her, but she's too fast.

She reaches into the basket and pulls Benjamin out. His crying gets even louder. They are angry wails that pierce my ears in the best kind of way.

I thought I'd never hear them again.

"Oh my God, you're alive." She hugs him to her chest and tips her head back, eyes squeezed closed. "You're alive."

He's alive. The information has barely had time to register.

I shift behind Piper and hold Benjamin's soft head in the palm of my hand. "He's alive. Thanks to you."

"Thanks to *you*. We were both going to die in here, Timofey. If you hadn't shown up—"

I press a kiss to the back of her head. The smell of iron is overwhelming. "Don't even talk about that. I did show up. It's all over."

"And Sergey?"

"Dead. As he should be."

Piper glances over her shoulder at Kreshnik's dead body and immediately looks away. "Can we... can we go somewhere else? There's so much blood. It's... Oh God, it's everywhere. It's on Benjamin, too."

Her voice is growing frantic, the words rushing out of her. Carefully, I pluck Benjamin from her arms.

"There's an employee locker room. There are showers. We can clean up there."

Her chin is wobbling with the effort not to cry. "Okay. Okay, we can... Yeah, it's okay. I'm okay."

"No, you're not," I repeat, pulling her tightly against my chest. "But you will be."

The locker room is at the end of the secret hallway and through another hidden door. This is the first time I've navigated these secret tunnels, but I know the layout of the rest of the building well enough to be able to reverse engineer a floor plan in my mind.

Thankfully, the locker room is empty when we enter. I lock the door behind us.

"Take off everything you're wearing and get into the shower —both of you. I can find you a spare uniform."

Piper pulls my ruined t-shirt over her head, and I know I'm going straight to hell. Because she looks incredible.

She's wearing nothing but a pair of pale pink panties, the rest of her body golden and lean. She's perfect.

"Maybe if I wasn't traumatized, I'd be able to see how hot this moment is." She meets my heated gaze with a self-deprecating smile.

"Don't worry. I'm used to this kind of thing, so I can see exactly how hot it is," I growl.

She chuckles and takes Benjamin from me. "I'm covered in blood."

She starts to pull away, but I catch her face in my hands and smear the blood with my thumbs, drawing patterns on her cheekbones. "You are covered in the blood of my enemy—in the blood of the man you fought to defend me and our children. Nothing will ever be hotter than that, Piper."

She smiles, her eyes going misty.

I want to revel in this moment, but there isn't time.

"Go shower." I point to the closest handicap stall. "I have to take care of some things."

She walks away, Benjamin in her arms, and I have to force myself to look away from the intoxicating sway of her hips.

I can still hear her confession to Kreshnik. *I was ready to spend the rest of my life with Timofey. I was going to give my entire self to him and our family. I... I love him.*

God, I love her, too.

"Later," I growl, reaching into my pocket for my phone.

I hear the shower kick on and the soft mutterings of Piper calming Benjamin. His crying has softened to a whimper now. Warm water always puts him at ease.

I move to the furthest corner of the locker room and dial Rooney. He picks up immediately.

"What the fuck are you doing, Viktorov? We just got a call that you're trespassing at your own company!"

"Fucking Manuel," I growl. He wouldn't stand in my way to keep me out, but he called the police. And after he claimed he didn't want to make a scene, no less. "Don't worry about that."

"Okay... If you're not calling about that, then why are you calling?"

I lower my voice. "There are going to be a lot more calls coming in to you guys soon. I suggest you get as close to Viktorov Industries as you can. I want you to take over the investigation."

"What investigation?"

"Bodies."

He sighs. "What happened to them?"

"I haven't fully decided yet."

He curses under his breath. "Fucking hell. Only you. Well, shit, I'd like some idea of what story to run with."

"I have to keep things interesting, Rooney. Otherwise, you might get bored of me."

"No chance of that," he mumbles. "Whatever it is, it must not be too bad. You sound chipper. Though... maybe the good mood is actually a bad sign. Oh fuck. It's bad, isn't it? The only thing worse than you in a rage is you being in a good mood."

On any other day, I'd tell Rooney to shut the fuck up and do as he's told, but I am in good spirits tonight. All things considered.

"Head this way and be ready to clean house."

"I've 'cleaned your house' a lot lately. I don't know how thorough I can be this time."

"Make it happen and you'll have an extended vacation from me," I tell him. "There might be a bonus in there for you, too."

Rooney whistles. "Wow. You really are in a good mood tonight."

"Do your part to make it last." I hang up and go to check on Piper and Benjamin.

The curtain to the shower is open, and Piper is standing just outside of the spray, shivering as she wraps Benjamin in a white towel. Streams of water twine around her hips and slip down her thighs.

"He's clean, but exhausted," she says, drawing my eyes back to her face. "The warm water put him right to sleep."

Blood is still smeared across her cheeks and dotted on her neck. I gently take Benjamin from her arms.

"I'll dry him off. You take care of yourself now."

She smiles down at Benjamin's pink face for another second before she can pull herself away and step back into the shower.

He really is exhausted. He barely moves as I take him. "Get your rest," I whisper. "You're safe now."

He yawns and then settles into a nest of clean towels I set up on the floor.

Once I'm sure he's content, I go back to the shower. Really, I'm drawn there. It's a compulsion. A better man than me might have given Piper her privacy, but I lean against the tiled doorway and watch her shower.

When she sees me, she blushes. "Is Benjamin sleeping?"

I nod. "He's as tired as I feel."

"He had a big few days. I doubt anyone was sticking to his sleep schedule." She frowns as if the idea just occurred to her. It probably did. Worrying if he was alive took precedence over whether he was napping. "I just hope he doesn't remember any of this."

"He won't."

Her brow pinches. "You don't know that."

"Yes, I do."

"How?"

There's a haze of anxiety around her like heat off an asphalt road. All I want to do is clear it.

I step closer, the spray from the shower misting onto my face. Piper leans her head back to look into my eyes. I can't help but wrap my hand around her delicate neck, rub my thumb along her pulse point.

"Because we are going to give him a life filled with miraculous, beautiful memories," I whisper. "There won't be room left in his head for the chaos he saw here today."

Her eyes flood with tears. "I can't believe I ever thought you were the wrong choice to be his father. Timofey, you're... He's going to love you so much. I know I do."

I smirk. "I caught that earlier. I hoped you weren't just saying it for Kreshnik's benefit."

"Fuck him," she hisses with a shocking amount of animosity. "That was for you, Timofey. I wanted you to know the truth just in case..."

I lean forward and press my lips to hers, ending the terrible thought before she can voice it. Her naked body arches into mine. I feel dampness soaking through my clothes, but I could care less.

I slide my hands down her arms, gripping her elbows. When I draw away, there's blood on my hands.

"Oh no, I'm sorry." Gently, Piper tries to scrub the blood from my hands.

But I shake my head and turn her to face the shower head. "Let's take care of you first."

I want to say I'm being selfless by washing the blood off of her, but there is no sacrifice at all involved in running my hands over her supple skin. She is warm and delicate in my large hands, and I never want to let her go.

When she turns to face me and then tips her head back into the spray, working her hands through her auburn hair, I have to bite my lip to keep from groaning.

Fucking hell, this woman is incredible.

I reach out with a finger and draw a line down her sternum to the barest hint of a bump in her lower abdomen.

She looks up at me sheepishly. "I'm sorry I told Kreshnik about our baby. I'm sorry I put your child at risk. I just wanted to be useful. I wanted to help."

I switch off the shower and grab the towel hanging behind me. I lay it over her shoulders and start drying her off. "Piper, you don't have to do anything to earn your place in my life. You help me by existing."

"I know." She lowers her head, staring down at her feet. "But your life is different. I don't want to be a burden. I don't want to be extra weight that you have to—"

"I don't *have to* do anything," I grit out. "I'm here with you because I want to be. You don't have to earn that, Piper."

"Neither do you," she says softly. "You have taken such good care of us, Timofey. You take care of everyone. But that's not why... I love you because of who you are. Because of how you make me feel. Even if one day, you aren't there when something bad is happening or—"

"I will be," I growl. "I'll always be there."

She lays a damp hand on my shoulder. "Even if you aren't, I'll still love you. Always."

I turn and kiss her knuckles. "Always."

Rooney was right on the phone. I am in a good mood. I have everything I need right now. Everything I could ever want.

Which is why I finally know exactly what I'm going to do next.

"Get dressed and be ready to go when I get back," I tell Piper. "I have one more thing to do."

As I turn, she grabs my arm and pulls me back to her. Our lips meet in an easy, sensual kiss. Then she pushes me towards the door.

"Give them hell."

I smile and hurry back into the hallway.

53

TIMOFEY

There isn't a single other sound in the long, echoey corridors. Whoever Kreshnik paid off to get into the building is doing their job. They are keeping the employee areas quiet.

I check three supply closets on my way back to the room where Kreshnik is lying dead. The first two are a bust—mostly seasonal wreaths and candle holders—but the third is precisely what I'm looking for.

Shelves and shelves of bulk chemicals sit in front of me. Industrial tubs of powdered bleach, dish soap, furniture polish, and other cleaning agents are stocked from floor to ceiling.

I grab any container I see with a flame printed on the side. It's meant as a warning, but it's a green light for what I have in mind.

I carry the containers all the way down the hall to the room where Sergey first took me. The door is cracked open. I see his legs splayed on the carpet, one of his shoes untied. I unscrew the cap from a metal container of acetone and splash it through the open door. Then, carefully, I trail it down the hallway to the storage room where I found Kreshnik holding Piper and Benjamin hostage.

The smell of the mixed chemicals is strong. My eyes burn, and I try to take shallow breaths.

When I finish one bottle of acetone, I toss the empty container into the room with Kreshnik and open another. I continue the trail down the hallway until it's a reasonable distance from the locker room where Piper and Benjamin are getting ready to leave.

The lighter slips out of my pocket like it's nothing. A flimsy piece of plastic, but one capable of toppling empires. I flick the lid open and press my thumb to the igniter.

Sergey did everything to protect his legacy. To lay claim to the company and the Bratva he built. It feels right that it should go down with him.

He'll be swallowed by his own creation.

And I'll be free.

I snap the flame to life and toss it down the hallway. Almost instantly, the bloom of heat is oppressive, sending sweat stinging down my spine. But the moment I see Piper step out of the locker room with Benjamin tucked into her arms, I don't feel a thing.

"Timofey," she breathes. "What did you—"

I squeeze her hand and pull her towards the door. "This place can burn. None of it matters as long as I have you."

She smiles, and we walk into the cool evening air as a family.

EPILOGUE I: TIMOFEY

"I'm feeling quite honored because this is the first anyone has done with either of you in over a year. Since before Viktorov Industries went up in flames." The reporter widens her eyes and takes us both in—the three of us, actually. "Since before you had a baby, too. Congratulations, by the way. He's an angel."

Piper adjusts Samuil in her arms. "Thank you. Hopefully, he'll stay sleeping just like this so you keep that opinion of him. You'd think differently if you were here last night."

"Not a sound sleeper?" the reporter asks.

Piper lowers her chin, eyebrow arched. "Monica, when I tell you he did not sleep for a single minute all night, I mean it literally."

"We could have rescheduled. I would have understood! Especially around this time of year." She gestures to the towering Christmas tree to our right. "It's a busy season."

"Every season is busy," I say. "No amount of exhaustion will keep us from promoting the Christmas auction."

Monica smiles. "Yes. And I promise we'll get to that, but you have to answer some other questions for me, too. My editor would fire me in a New York minute if I let you get away without answering some questions."

I sense Piper stiffen next to me.

There are countless reasons we haven't done any interviews in the last year. One of them being that Piper wasn't ready. Overnight, her life changed. She went from a single woman scraping by to a mother in a relationship with a Bratva don. She's been the target of attacks. She's seen death.

I wanted to allow her as much time as she needed to process all of that trauma and revel in our little family before I opened us up to the world again.

She reaches over and squeezes my hand, a gesture the eagle-eyed interviewer doesn't miss. She jots something down in her notebook.

"We finally can answer some questions," Piper says softly. "With the ongoing trials, our attorneys rightfully asked us not to speak out. Now that they've ended, we have more freedom."

"It was hard to stay quiet with so many nasty rumors swirling," I add.

Nasty, definitely. But rumors? Hardly.

I killed Kreshnik Xhuvani and Sergey Viktorov with my bare hands and set Viktorov Industries on fire. I'd do it again, too, if given the chance.

But that's not the story we went with.

"That's a good place to start," Monica says. "There is maybe no name more likely to split a crowd than Timofey Viktorov. People either love you or loathe you. There doesn't seem to be a middle ground."

Piper loops her arm around mine and snuggles close. "Count me with the 'love' crowd."

Monica smiles. "Some people call you a hero. They say you walked away from your father's tarnished legacy and started again. Rising from the ashes, you could say. Others think maybe your hands aren't so clean. Why do you think you divide people like that?"

I shrug. "Powerful men always draw detractors. It doesn't matter what kind of good you try to do in this world, there will always be people who think it's an act. And I don't want to point the finger at you, Monica, but—"

"Uh-oh," she chuckles. "I feel like you're going to point the finger at me."

Piper pats my arm, taking over the conversation. "Not you specifically, but the news has been running so many wild stories over the last year. One article hinted that I sent my family to Mexico to escape Timofey's reach and that he is holding me captive."

I gesture around at the lush garland hanging from the roaring fireplace and the tray of peppermint chocolate cookies Akim made for the interviewer. "Does this look like a prison?"

"If it is, it's the nicest prison I ever saw." Monica laughs appreciatively.

"We're just a little dubious about allowing press into our baby bubble," Piper continues. "We don't want anything to ruin it."

I drape an arm around her shoulder and pull her and Samuil close. "Nothing could ruin this."

"I believe you," Monica says. "Especially given everything the two of you have been through this year. Is it true you've left Viktorov Industries, Timofey?"

As nice as Monica seems, I know a *gotcha* question when I hear one. "I was removed as CEO in a board vote just prior to the fire, actually. I didn't walk away willingly."

"You're referencing the fire that killed your adoptive father?"

I nod. "Yes. Unfortunately, he was one of the men lost in that tragedy."

"This is where those nasty rumors come in," she says. "Some people think the fire was a cover up."

"People love to gossip," Piper says.

Samuil is stirring in her arms, but she strokes her finger down his chubby cheek. He has her coloring—pale, peachy skin, and a head full of red waves.

Monica nods in agreement. "It's not hard to see where the roots of these rumors stem from, though. Two of the wealthiest men in the city dead in the same fire? It's almost unbelievable."

"Backroom deals have to happen somewhere, don't they? My father and Kreshnik Xhuvani were working together, forging an alliance during the annual Viktorov Industries gala. They couldn't have known death was lurking just around the corner."

I find great joy in repackaging the truth. Nothing I said is a direct lie, but there is some pertinent information missing.

Most importantly, that I was 'Death.'

"Did you support your father's alliance with one of his biggest competitors?" Monica asks shrewdly. "If you'd remained with Viktorov Industries, would you have seen that deal through to the end?"

"I haven't considered it. I'm not with Viktorov Industries, so that decision is out of my purview. I am happy to look to the future."

Monica's mouth puckers. We aren't quite giving her the hot and juicy story she was hoping for, I can tell. She turns to Piper.

"While you haven't done any interviews for the last year, your father certainly has. I have noted here, let's see… fourteen separate interviews he has done with the press. Most of them complain that he has been cut out of your life."

Piper blinks placidly. "I'm not here to answer for the actions of my father. He is my blood relation, but I can't control him anymore than he has controlled me."

Not anymore, I think.

"'Blood relation?'" Monica wrinkles her nose. "That's a little cold."

Piper sighs. "I just don't want to—"

"Next question," I interject.

"I know family can be difficult, but wouldn't you rather answer some of these questions and dispense the rumors?"

I narrow my eyes. "Next question, Monica."

The reporter looks from me to Piper and back again, searching for a way through our strong front. But Piper circles her finger across my bicep and presses her leg closer to mine. We're as close as possible without her being in my lap.

We're impenetrable, and Monica knows it.

She flicks her dark hair over her shoulder and glances down at her notes. "Let's go back to the trial. That just wrapped up and your former best friend was sentenced to prison. How do you feel about that?"

I'm half-poised to jump in for Piper and shut down the line of questioning, but she lifts her chin and faces it head on. "I love the people in my life and want what is best for them, but I will not excuse illegal behavior. Noelle and her boyfriend broke the law, and I'm satisfied that they are being appropriately punished."

"With fraudulent activity so close to you, what do you say to people who are concerned with your new charity?"

"Why would people be concerned with her charity?" I ask. "Piper wasn't the one on trial."

Monica swallows nervously. "No. But she was friends with—"

"She's not going to be held accountable for the actions of her *friend*."

Piper pats my arm and sits forward. "Timofey is protective of me. We've had death threats, you know? People who think I'm taking donated money for myself and buying cars and expensive trips. But every penny that is donated goes directly to finding long-term placements for children in need. Bringing together families is my only goal."

"You say you want to bring together families, but your father was quoted just last week telling NewsCannon's Linda Pho, and I quote, 'Piper wants to bring together families? Why did she rip mine apart? She won't return my calls or letters. She has drawn away from me and refused to help me pay for the medical bills that are—'"

"If you wanted a quote from her father, you could have gone to interview him instead of us," I interrupt. "God knows he'll spout off at the mouth about nonsense for next to nothing. Anything to feed his alcohol addiction and keep him from having to take care of himself."

Monica's eyebrows raise. "You don't have a kind word to say about your father-in-law."

Another *gotcha* question. I smile. "He isn't my father-in-law."

Monica grins back, and a moment of mutual respect passes between us. "Excellent segue. I was wondering if there was any validity to those rumors."

Piper looks over at me, a perfect mask of confusion on her face. "People are saying we're married?"

I smile at her slyly. "In the same article in which NewsCannon quoted your father, they also reported that you and I were married in a secret ceremony before Samuil was born. We had a fire eater at the reception, did you know?"

"I had no idea! It must have been hard for me to plan a wedding while I was eight months pregnant." Piper smirks at me. "It really has been a big year for us."

"Is this a confirmation?" Monica asks. "I'd love to get the exclusive scoop on this story."

Piper rocks a fussy Samuil back and forth, trying to keep him asleep. Based on his crumpled face, we have three minutes before this interview ends in a flood of newborn tears.

"I'm afraid the only exclusive I have for you is that my charity is hosting their first annual Christmas silent auction," Piper says, seamlessly circling the conversation back around to the entire reason we accepted this interview in the first place. "There will be massages, weekend staycations—"

"A free round of golf at exclusive clubs," I add.

Piper nods. "Golf, tennis lessons with a pro, a date with a fireman. Basically anything you can imagine is on the bidding block. And every single cent goes towards placing children in loving homes where they can grow and prosper."

Monica jots all of this down, but her heart isn't in it. Right now, she has a boring story in front of her. She knows it, and I know it.

"I'm here to help you promote your charity. I think it's a great idea, and I want to help however I can," Monica says. "But between you and me, you'll get more clicks on this article if it's a marriage announcement."

At this point, I'm annoyed. I'm beyond being nice to Monica. I'm ready to toss her on her ass and slam the door in her face.

But this is why Piper and I are perfect together.

She picks up my slack.

"There's no marriage to announce. Timofey and I are over the moon about Samuil entering the world, healthy and perfect. And we have our hands full with Benjamin."

"That's right," Monica says, looking around as if she might have missed the whirlwind that is our fifteen-month-old. He's with the nanny in the opposite corner of the house. "Two under two is quite the feat."

Piper nods. "We are busy. I'm starting a business and we have a newborn and a toddler running around. I'm still trying to feel grounded in my role as a mother. Getting married is the last thing on our list right now."

"The absolute last thing," I agree.

"Will you get married one day?" Monica asks.

Piper and I turn to look at each other. Her green eyes are sparkling in the Christmas lights hanging from the tree, her full lips turned into a delicate smile. I just know I'm beaming a goofy grin back at her. Which is probably why Monica chooses this moment to pull out her camera and snap a shot of the two of us.

"If we were going to tell any reporter about our potential wedding day, it would be you, Monica. I can assure you that."

I turn back to the interviewer, pleased with my latest reshaping of the truth.

"I'm honored," Monica says. "And if you're in a pinch, I married my sister and brother-in-law last year. I am ordained."

Piper laughs and twines her fingers through mine. "We'll remember that if life ever slows down enough for us to tie the knot. But we're beyond happy without the tax write-off. We may never get married."

"There's the latest scoop for you," I say, snapping at Monica. "Piper Quinn and Timofey Viktorov may never get married."

Monica jots it down.

While she's writing, I look at Piper and wink.

EPILOGUE II: PIPER

Ashley holds up her phone with the article displayed on it and cackles. "You two are cruel! Absolutely ruthless!"

Akim is leaning over the back of her seat in flagrant disregard of the flight attendant who just told us to buckle our seatbelts. He shakes his head. "This was supposed to be your make-nice with the press. I think you're about to make an enemy of Monica Pruitt."

Timofey waves a dismissive hand. "So I fibbed a little. She'll get over it."

"A little? We fibbed a lot!" I grab Ashley's phone and read the headline aloud. "**Piper Quinn and Timofey Viktorov Don't Need the Tax Write-Off; Couple Forgoes Marriage to Focus on Charity.**"

Timofey winces, obvious amusement written all over his face. "If she wanted the truth from us, she shouldn't have peppered you with questions about your dad."

My dad has been raking in checks from every trashy magazine and online blog he can get a hold of. I know stories about me will stop paying his bills eventually, but I don't want to drag out his press relevance any more than I have to.

There is no story to tell.

He isn't in my life, and he never will be.

"Oh my God. What a bitch!" Ashley starts reading another excerpt out loud. *"Piper Quinn is cagey when it comes to questions about her father. I'm not surprised; someone in the family has to be. Her father has aired all of their dirty laundry in the last twelve months, and the youngest Quinn isn't a fan of the public therapy. If what the elder Quinn says is true, Quinn's beau, ousted CEO of Viktorov Industries Timofey Viktorov, paid her father fifty-thousand dollars to stay away from her. How's that for bringing families together?"*

Akim drops down into his seat when the middle-aged attendant glares at him from the doorway of the cockpit. "Yeah, I take it back. Don't make nice with the media. They suck."

"She really was okay," I say, defending the woman. "She was just doing her job. It just so happens that I hate her job. I want my privacy."

Ashley spins around and wags her brows at me. "I'm sure you do. You just had your six-week postpartum appointment last week, right? Did she give you the all-clear to—" Ashley makes a crude gesture with her hands.

I gasp and turn to make sure Benjamin isn't paying any attention. He's happily tapping away at the buttons that adjust his seat. He buzzes forward and back over and over again, giggling all the while.

"He doesn't know what this means," Ashley says, doing the gesture again with a little more vigor.

I glare at her. "No, but other people might. I don't want his nanny to see him doing that. It would make us look bad."

"Imagine what the press would say about us then?" Timofey says it softly in my ear, goosebumps blooming all over my skin.

Ashley is crude, but she sure as hell isn't wrong.

Everything about Timofey calls to me. Those first few weeks, I was beyond exhausted and enamored with the new little bundle we brought into the world.

But it's been eight weeks and things are starting to settle into something resembling a manageable routine. Which means, between nursing sessions and middle-of-the-night crying fits and keeping Benjamin from coloring on the walls with his chunky toddler crayons, I occasionally have five minutes of free time in which all I want to do is tear Timofey's clothes from his body.

"Easy," I whisper. "I thought we wanted to wait until after the wedding."

Timofey groans softly. "You wanted to wait. But that's hours and hours away. And it has been two long, torturous months."

"Torturous?" I raise my brows. "I'll be sure to tell Samuil when he's older that you found his newborn days 'torturous.'"

"Tell him whatever you want. So long as you end my celibacy. I'm starved for you, baby."

Heat floods through me, pooling between my legs. I press my thighs together and readjust in my seat.

When I look back at Ashley, she's staring at me with one eyebrow raised. "And you think *I'm* inappropriate?"

I discreetly flip her the bird, and she blows me a kiss.

The next twenty minutes are a haze of takeoff procedures and nursing Samuil. He does better during takeoff when I nurse him. The added bonus is that he's in a milk coma for at least the first hour of the flight.

I settle him into his travel bassinet, which buckled into the plane seat next to Akim. Ashley unbuckles and scoops Benjamin into her arms the moment the attendant tells us we can remove our seatbelts.

"As the bestest godmother in the world, I packed copious amounts of snacks." She unzips a duffel bag and reveals a stash of mini muffins, cheese crackers, and gummy worms.

Akim frowns and points to a cooler in the corner. "As the bestest godfather in the world, I baked chocolate chip cookies, mixed berry scones, and made strawberry lemonade with basil."

Ashley wrinkles her nose. "Have you ever been near a child, Akim? Do you have any idea what kids actually like?"

"I know what kids like! I basically raised Benjamin right after he was born!"

Timofey swats the back of his head. "You were a *temporary* nanny. As his father, I raised him."

Akim rolls his eyes and turns back to his face-off with Ashley. "Put all the snacks in front of Benji and see which ones he picks if you're so confident."

"Oh, you are so on, pretty boy," Ashley says with a sultry wink.

For a long time, Ashley was almost always drunk or high or both. Her flirting was sloppy. Ever since we asked her to be the godmother to the kids, she's been stone cold sober.

It looks very good on her.

Akim must think so, too, because he blushes from head to toe. He doesn't get tongue-tied around anyone—anyone but *her,* that is.

Benjamin, ever the little people pleaser, politely takes Ashley's mini muffin and Akim's cookie from the spread in front of him.

"We tied!" Ashley is outraged.

I laugh. "You know what that means."

"Your kid needs to be more decisive?"

I pucker up, blowing air kisses her way. "When you tie, you have to kiss."

Ashley and Akim both turn to me, faces puckered in confusion.

"You know, the kissing cousins thing," I remind them. "It's a saying."

Timofey leans in. "The phrase is, 'A tie is worse than kissing your sister.' I don't think it's a suggestion."

"Oh... Well, whatever." I wave my hand in the air. "Kiss and make up, anyway."

Akim seems partially interested in the idea. He turns towards Ashley just as she throws a bag of gummy worms at me.

"Akim and I are godparents. It would confuse the children if we kissed."

I've known Ashley long enough to know when she's playing hard to get. And boy oh boy, is she playing with Akim now.

The two of them have been dancing around each other for months. I wouldn't be surprised to find out they've secretly hooked up once or twice, but if they have, Ashley hasn't breathed a word of it to me. Which is very unlike her.

"Nice try," Timofey mutters out of the side of his mouth.

"They'll get together one of these days and thank me."

He kisses my temple. "You're usually right about these kinds of things."

I stroke my fingers through his hair. "I am, aren't I?"

His blue eyes are molten, his gaze dripping over my skin like hot wax. God, I want him.

As the thought solidifies, Timofey turns away and stands up. "What's the guest list look like, Akim?"

Maybe Ashley isn't the only one playing hard to get, I think.

"The younger guys are hanging back to keep things running smoothly, but all of the older Vors will be there."

Timofey raises his brows. "All of them?"

A knowing smile crosses Akim's face. "A few will be arriving with *very* generous wedding gifts. It's the start of what I expect to be a very long apology tour."

Akim and Timofey seem to be speaking their own language, but I need it said plainly.

"So they all believe that Sergey is a traitorous piece of shit now?"

Akim snorts. "That's one way to put it."

"The DNA test proving Rodion was Sergey's son helped a lot," Timofey adds. "But convincing everyone he willingly worked with the Albanians to conspire against the Bratva was the last puzzle piece."

I wrinkle my nose. "They're okay with filicide, but working with the Albanians is where they draw the line? The Bratva life really is another world."

"You're not having second thoughts about marrying into it, are you?" Timofey is teasing, but there's a subtle, underlying anxiety I've learned to pick up on. There's a thread of truth beneath the question.

I stand up and wrap my arms around his waist. "Whatever world you're living in, that's where I want to be."

Timofey brings my knuckles to his lips, pressing a long kiss there.

Ashley complains that we're spoiling her appetite, but I barely hear her. My heart is beating too loud.

The kids are asleep and Ashley and Akim are hunched together watching some movie on her laptop. My heart is still racing.

Timofey is drawing circles on my thigh, his calloused finger smoothing new sensations into my skin while he reads.

We decided to wait until the wedding to have sex again. Given Samuil's existence, everyone knows I'm no virgin. But I thought, since we already had to abstain for six weeks after Samuil was born, why not tack on two extra weeks?

"It will make it more exciting, won't it?" I told him, a three-day-old baby laying on my chest.

What an idiot I was.

I'm not excited right now. I'm in agony.

Timofey is sitting next to me, all broad shoulders and muscular legs and chiseled jawbone, and we have hours to kill. Not to mention a full-sized bed and a couch in the private room two feet away.

Fantasies fill my mind as Timofey's finger circles closer and closer to the inside of my leg. I try to bat them away, but why?

It's my wedding day. If I want to get absolutely railed by my future husband before my wedding, why shouldn't I? Everyone has told me repeatedly that this is my day, after all.

Before I can consider it anymore, I jump up.

Timofey's hand falls away, and he glances up at me. Without a word, I grab his hand and walk into the aisle, pulling him with me.

"Why am I not surprised?" he chuckles, though I notice he doesn't waste any time hurrying after me.

Samuil is asleep in his bassinet and Benjamin is asleep in the seat next to Ashley, his chubby fingers loosely wrapped around her index finger.

I have no regrets at all as I silently pull Timofey into the back room and close and lock the door.

Beyond the hum of the airplane, the room is silent. I lean back against the door and face Timofey. Some of my confidence fades in the face of how truly magnificent he is. Even in jeans and a plain long sleeved tee, he is devastating. How am I going to handle him in a tux? On an altar?

He smirks. "Did you wish to speak to me, Piper?"

"Are you going to be smug now?"

"Smug about what?" he asks, playing dumb.

I should turn around and leave him here alone. That would teach him.

But who am I kidding? I can't walk away.

I meet his eyes "You know why damn well we're here, *Mr. Viktorov.*"

"I know it must be important for you to tempt yourself like this, *Ms. Quinn.*" He looks around at the bed and the couch. "We only have a few hours left until the wedding, and I know how important it is for you that we wait until after we're married to have sex. Walking into this room must be difficult for you."

"Difficult for me?" I shake my head as I shrug out of my jacket. "No. It isn't difficult for me. It is a little hot, though. Are you hot?"

Timofey is still smiling, but he's watching my movements with suspicion now. "No. I'm not hot."

"Really?" I fan my face and pull at the already low-cut neckline of my shirt. "I'm roasting."

"Then say what you need to say so we can get out of this room."

Is that a note of panic in my husband-to-be's voice? It's rare to see Timofey on the defensive. He's used to controlling whatever narrative he's a part of. But the last eight weeks have been painfully long for him, too.

He's every bit as tempted as I am.

"I would, but I can't think back here. It is so hot." In one move, I grab the hem of my shirt and lift it over my head.

I just had a baby eight weeks ago, so I know I look different. My body is soft in new places and stretched in others. But based on the look on Timofey's face, he doesn't mind one bit.

His smile is gone now. His eyes are black holes of desire, raking over every inch of exposed skin. He grits his teeth. "Piper."

"Yes?" I run a hand over my chest and lower, fiddling with the button of my high-waisted jeans until they pop open. "It's so hot in here… I'm dripping."

Timofey doesn't miss the double entendre. His gaze slips lower. "What are you doing, Piper?"

I hook my fingers in the waist of my jeans and shimmy them over my hips. "I know you were playing dumb before, but this is getting ridiculous. You know what I'm doing, Timofey."

"Then tell me."

I kick my jeans off and stand in front of him in nothing but his favorite lacy green lingerie. Maybe this isn't as spontaneous as I thought. I might have had a plan when I got dressed this morning.

"Do we have to play the 'I told you so' game? Am I supposed to admit that I was wrong and you were right? Will that please you? Will that make you hard, my don?"

He groans and licks his lower lip. "Say it, Piper. Say you need me. Tell me that you can't wait another fucking second."

"I could do that." I walk towards him slowly, one foot in front of the other. I stop in front of him and drag a hand over his muscled chest. Then I drop to my knees, my fingers tracing the bulge in his pants. "But I think actions speak louder than words."

Timofey is vibrating by the time I slide his zipper down. When I wrap my lips around his length, he leans his head back, a deep moan unfurling from his chest.

I work my tongue over him, swirling and sucking. His hand rests gently on the back of my head, but as I continue, the pressure becomes firmer. He pulls me towards him as he bucks into my mouth. I grip his hips as he gently fucks my face, taking what I know he wants.

"Holy shit, Piper." My name sounds like a prayer on his lips. I answer by taking him deeper, by choking on him.

He curses again and pulls back, panting.

I wipe my mouth and smile up at him. Before I can stand, Timofey carries me back to the bed and settles between my legs.

He is feverish, ripping my panties away and burying his face between my thighs. I bite down on my hand to keep from crying out.

He laps at my wetness and sucks on my clit. He drives me to a leg-shaking, earthquaking orgasm faster than I would have thought possible.

I grip his hair in my fist and ride his gorgeous mouth.

When he sits up, he's grinning. "I knew you'd never be able to wait."

He's so right. I can't believe I made it this long, actually.

"Careful," I warn him. "I'm the one who was just satisfied. I could walk out of here and leave you high and dry."

He draws back, looking offended. "You consider yourself satisfied?"

No way. Not even close. Never.

I shrug. "It was a good orgasm."

His eyes narrow as he stands up.

For a second, I think I might have pushed him too far. Maybe he really is going to walk away and leave me here. It would be so like Timofey to take the power back and torture me.

Then he grabs my hand and yanks me off the bed.

I slap against his solid chest, off-balance and helpless in his arms. He holds me for a second, his lips hovering over mine. I let my eyes flutter closed and my mouth part. His breath is warm against my skin.

"I can do a hell of a lot better than 'good,' Piper."

Then the world tips.

He whips me around and positions me on the couch opposite the bed. My hands grip the back of the couch, and I'm looking into the twelve-inch strip of mirror that runs the entire length of the wall. I've never paid much attention to it before, but my eyes are locked on it now.

I can see Timofey standing behind me, his heated gaze raking over the curve of my jutting hips. He grabs my leg and positions my knee on the cushioned bench. Then he does the same with the other, splaying me open in front of him.

I turn my head to look back at him, but he presses on my jaw and forces me to look straight ahead. Directly in his eyes.

He presses himself to my entrance and thrusts, filling me from behind in one slick motion.

I arch against him, taking him even deeper.

"What do you think?" he asks, stroking a finger down the curve of my spine. "Are you satisfied?"

There's no time for games now. Not when my body is craving his touch.

I shake my head. "Never."

"Good girl."

I'm rewarded for my honesty with another slow, sensual stroke. Timofey fills me with purpose. Every brush of skin is important and worth savoring.

He spreads his hands over my hips and groans. "This is going to be mine. All of it. All of you."

I meet his eyes in the mirror. "I already am yours."

Immediately, I realize how silly it was to try to wait for our wedding. What is a minister going to make official about our relationship? What can any piece of paper say about the two of us that hasn't already been said?

Timofey must feel the same way, because his eyes glaze over with a primal kind of lust. He claims me, marking me as his until I'm crying out.

Then, just as suddenly, Timofey sits down on the couch next to me and pulls me into his lap. His hands ghost over my peaked nipples and caress the soft skin of my belly. He bites my jaw and sheaths himself inside of me again.

"You're it for me, Timofey," I gasp, riding him. "You're everything—my lust, my love, my don."

He growls and increases our pace, driving into me until I'm shaking around him. My body clenches down hard, pulsating with a bone-deep pleasure I've rarely known.

"Like that, Timofey," I cry. "Don't stop. I—I—I love you."

Words tumble out of my mouth incoherently as the orgasm lifts me up and wrings me out.

When I'm done and lying limply on his chest, Timofey carries me to the bed, curls around me, and enters me from behind.

It's a gentle finish. Timofey spills inside of me and then stays there, cuddling me until my heart stops racing.

"I could stay here forever with you." He lifts my hair and kisses my damp neck. "Actually, let's do exactly that. Forget the wedding. You're my wife already, and we're going to stay in this bed forever."

I laugh and turn to him. "The government might have something to say about the legality of this arrangement."

He wrinkles his nose. "Forget the government, too. You're my wife in every way that matters, Piper. I'm going to honor you and love you and worship you and fuck you—"

"I don't remember those vows," I laugh.

"I'll make my own," he says in all seriousness. "I'm going to spend every second of the rest of my life making you happy."

"Do you have that kind of stamina?"

He presses a hand to his chest in offense. "Is that your subtle way of seducing me into round two? I'll do it. I just don't want to wear you out before tonight."

I'm still buzzing with an orgasm, but I feel butterflies in my stomach at the idea of being with Timofey again.

I'm not sure that feeling will ever go away.

"I want a round two and a round three and a round four…"

He groans and spans his large hand across my hip, drawing me close to him.

"But," I interrupt, kissing his nose, "we have children to take care of."

He sighs, his full lower lip pouting out. "So staying in this bed forever is off the table?"

"For now. But ask me again in… twenty years?"

"Two decades is a long time. Are you sure you'll still feel the same way?"

I stroke his stubbly cheek and nod. "I'm positive."

He grins, and I feel the force of it all the way down to my toes. "Okay, then. You, me, a bed, and the rest of our lives. It's a date."

EXTENDED EPILOGUE: PIPER

Check out the exclusive Extended Epilogue to WHISKEY PAIN!
Five years into the future, see babies, weddings, and more!

CLICK HERE TO DOWNLOAD

Printed in Great Britain
by Amazon

22677594R00215